BAD NEIGHBORS

BAD NEIGHBORS

KATHRINE BECK

DOUBLEDAY

NEW YORK LONDON TORONTO SYDNEY AUCKLAND

PUBLISHED BY DOUBLEDAY
a division of Bantam Doubleday Dell Publishing Group, Inc.
1540 Broadway, New York, New York 10036

DOUBLEDAY and the portrayal of an anchor with a dolphin are trademarks of
Doubleday, a division of Bantam Doubleday Dell Publishing Group, Inc.

All of the characters in this book are fictitious, and any resemblance to actual
persons, living or dead, is purely coincidental.

Book design by Jessica Shatan

Library of Congress Cataloging-in-Publication Data
Beck, K. K.
    Bad neighbors / Kathrine Beck. — 1st ed.
        p.   cm.
    1. Working mothers—United States—Fiction.   2. Neighborhood—
United States—Fiction.   I. Title.
PS3552.E248B3   1996
813'.54—dc20   96-10616
                                                                       CIP

ISBN 0-385-48346-5

Printed in the United States of America
October 1996

1   3   5   7   9   10   8   6   4   2

First Edition

FOR MICHAEL,

a good neighbor

"The mere presence of a coward, however passive, brings an element of treachery into a dangerous situation."

—JOSEPH CONRAD

BAD
NEIGHBORS

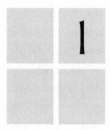

HE MORNING OF THE DAY SHE WAS GOING TO have lunch with Frank Shaw, Anita made sure her underwear was especially pretty. She dressed as she always did, in the half-light, so as not to wake David. She stood admiring herself in her beige lace camisole and matching slip in the full-length mirror inside the closet door, glancing over briefly, guiltily, at the motionless lump beneath the covers.

She went to the window to see what kind of a day it would be, what she should wear. A spring day in Seattle could be cold or very mild. She twirled the plastic wand on the blinds for a quick look outside into the backyard. The lawn and the shrubs were drenched with glistening dew. A small ornamental cherry tree had blossomed out in cotton candy pink for its one attractive week a year. The sky was pale, almost white, but streaked with feathery gray clouds that were lit at the edges with a promising golden peach. It was going to be nice.

Without warning, a window shade in the second story of the house opposite hers flew up. Anita was startled. The whole time she had lived here, the windows in that house had been blank rectangles. The old couple living there had never raised the old-fashioned yellowish shades. There were two windows on the top floor and a big one placed centrally on the first level, giving the impression of two eyes and a mouth. With the shades down all those years, it had looked like a blind or sleeping face. Now it was as if it had opened one eye in an impudent wink.

Self-conscious in her underwear, Anita stepped to one side and fiddled with the blinds so she could look out a little without being seen. The window opposite had been dressed up with white flouncy ruffled curtains with tiebacks. Framed between them, Anita observed a blond woman in a fuzzy pink bathrobe making a bed. The woman tossed the sheets and blankets up gracefully and vigorously. They fell neatly back down, and she bent over and smoothed the bedclothes with the palm of her hand in a large, circular motion.

Anita, small and dark, with a tendency to make quick, delicate, darting movements, found herself intimidated by this unknown woman. There was something very capable about the calm and practiced way she was now fluffing up pillows. She didn't seem to be in any hurry. In fact, she actually seemed to be enjoying what she was doing. Anita felt a stab of shame and envy. Most nights, she and David got into an unmade bed.

Anita closed the blinds firmly and went to her closet. One of the old people over there had died, she knew, and the other one—she thought it was the woman—had gone to live in a retirement home. The house had been listed at two hundred thousand. When Anita and David had bought here thirteen years ago, they paid eighty thousand for their house. The neighborhood was definitely moving up.

She slid hangers to one side and picked out something to wear, chiding herself for the messy collection of empty dry cleaner bags cluttering things up. On top of the beige lace went a plain dark skirt and an opaque, wine-colored silk blouse. Probably nothing would happen. No one, least of all Frank Shaw, would ever know that she would be sitting in the restaurant feeling the scratchy lace and smooth silk of the camisole against her breasts and torso as she shifted in her chair.

As far as Anita knew, her mother had never had a lunch date with a man other than her husband in her whole life. How could she have? The only other men around had been her husband's fellow air force officers. She had lunch with the other officers' wives. The sexes had been strictly segregated. Even after Anita's father had retired, and later, after he had died, her mother only seemed to have female friends. Even if Anita's mother had arranged to meet an interesting man for lunch, Anita could hardly imagine her thinking about her underwear beforehand. Lately, Anita had found herself giving her mother's life a lot of thought.

She watched David toss over in his sleep and lay on his back. He still had that rangy, boyish, open-faced look he'd had when they'd met. Thick golden brown wavy hair, straight nose, nicely shaped chin. Realistically, she knew that Frank Shaw wasn't nearly as handsome. He was shorter, and his hair was thinning and there was kind of a bump in the bridge of his nose. But his green eyes were shiny and glowing and always tracking, and there was something disciplined yet sexy about the way he held his mouth.

Since meeting him at Julie's party, Anita had met him for lunch four times. She could repeat most of the dialogue from each encounter, and relived in her mind the tiny gestures or phrases that might be construed as evidence of lust on his part. The time he had let his hand linger on her shoulder just slightly as he helped her off with her coat. The time he had once tapped the back of her hand for emphasis as she laid it on the tablecloth before him like some kind of offering. The way he had greedily eyed her throat as she exposed it by sliding away a silk scarf. The way his face lit up with relief as he scrambled eagerly to his feet to greet her when she walked into the restaurant ten minutes late. And the last and most riveting time, when he had looked disturbed and slightly bitter as she kissed him hello on the cheek instead of offering him the usual handshake.

She'd meant it to appear simply friendly. After all, their conversations were becoming increasingly intimate. They had discussed all kinds of things, like the pain of his divorce, and how at their age life often seemed not to have turned out as they might have thought when younger, and how men and women saw life differently. A kiss instead of a handshake seemed in order. Although she had made a point of clearly grazing his cheek with her lips, it was almost an air kiss, with an accompanying pat on the shoulder.

But when she pulled back and saw the slightly resentful look on his face, she felt like some kind of a tease. If, as she hoped, he wanted her passionately, that pat on the shoulder probably came off as patronizing and cruel.

Anita spent a lot of time lately fantasizing about Frank Shaw. Sometimes, they were tearing each other's clothes off in a frenzy. Sometimes, he was seducing her slowly and delicately, and she was trembling with anticipation, trying to fight it, then succumbing. These imaginary encounters took place in a dark, shadowy setting. Anita hadn't bothered to mentally decorate his apartment, where she had never been.

What surprised her was that she saw all this not as if through her own eyes, but rather like a third person, watching. She tried unsuccessfully to imagine it all from her own point of view, thinking this would ultimately be more satisfying. Instead, she saw their limbs entwined, saw him wrap her hair in his fingers, saw her own orgasmic face, head tilted back, mouth open and glistening from his kisses.

But while she saw this from outside her body, she felt his hot breath at her ear, his tongue at her nipples, his hands running down the sides of her body to the curve of her waist and hips, his penis pushing inside her.

These fantasies shocked Anita. She hadn't felt sexy for a very long time. At first, she had felt guilty about her lack of interest, knowing how hard it must be on David. After all, when they were first married they were incredibly passionate. She remembered whole weekends in bed with both of them telling each other that they had never imagined such happiness. She couldn't, however, remember the actual physical sensations, any more than she could recall the pain of childbirth.

Eventually, she lost regret for her vanished passion just as surely as she had lost the passion itself. When she came across a magazine article about rekindling desire, she just frowned and flipped past it. After all, you couldn't will yourself to be hungry or thirsty, either. She consoled herself with the thought that indifference was certainly better than wanting something you couldn't have.

She had been right. Wanting Frank Shaw was depressing and painful and left her in a reckless, reeling state. Maybe it was just the beginning of some more general midlife crisis. When she had first become aware of him, standing with the other parents at softball games in which both their daughters were playing, she hadn't even noticed him, other than to think he seemed aloof and as if he didn't want to be at some kid's softball game. She hadn't actually talked to him at all until Julie's party.

And now, she was obsessed. She had also taken recently to driving too fast with the radio blaring, like a sixteen-year-old who had just got her license.

DAVID WAITED UNTIL HE HEARD THE FRONT DOOR slam and Anita's heels walking up the street to the bus stop, then he rolled over, propped himself up halfway on the pillows, and turned off the clock radio's alarm before its horrible blips began. He had fifteen minutes to lie here in the warmth of the down comforter, to wake up slowly, plan his day. He ran a hand along his jaw. After he dropped the kids off, he'd shave. He always felt better about things if he shaved.

The girls were already up, filling the house with the familiar sounds of flushing toilets, slamming doors, running showers, blaring television cartoons and rock music. As soon as he'd gotten them off to school, David promised himself he'd go down to the office and start on the new project he'd thought of two days earlier. He'd had the germ of the idea as soon as he'd walked out of the meeting with the Conway's Home and Garden Center people ten days ago, but he'd had to let it percolate awhile. He hadn't told Anita anything about that meeting. He'd been afraid the old inertia would set in, and instead of offering him the support he always hoped for, she'd end up nagging him about it with that tense, frightened, clench-jawed expression on her face. Now, she'd be happily surprised.

He checked the clock and snuggled back for another ten minutes. For the first time in as long as he could remember, he felt incredibly optimistic. The old creative juices were flowing again. It had all been made clear to him in one great insightful burst. The way to sell hardware was with feelings. Good feelings. Feelings about home and family. But not the old patriarchal, oppressive family. A new kind of family to-day's customers could relate to.

He knew his concept was sound. A few little insights he'd had lately seemed to reinforce it. For instance, the tender-ness he'd felt one afternoon looking out at his youngest daughter twirling around and around on the lawn. Her white arms and legs flashed against the background of the hedge that ran across the end of the garden. The tender bright green of the hedge's new growth stood out, young and sassy, against the sober, darker leaves.

And there was the satisfaction he'd felt at that party when Anita introduced him to that high-powered lawyer with the hatchety face, Frank somebody, whose kid was on Lily's soft-ball team last year. David saw envy in his eyes.

"David works at home and looks after the girls," his wife had announced to this stranger. In the past, she'd always acted vaguely ashamed of his status when they socialized, even though she invariably denied it later.

That night, David had thought that after all this time Anita was finally beginning to accept his staying home. For one thing, after that party he'd reached over and touched her in bed and she'd rolled right over on her side and put her arms around him and kissed him and they'd had sex for the first time in a long time—and without first talking about whether it was a good idea or not.

Even more important to David was the fact that he hadn't felt put down at all when she'd told that lawyer he was a part-time househusband. Just the reverse. David had felt smug, as if he knew something this guy didn't.

"Yes," he'd said in a self-assured way, putting a proprietary arm around Anita's slim, silk-clad shoulder. "My own rela-tionship with my father was a blur. It's very rewarding to be a hands-on parent."

The lawyer had smiled wistfully, looking back and forth at

him and Anita with what David was sure was envy. Other people's envy was so satisfying. It was a validation of the choices one had made.

"The great thing about working freelance," David had explained, "is that I don't have to work with anyone I don't respect. I limit myself to clients I feel are contributing something of value to the culture at large. There's a lot of crappy advertising out there that sends the wrong message about what life today is all about."

"That's very interesting," the man had said. He clearly didn't get what David was talking about. But that conversation, wasted as it was on the gloomy-looking lawyer at Julie's party, had inspired David himself when it came time to come up with the Conway's campaign.

It wasn't about hardware. It was about family in its broadest sense: how the ever-changing needs of a growing family required constant, nurturing adaptation, and how the rewards were a sense of belonging and peace.

His thoughts were interrupted by a fierce yowl from the kitchen below. Lily was screaming, "Fuck you, you little brat!" at her sister.

"Hey," David yelled halfheartedly. "Pipe down, will you?"

Sylvie's outraged wail floated up the stairs, followed by an indignant, two-syllable *"Da-ad."*

"Goddamnit!" said David, swinging his feet out from underneath the warm covers. Couldn't they even pour out a couple of bowls of cereal without going ballistic? And did Lily have to use language like that? It sounded so sleazy coming from a fourteen-year-old.

He went downstairs in his bare feet and stood in his rumpled pajamas in the doorway to the kitchen, hands in fists. He told himself to relax, to let the hands open.

"She pushed me," said Sylvie, pointing to the older girl.

"Don't pick on your sister," he told Lily firmly. "She's only eight, for Christ's sake."

Lily folded her arms underneath her breasts and slouched, putting all her weight on one foot so her hip stuck out. She gave her father a cold sneer. David looked at her and thought how unattractive she had become. Her face looked coarser somehow, heavier and thicker. Fourteen-year-olds were supposed to be coltish and gamine, for God's sake, and here was his daughter in a pair of ugly, baggy shorts that showed off her piano legs, and a tired old T-shirt stretched tight across her burgeoning chest.

"Why did you push her?" he demanded.

"She went into my room without my permission," said Lily, flicking back her glassy brown hair with a dismissive, whip-like gesture.

He turned to Sylvie. "We've talked about how important everyone's personal space is." He wondered bleakly if she would turn into a big sulky girl like her sister in just a few years. She was cute enough now, with narrow, watchful eyes with thick lashes, and crisp dark curls just like her mother's.

"I was looking for my Hello Kitty pencil sharpener," Sylvie said, twisting the hem of her cardigan sweater in her hands while she talked. "I want to show it to April." She gave him a sweet little smile that he suspected was masking sly triumph at having provoked her big sister.

David went over to the cupboard and pulled out a box of cereal. "Get the milk, will you?" he said to Sylvie.

"Why do you have to buy those cheap generic cereals?" asked Lily. "They taste like cardboard. Why can't we get real Honey Nut Cheerios?"

"Mom does when she shops," said Sylvie. "I like it when she shops. She gets better stuff." She yanked a half gallon of milk in a big plastic container from the top shelf of the fridge and thumped it down on the table with such force that a lot of milk gushed out the top.

"Where's the lid to that?" David demanded, his voice rising a little. "Why do you put the milk back in there without the cap? When I see the caps lying around I throw them out because I think they're from milk we already used up."

"Chill, Dad," said Lily contemptuously, pouring out a stream of cereal into two ceramic bowls. He hated that dry rattling sound. He hated the bowls, half full of milk and floating, soggy cereal that would sit in the sink all morning. It was all terribly depressing. He remembered from just a few years earlier that circle of sticky food that developed on the floor around the high chair. Now the debris was up here on the table. The only difference was that he didn't have to bend down to clean it up.

The girls sat down and ate together in silence, elbows on the table, faces hovering over the bowls. He was horrified to discover himself thinking that they looked like animals feeding.

David went upstairs to get dressed. Anita used to get the girls ready for school before work, but she'd been promoted again about a year ago and liked to go into the office early and take calls from the East Coast. David wondered if that was just an excuse to ditch out on what he considered a particularly grim part of the day. She knew how difficult the mornings were for him. He thought enviously of her on the phone at her desk, drinking Starbucks coffee and eating a brioche or something while he had to face all this. It really wasn't fair.

He just had time to shave before he drove them to school. Inspecting himself in the bathroom mirror, he decided he was looking pretty good for his age. He figured he probably had a good fifteen years on the creative directors from the two agencies who were also pitching the Conway's Home and Garden Center account, but that could cut both ways. Sam and Bob Conway and their sister, Sandy, who had just taken over from their father, were about David's own age— early forties. They might resent some pushy Generation X types telling them what to do. Maybe he should update his haircut for the presentation, though.

There was the usual last-minute scramble for homework and lunch money while he waited at the door jangling keys, then the drive to Sylvie's elementary school, and on to Lily's middle school. He wasn't quite sure how they'd gotten into the driving routine, instead of having the girls walk or take the bus. Anita had insisted way back when, and he generally let Anita call the shots, even if he thought she was overprotective. It seemed so much more important to her.

But today, watching Lily walk round-shouldered and hunched over the books she carried against her body like armor, her thick legs carrying her laboriously up the steps, it occurred to him that walking to school would have been good for her. There were some other girls on the steps of the school, prancing and teasing each other and skipping up the stairs like little gazelles. Lily looked stolid and middle-aged compared to them. He was suddenly overcome by a sense of pain and protective love edged with panic. She looked so terribly sad.

He remembered her as a sprite-like toddler, climbing to the top of the jungle gym. She had been cheerful and energetic with a lot of unselfconscious charm. That little girl had to be the authentic Lily. This sullen girl was a delusion. Her personality had been temporarily veiled by adolescence.

It was too painful to believe that people were like cats, starting out like cute and cuddly kittens, and later growing into unattractive neurotics who bred with other screwed-up, unattractive people and made more cute babies who turned into gangly, homely, witless people.

He'd made a mental note to remember the idea that the authentic personality went into hibernation during adolescence. He could work a cute TV ad around that idea. Father and sulky daughter working on some household project together—a real-looking teenaged kid, not some cheerleader. Give it a happy ending, some sense that the kid is turning back into a recognizable human being. It was a thought that would cheer people up and help them deal with one of life's rougher patches. They didn't want to hear that they'd been suckered by cute little babies, then Bam! and you're living with the teenager from hell.

Back at home, he went into the kitchen to make coffee, flinging yesterday's grounds on top of the morose-looking cereal bowls sitting in the sink. He stood there for a moment and took his first sip as he gazed out the window into the backyard. From behind the glossy green hedge flecked with spring growth came a horrible mechanical sound, like a speedboat tearing across a quiet lake.

He wasn't quite sure who lived over there now. The sold sign had gone up a few weeks ago. Since then there had been some signs of life from beyond the hedge—the *blonk* of a basketball on concrete, the squeak of a swing set, and two yelling little boy voices and a mother voice with a sweet and patient tone, at a decibel level just too low to hear the actual words. And now, this horrible racket that he hoped wouldn't go on all morning—the very morning he was planning to start work.

Frowning, David went downstairs to his office. Actually, it wasn't really his office anymore. Since the girls had grown bigger, it was now also a room for Sylvie and her friends to play, as well as Lily's favorite spot to watch MTV and do her homework. It had also become a catchall for everything that didn't have a place—like the boxes of crap his sister and mother had sent him after they cleaned out Aunt Martha's house in Muncie a few months ago. Anita had been after him to do something about those boxes, but it would have to wait now that he was creatively inspired.

He picked his way through a litter of fashion magazines and glittery Barbie doll dresses and shoes, a half-done puzzle, and coloring books surrounded by a spray of crayons. At the back of the room was a row of bookshelves, a bulletin board with a Sierra Club calendar, and a desk with his ancient and bulky computer.

He turned it on and waited patiently while it labored to life, then watched the pale green letters jump on the black background. His fingers hovered over the keyboard, and he felt pleasant anticipation at the idea of work. At those competing agencies, they were screwing around with research and focus groups and spending a lot of time and money creating fancy charts and spreadsheets on brand-new computers with full-color printers. David shut out those thoughts and told himself that all he really needed would come from within—from a mind and heart focused on people and their needs. It's what had made him a star in the past. The idea was right. The creative element would be right, too, and that would guarantee that the Conways, who seemed like bright, perceptive people, would get it in a visceral way.

He began drafting a statement of the creative philosophy. The ease with which he worked was proof enough to him that he was on the right track. Of course it would have to be honed and polished, but he was definitely back in business.

While pausing briefly, he realized that the horrible mechanical noise rattling through the glass doors that led out to the backyard was still going full force. David rose from the desk and went over and pulled back the curtain. Some glossy-leafed branches had fallen at the back of his yard,

dark against the lighter green of the lawn. Apparently someone was trimming the hedge. At least that shouldn't take all
day.

He managed to get a few more choice lines done despite
the noise. No doubt about it, he was on a roll again. Anita
would be so surprised when she got home from work. They
could go out to dinner, just the two of them, and he'd tell
her all about his new concept. The kids could order a pizza.

Anita had been a pretty good sport these last years when
he hadn't really done all that much, but now that he was
working again he realized he'd been repressing the knowledge that she was actually disappointed in him. That would
be remedied soon enough, he thought happily. He'd always
told her she should have a little more faith.

He decided he deserved another coffee and picked his
way back through the minefield of kid detritus. Today, he'd
insist the girls clean this mess up. After all, this was his work
area. Maybe he'd been too slack.

While pouring his fresh cup, he glanced out the kitchen
window. Something was different, but it took him a second
to figure out just what. The hedge, formerly eight feet or so,
was now down to about six and a half feet. Above it, he
could see the top of a stepladder along with the crown of a
sandy-haired head.

He raced down the back steps and yelled, "Hey!" The
clamor went on, and he shouted, "Hey," again, a lot louder.
The sound faded out just as he raised his voice even louder
and so he heard himself scream, "Stop it!" like someone in a
bad movie.

A little female cry of surprise came from behind the
hedge. He'd somehow expected a burly young male gar-
dener. Then he heard the ladder squeak twice, and the head
rose, in two stages, until he was confronting a woman in her

mid-thirties with a heart-shaped face peering over the hedge at him like a giantess.

"How far down are you planning to take that?" he demanded angrily.

"I'm Sue Heffernan," the woman said, looking nervous but brave. "Your new neighbor," she added in more confident tones—like a teacher getting an obstreperous child to be polite by her own patient example.

"David Jamison," he said, giving her a tight smile. "Listen, can we talk about this hedge? We kind of enjoy our privacy."

"Wow," said Sue, looking down at him with the comic air of someone on stilts, "I'm sorry. You see, my husband's in the insurance business and he's very safety-conscious. A tall hedge like this makes it easy for burglars. I thought if visibility was increased . . ."

"You mean you want it even shorter?"

"Just so you can see an adult over the top of it."

"Sorry," David snapped. "That's out of the question. Anyway," he added, "I can keep an eye on things because I work at home."

"Really? How interesting!" Sue Heffernan leaned over so far on the ladder that David thought with malicious hopefulness that she might tumble into the hedge. "I work at home, too."

"Well, in that case," he said, "I think we'll be pretty safe here. So let's keep the hedge where it is, all right?"

"All right," she said. "I'll be by later to rake up the stuff that fell on your side."

"Thank you," he said stiffly. "I appreciate it."

"We just moved here from Wisconsin," she said, apropos of nothing. "My husband was transferred."

"I'm afraid we may not be as friendly here as they are in the Midwest." David smiled to let her know he wasn't really being hostile. "We like our hedges. I really appreciate your restraint."

He nodded curtly and went back to the house. Jesus Christ! That was a near miss. Another foot or two and they would have been treated to the sight of Sue and family all summer long.

David himself had grown up in the Midwest and reflected with loathing upon the endless progression of immaculate lawns that surrounded the houses on his block in suburban Indianapolis, like a commons where sheep could graze. Instead, children had roamed there, while mothers kept an eye out over the vast terrain, drifting in and out of one anothers' kitchens for coffee as they shepherded their flocks.

David had found his family oppressive in large part because of the way it clung to normalcy and its ignorant suspicion of anything introspective or artistic. He'd left for college at the University of Michigan with a heady feeling of liberation, and got a summer job in Ann Arbor right after his freshman year and every summer thereafter so he'd never have to return.

Where he'd grown up, a hedge or a fence would have been seen as un-neighborly if not actually hostile. Maybe Sue felt the same way. The sooner she got with the program, the better.

His new neighbor was rather attractive, he thought. All the more reason not to let her think she could pull anything over on him. Anyway, she'd backed right off, which was a good thing. He felt pleased that he'd been so forceful, and went back to the house whistling and eager to get back to work.

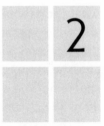

2

ANITA CIRCLED THE BLOCK A FEW TIMES BE-fore pulling into the driveway. When the girls were smaller, she used to rush up onto the porch to hug them and they'd flap around her like little birds. Now, the solitude of the car had come to mean a lot to her. It was her only chance to decompress after a hectic day at work and before facing the evening's rigors.

When her father had come home from work, she had been shooed out of the living room while he smoked and read the paper until dinner was ready. Only then, after neatly folding the paper, would he join the family for a hot, home-cooked meal.

Of course, she couldn't expect anything like that. The girls always had a million things to tell her, or more often, an argument for her to arbitrate. She supposed it was their way of getting some of her attention after her long absence. And then there was David, usually collapsed on the sofa with a glass of wine, watching the news while they argued about what they should have for dinner and who should make it. If she were organized, she'd make a bunch of casseroles over the weekend that they could nuke during the week. Long ago she stopped expecting him to have a meal ready when she came home, even though that was the official arrangement they'd made.

If she were a better person, she'd be able to handle it. She should want to come home and be warm and nurturant and make everybody happy to see her again. But it was getting harder and harder to be a nice person. Sometimes she heard herself brush off the girls and tell them in a defeated little voice that she was too tired to help them with some project just now—too weak to summon up the cheerful patience she needed to make sure they knew she loved them.

Sometimes she heard herself snap at David, or make gratuitous critical remarks to him. He didn't even seem to notice, but she shocked herself. All her woman friends who had stayed at home with their kids admitted they were often wrecks by the time their husbands came home. It wasn't fair for her to have a different standard for David.

She tried to change her attitude as she approached the front door. If those damn cereal bowls were still in the sink today, she was afraid she'd burst into tears.

She pushed open the door.

David was standing in the hall, smiling and holding out his arms. "Hello, sweetheart," he said. "How was your day?" He really was very handsome, she thought. Especially when he smiled. He moved toward her with the skating, insouciant light step he exhibited when he was feeling festive, a step that never failed to charm, and wrapped his arms around her.

"Fine," she said, hugging him rather fiercely. "Just fine." She pulled back and looked into his face. "Oh, David, I love you." She sounded so intense. She laughed a little. That kiss in the taxi hadn't really meant anything, she told herself. At the time, she had leaned into Frank's body with an overwhelming sense of relief and let him kiss her as if it were all meant to be. But now, she told herself she'd kissed him back out of vanity, just so he'd know what a good kisser she was.

"Of course you love me," David said happily. "Sit down in the living room and I'll bring you a glass of wine and I'll tell you why today is a terrific day."

"You're awfully chirpy," she said, ignoring his instructions and following him into the kitchen. She felt so relieved. Somehow, she had imagined her husband would be able to tell she had kissed Frank just by looking at her. "Did you win the lottery?"

"Close." He was poking around in the fridge. She went to get herself a glass. The kitchen was immaculate. The sink was free of cereal bowls. The electronic message on the dishwasher said "CLEAN."

He turned toward her with a bottle of white wine in one hand, the other stretched out in a "ta-da" gesture. "I'm pitching a big account. A very big account. It's just me and two downtown shops. And I think I've got a really good chance, because I've got a hell of a concept."

"Who is it?" she said, startled. She hadn't seen him so energetic and confident in ages.

"Conway's Home and Garden Center."

"You mean you followed up on that?" Anita was amazed. She'd given David a story about Conway's that she'd clipped out of the *Puget Sound Business Journal*. With a yellow Hi-Liter she had carefully marked the part that said they were thinking about taking their advertising outside. The chain wasn't very glamorous—a lot of smallish neighborhood hardware stores with kind of sad nurseries attached. She imagined they were getting slaughtered by warehouse stores like Costco. They'd been around forever, though, and had some great locations. If David could spruce up their image, maybe they'd be able to grab a respectable market share.

David waved his hand dismissively. "I had a very productive meeting with them last week. The younger generation has just taken over and they're ready to clean up their act. They've screwed around with an in-house agency for years. Really pathetic stuff—all price-item newspaper inserts. I've got some ideas that'll really knock their socks off. We're going out to dinner to celebrate."

Her face fell a little. "But I had lunch out. Can't we have a quiet dinner at home?" The world outside seemed suddenly threatening and full of nameless perils. Then she realized the significance of what he'd said. He was finally pitching a big account. He'd met with them. If he actually got it, they'd have two incomes again. David would have to hire people. Maybe get an office somewhere. A big retail account like that would be nice and steady.

"But I've already ordered a pizza for the girls," he said, looking hurt.

"Of course we'll go out," she said, suddenly ashamed at her lack of apparent enthusiasm. "I'm sorry. I was just a little tired. But if you drive and order and do everything, it will be wonderful to go out. And you can tell me all about the pitch. You never even told me you followed up on that lead I gave you. When was the meeting?"

He smiled again and filled her glass. "I lined it up last week, but I didn't really know whether I was interested in fighting for the business until today. I just woke up, ready to compete and feeling like some kind of cloud had lifted." He topped off his own glass and clinked it against hers, then stood very close to her, bracing himself with one hand on the Formica counter while he leaned over and kissed her forehead. "I've already got a draft of the underlying creative philosophy. I think they'll be pretty receptive. We established a good rapport when I met with them. A couple of brothers and a sister. They're really open to a fresh approach."

He'd actually started.

All at once Anita felt that safety and a sense of stability were possible. Everything would be all right now. She didn't want to fall into a dark abyss with Frank Shaw. She'd known that all along. She'd struggled and fought the attraction and just when she was about to succumb, David had pulled himself together. She'd been tested and she'd managed, just barely, to pass the test.

She would tell Frank she'd changed her mind about meeting him tomorrow. Someday, she would look back and realize how silly this had all been. She wasn't the type to sneak around town having an affair. It was some stupid midlife crisis that might even seem funny years from now, just as her adolescent anguish now seemed mildly comic. She was so grateful at having been saved, she thought she might cry.

"Darling!" said David sympathetically. He had always been able to tell when she was about to cry, bless his heart.

"I'm just so happy," said Anita. "I'm being silly."

"I didn't realize how important it was to you," he said. "I know it's been hard, me blocked like that. You've been so patient. A saint."

Anita wanted to blurt out that she wasn't a saint at all, she was a middle-aged woman who all of a sudden felt like a sex-starved teenager, a woman who was prepared to betray her family and do something that would certainly hurt the girls and David a lot if they ever found out.

"Tell me about your ideas, David." Anita didn't care about his ideas. She just wanted him to collect nice 15 percent agency commissions on the ads he placed, year in and year out. Then, they could actually save some money, invest it, get a little interest income, get some college funds going for the girls. Maybe replace that awful cracked concrete patio in the backyard with brick. She could feel all right again.

David kissed her on the forehead again and said, "It's about families. It's all about a feeling of what home really means. We'll sell hardware and garden stuff by selling new ideas about family and the spiritual value of domestic life. I'm working my way into it. I think it's really got fabulous potential."

Anita looked dubious. "You mean like a feel-good, heartwarming thing about families? Like a nostalgic Norman Rockwell kind of thing? You think they'll go for that?"

Lily had come into the kitchen. "Hi, Mom," she said.

Anita gave her daughter a distracted smile. "Hello, sweetie."

David stepped back and leaned against the fridge. "Not nostalgia," he said sharply. "It's a way to follow the demographic bulge of us boomers into our middle years. You know. Inspirational stuff about family life that's hip and cool. A new way to talk about domestic life. After all, I've been home for six years now. I've got a real take on running a household."

"Yeah, right," said Lily. "The laundry's whiter than white. Fresher than fresh." She looked childishly pleased with her sarcasm as she reached for the cookie jar.

"Oh, Lily," said Anita. "Your father is starting a new project. Remarks like that aren't very helpful."

"Judging by the way you're filling out lately, I don't think you *really* need those cookies," said David.

"Leave her alone," Anita said. "She's filling out a little before she shoots up." She went over to her daughter to give her a reassuring hug, but Lily had flounced out of the room. They heard her heavy tread on the stairs and a door slamming.

"Great!" said Anita, setting down her glass and heading after her. "That's just what she needs right now, put-downs about her appearance. Next thing you know, she'll go bulimic on us!"

Anita went upstairs and knocked softly on Lily's door.

"What is it?" Lily barked from behind the door. Anita heard a certain pleading in that bark. She opened the door and walked in. Lily was sprawled on her back on her unmade bed, staring up at a picture of Keanu Reeves taped to the ceiling.

"Don't pay any attention to Daddy." Anita sat gingerly on the edge of the bed and ran her fingers over her daughter's forehead, feeling the smooth, warm skin and the soft hair along the brow. Lily turned away a little, but she let her mother continue to stroke her.

"He's worried about his work," Anita went on. "We have to encourage him. He's trying to get a pretty big account. He's probably a little nervous. It's understandable."

"Yeah, right," said Lily, rolling her eyes.

"We want it to work out," said Anita. "You know, Lily, your father is very talented and creative."

"Yeah, but he's a slacker, too," said Lily.

DOWNSTAIRS, DAVID WAS POLISHING OFF HIS wine, and feeling angry. Just when he needs her support, Anita acts skeptical about his new project, then abandons him for the sulky child. If Anita hadn't been giving him lots of little digs lately, Lily wouldn't be getting into the act, too. Suddenly, he had a vision of Lily, galumphing into womanhood, joining her mother in a campaign to put him down in lots of tiny, mean-spirited ways.

Sylvie walked into the kitchen. "Hi, Daddy," she said cheerily. She was wearing her Brownie sash over her sweater and her brown felt beanie was attached to her head with two bobby pins. Great, he thought, letting his anger get the better of him. Another little soldier in the battle of the sexes. God knows what she was learning from the hearty young lesbian with the crew cut and the nose ring who ran the Brownie troop. How to geld every male who came into her orbit, no doubt.

"It's Brownies tonight," she said.

"I gathered that."

"We're taking Melissa and Sara," she continued. "And it's our turn to bring a snack."

"Oh, hell!" said David. "Can't Mom deal with it?" Without waiting for any reply, he plunged out the back door clutching his wineglass. He went into the yard, flapped open an aluminum webbed lawn chair with a squeak, and plunked down into it.

What he saw as he glared out into the dimming light replaced his dull, general bitterness with an entirely new, specific, adrenaline-laced anger. There, cut into one end of the hedge, was a curved portal, a little archway leading to his neighbor's yard. It looked like something a Beatrix Potter character might toddle through at any moment. In the opening he saw an unwelcome glimpse of a sandbox and a swing set. He had a hideous vision of a whole checkerboard of houses and yards, fenced off by a maze of hedges, linked by these round little arches, connecting all the miserable, pointless clusters of men, women, and children pretending to be happy all over America.

He was certainly going to confront them about this.

ANITA AND SYLVIE WERE PEERING DESPERATELY into the refrigerator when David burst back into the house a few seconds later. Why couldn't he have told her about the snack, Anita thought angrily. She could have picked up something on the way home from work. While he was at it, he could have cleaned out the fridge. There was a dried, brownish pool of ketchup on the top shelf that looked like congealed blood.

"There's twelve of us," said Sylvie. "And it doesn't have to be healthy or anything. Just good. Like Fruit Roll-Ups or Cheez-Its and Capri Sun Maui Punch."

"We'll bring some real food," said Anita with grim determination, consulting her watch. "Maybe fruit and string cheese and whole wheat crackers." She turned to David, who was staring out the window into the yard. "I wish you'd taken care of this snack thing," she said coldly.

"Look out there and see what the new neighbors have done!" said David. "They've carved a big hole in the hedge so they can troop in here anytime."

She went over to the window. It looked very odd to see that doorway in the hedge. In fact, there was something creepy about it. It reminded Anita of the vivid, unsettling dreams she sometimes had in which details of familiar places were altered. She always awoke from them disturbed, as if she had slipped into another dimension, equally real but very threatening.

Sylvie went over and looked out the window, too. "It's cute," she said. "Like a cartoon door. I want to go through it."

"I'm going to go over there right now and give them hell," declared David through clenched teeth.

With panic in her voice, Anita said, "Don't do that."

"Your problem," said David, "is you're afraid of confrontation."

"Well it's not as if they can undo it," Anita pointed out reasonably. "It'll take ages to grow back."

"They need to be told that they can't just do whatever they want."

"Maybe we can plant something in front of it. I'd hate to get off on the wrong foot with them. It could lead to years of trouble."

David snorted. "The thing to do is to be firm right from the very beginning. Let them know they can't screw us around."

"Please don't go," Anita pleaded. "We have this Brownie thing to deal with."

"Yeah," interjected Sylvie.

"Fuck the Brownies!" said David, heading back out into the yard, not noticing that Sylvie looked shocked at his language. "I'm going to go right over there and give those people hell."

"I'm coming with you." Anita hoped she could dissuade him from a confrontation, or at least tone it down.

"Fine, but I'll do the talking."

"Why don't you leave the wineglass here? It'll make a better impression." She was trotting after him, wishing she'd had time to get out of her heels. "Call Melissa and Sara and tell them we'll be a little late," she called back to Sylvie.

"Mom! Where are you going?"

"Just over to meet the new neighbors," Anita explained, slightly out of breath.

"I'm coming, too!" Sylvie said. "I want to go through that cute door!"

Anita started to say no, then reflected that Sylvie's presence might put the brakes on David's behavior. "Okay, come on," she said, holding out her hand. They followed David through the hedge and the neighbor's backyard, where Sylvie noted the swing set with interest, and around the house to the front door facing the street. A shiny brand-new silver van sat in the driveway. They caught up with him on the front porch, where he was urgently pounding a handsome brass knocker. Anita admired a big green glazed ceramic pot full of cascading lobelia and ivy and little white flowers that sat right under the mailbox, and the light coming serenely through a heavy lace curtain in the glass door. How could David *blam* insistently like that on the door of someone who'd taken the trouble to make the entry to their house so pretty and inviting? Even the big bristly orange doormat looked attractive—plump and generous, somehow.

"Be polite, for God's sake," Anita whispered to David. The door opened. Four people stood there looking out at them like a family portrait. There was a florid-looking middle-aged man in a cardigan sweater and gold-rimmed aviator glasses with thick lenses that made his light brown eyes look huge. Next to him stood a smiling woman with a happy, relaxed expression, and a straight, simple haircut. Her hair was streaked with blond that could only come from the sun itself or a really fabulous hairdresser. Her almond-shaped eyes, a very soft blue, made her look piquant and slightly feline, and she wore a rosy, old-fashioned chintz smock like something an Edwardian lady might wear to arrange flowers.

In front of the two adults stood two little boys in immaculate Cub Scout uniforms. The smaller boy wore glasses. Anita had a bizarre image of all of them walking lockstep to the door so they could present a collective appearance for the visitors.

"About that hedge . . ." began David.

Anita smiled nervously and interrupted him. "I'm Anita Jamison," she began.

"Hello, Anita! I'm Sue. I've already met David," said the woman pleasantly. Anita was surprised. David hadn't said anything about meeting this woman. "This is my husband, Roger," she went on. "And our sons, Chris and Matt." Anita almost expected the boys to salute. Their uniforms were handbook perfect. In fact, they looked starched and pressed with rigid creases, just like Anita's father's uniform. Both boys, blond, gap-toothed and freckled, were emblazoned with merit badges. Anita was suddenly slightly embarrassed that Sylvie, like most of the girls in the troop, just wore part of her Brownie uniform.

"And who's this?" Sue put her hands on her knees and bent down to Sylvie's level. Anita caught a whiff of Yardley English Lavender.

Now Anita was embarrassed that Sylvie's merit badges were attached to her sash with safety pins. They were supposed to iron on, but they never seemed to stick.

"This is our daughter Sylvie," said David impatiently.

"I wish I could invite you in," said Sue with what sounded like real regret, "but we're off to a Cub Scout meeting over at the school."

"I know. The Brownies meet there, too," said Anita. "In fact, I should be driving Sylvie there right now."

"Yes," said David, frowning, as if the fact that Anita was here instead was Sue's fault. "But we noticed . . ."

"It's real neighborly of you to come over and meet us," said Roger, without much enthusiasm.

David plunged right over him. "We noticed," he repeated in a louder voice, "that you cut a big opening in the hedge."

Sue's face collapsed. Anita felt terrible for her. She knew she herself would just die if her neighbors complained about anything like that.

"I'm so sorry!" Sue said, sounding anguished. "You said you didn't want it lower, so I thought it would be a nice compromise—and increase visibility. I guess I should have asked you, but to be honest, I didn't want to disturb you anymore."

Roger looked at his watch and interjected, "Maybe we can discuss this later?"

"We can give Sylvie a ride over to the school if you want," said Sue, as if trying to make up for her faux pas.

"That's all right," said Anita. "I have to take two other little girls, too."

"No problem," said Sue. "We've got a big van."

"Carries a whole Little League team," added Roger proudly.

Sue covered her face with her hands and peered out coyly between her fingers. "It would make me feel better about the hedge. I guess I really blew it." The hands fell away and she bit her lower lip and wrinkled up her forehead in a classic expression of contrition that seemed a little overdone but also made it clear she really was sorry.

David looked over at Anita. "Let's take them up on it," he said. "Then we can go out to dinner, like we planned."

Anita had completely forgotten about the celebratory dinner they were supposed to be having. She smiled at Sue. "I couldn't possibly let you do that."

Sylvie piped up. "What about snack? My dad forgot it was our turn," she added, looking up at Sue.

"We can take care of that right away," said Sue, leading Sylvie down the front hallway and into the house. David and Anita looked at each other quizzically for a second, then followed.

The layout of the interior was a mirror image of their own. "We have twin houses," Anita said, startled. It was as if someone had removed all her furniture and replaced it with something better. "I knew there were a lot of them around here, but I'd never been inside this house before."

"You didn't know the Hansens?" said Sue.

"In this neighborhood, people like their privacy," David said pointedly.

Anita shot him a dirty look. Sue and Roger did seem overly friendly, but the decor—soft, simple curtains, gleaming hardwood floors, pretty country antiques mixed with some modern pieces—was so tasteful and gently pretty that his rudeness seemed amplified by contrast.

"How many girls in the troop?" Sue was asking.

"Twelve," said Sylvie, staring at the two boys who had come into the kitchen behind them.

"No problem. I've got just the thing," said Sue, opening the fridge and taking out a brown earthenware crock. "Spreadable cheese, and crackers. I've got some grapes, too."

Sylvie looked grateful.

"Hey, that's great," David said to Sue. He then made what Anita felt was a theatrical big deal of consulting his watch. "Actually, we were on our way out. We have dinner reservations," he lied. "Sylvie can tell you where her friends live."

Anita cast what she hoped was a subtle eye around the kitchen, shaped just like her own, but much cleaner. There was a homey baking smell here, like cinnamon. A row of gleaming copper pots hung over the stainless steel stove with six burners. It looked like a restaurant stove. A big antique wooden table had a bowl of green apples on it. Immaculate blue-and-white-checked dish towels were folded so the monogrammed *H* was centered perfectly. On the windowsill was a sweet potato suspended by toothpicks in a glass of water, sprouting leaves. Anita remembered that trick from kindergarten, and how much it had pleased her. Maybe Sylvie would think that was fun, too.

"I may as well run them all home, too," said Sue. "I stay for the whole thing anyway because I'm the assistant den mother." She started showing Sylvie just how thick to spread the cheese on the crackers before smashing them together.

"Oh, David," Anita said, "we can't let Sue do all this!"

"Oh, you two run along!" said Sue with a perky little wave of her hand. "It's great to be alone with each other once in a while, isn't it?" she added with a jokey, arch look. Much to Anita's relief, the hedge incident seemed to be receding.

"Well, thank you," said Anita. "It's really nice of you."

David started to lead Anita toward the front door, but Sue looked up, surprised. "No need to go all the way around!" she said. She pointed out the window. "You guys can just go through the hedge."

3

IN THE HEFFERNANS' BACKYARD, DAVID TOOK
Anita's hand, and laughed quietly. "Hey," he said, "that
worked out great."

"Do you think it's okay?" said Anita. "We don't even know
them. I mean, they seem so wholesome, but we really don't
know . . ." The swing set and sandbox loomed up in the
dusk. A little breeze set one of the swings creaking. They
made their way around them across a square, closely cropped
lawn edged in brick.

"Wholesome! They make Ozzie and Harriet look like the
Addams family," said David. "The place is a magazine layout.
Anyway, she seems like she loves schlepping kids around."
He led her through the archway in the hedge, inspecting
Sue's handiwork. "She did a good job hacking through here,
anyway," he said.

"She's obviously a supermom. The whole place was completely under control," said Anita. "Right down to the color of the apples on that rustic kitchen table."

"The husband looked like kind of a jerk, though," said David. "I bet he just stands back and lets her run around monogramming everything that's not nailed down. Did you get a look at those dish towels?"

Anita giggled and took her husband's arm, feeling the warm glow of shared bitchery. She was grateful for the dish towel remark. Her brief exposure to Sue Heffernan had made her feel hopelessly inadequate. Their houses may have been identical, but next to Sue's, their own house seemed unwelcoming, worn, and a little sad.

Lily was sitting at the kitchen table with the open pizza box and what looked like her math homework splayed out in front of her. Anita was relieved to see that she seemed to be over her sulks. Their daughter gazed up at them without animation, but without rancor, either, which was a plus.

"Thanks for ditching without leaving me money to pay the guy," she said, reaching for another slice. "You owe me from my baby-sitting money."

"Listen, we're going out for a quiet dinner for two," said David.

Lily bent her head way back and guided the point of a pizza triangle, dripping with double cheese, toward her mouth, pausing to say, "Trying to put a little zing back in the old marriage?"

THE NEXT MORNING, DAVID LAY IN THAT DELI-cious but tense state between sleep and actually having to get up and deal with the children. The fact that he and Anita had actually made love last night—kind of a quickie, maybe, but the real thing nevertheless—after a fabulous meal in an

Italian restaurant on Queen Anne Hill had reminded him how important sex really was. In the warmth of the down comforter, David absentmindedly reached into his pajamas and caressed his cock in the manner of a coach patting his star player after a good game.

It wouldn't kill Anita to go in to work a little later and get them off to school herself, he thought. After all, he always got his best ideas just as he was waking up. He felt a sudden burst of resentment. He'd let himself become beaten down. He'd talk about it with her as soon as she came home from work.

Just then it came to him—a sexy ad for the Conway's presentation. A couple, obviously great together in the sack, working together on a home improvement project in the bedroom. Then a neat little transition from wallpapering to nighttime—the couple getting between the sheets. The transition could come from the changing light in the window. It could end with the man putting out the light and the woman putting it back on—she wants to keep admiring the new wallpaper. He turns the light off again. To black. Some giggly, contented sounds from the woman. Then the voice-over and slogan in an updated typeface. All he needed now was some kind of slogan for the whole campaign.

David was beginning to see a whole series of TV ads. He'd get Mark Miller to do some fabulous storyboards for him. No one had ever sold hardware like he was going to. These would be ads about the things that are really important to people. Home. Work. Kids. Love. Sex.

Let's face it, sex took all the kinks out of things, stripped it all back down to the bare essentials. That was his idea—cut through the claptrap of modern life and find out what really made people happy. Then use it to sell them hot water heaters and doorknobs.

He had just rolled over on his stomach and promised himself ten more minutes when he heard a shrill and outraged scream from downstairs. It was Sylvie. Lily's screams were more like bellows. He put the covers over his head, hoping it was a temporary outburst. Then he heard feet pounding up the stairs, and Sylvie ran into the room. "Daddy, Daddy, come quick!" She was gasping.

"What is it?" he snapped, sitting up in bed.

She stood there rigid, her arms held straight, her little hands in fists. "There's something really icky on the ceiling!" When he didn't respond, she added frantically, "It's getting bigger."

"Calm down," he said, taking his time getting into his slippers. He followed her downstairs with a heavy sigh. "Bugs can't hurt you," he said.

"It's not a bug," she said, leading him into the living room and pointing up.

There, hanging from the beige ceiling, was a big bubble. The latex paint had formed a round sack that appeared to be full of liquid.

Lily wandered in from the kitchen. "It looks like a water balloon," she said, examining it thoughtfully. Then she looked at David. "New pajamas!" she said, examining his red and white checks. "They look like a tablecloth."

"It must be a plumbing leak," said David. "And we just painted, so the paint is nice and stretchy and holds the water."

"Do something," said Sylvie, wringing her hands.

It did look hideous. Because of the beige color, it resembled some kind of pustule on human skin. David decided he should lance it before it burst on its own.

"Get a bucket," he said to Lily. "And a fork."

He stood on the coffee table, with the bucket in one hand, and poked at the thing. Rusty water gushed out. He stepped down and positioned the plastic bucket beneath the spot, which was now a wet circle with some flaps of latex paint hanging down. A drip fell loudly into the bucket.

"Mom will be really pissed off," said Lily. "She just painted that ceiling."

"We'll get a plumber in here, and when they finish we can get out the paint and touch up that spot," said David airily. "Poking a hole in it like that ensures the spot won't get any bigger. The water needs a way out." The three of them stood there and watched another drip fall.

DAVID SAT AT HIS COMPUTER WEARING THE EAR-phones to Lily's Walkman, and reworked his creative philosophy, expanding it into a media rationale. TV was definitely the way to go, with maybe some very classy print to back it up. None of that depressing price-item shit. Mood stuff. It was an absolutely revolutionary approach to selling hardware, real cutting edge material. David thought maybe he should submit some of it for national awards. That'd keep the client impressed.

He'd been at it about an hour when he heard, over the music, the banging at the glass doors next to the desk. He pulled off his earphones. He glanced over nervously at the window and saw a vague shape there through the semi-opaque curtain. Some burglar, checking the place out? He thought about his paranoid, hedge-slashing new neighbors. David flicked back the curtain nervously. Sue Heffernan stood there in flowered chintz, head tilted a little shyly, smiling up at him. She held up a large cake for his inspection like someone in the final product shot of a commercial. It was a fluffy, frosted cake, wrapped in gleaming Saran Wrap.

David unfastened the latch and slid back the door.

"Hi!" Sue said cheerily. "I rang the doorbell but I guess you couldn't hear me. I felt so bad about the hedge, I've baked you a little peace offering."

Sure enough, as soon as she'd made that hole, she'd plunged right on through it, he thought. It was just as he had predicted. "Oh, you shouldn't have," he said, meaning it literally. He should have been more unpleasant last night. But then he remembered she'd taken Sylvie off their hands.

"Thanks for running the kids to Brownies," he said begrudgingly.

"No problem! She's a real little doll. I love little girls." Sue had worked her way halfway into the house now, and was glancing over at his computer. "Oh!" she said eagerly. "Are you working?"

"Trying to." David insinuated himself between her eyes and the screen. He hated to have people look at work in progress.

She set the cake down on the desk. "What do you do, exactly?"

"I'm in advertising," he said.

She nodded, and looked disappointed, which annoyed him. Most people thought advertising was glamorous. "Right now, I'm working on a campaign that revolves around family life in the nineties. Like how to incorporate traditional values in a modern setting," he said. "Working at home, raising kids, I've developed some insights that guys in offices just don't have." He realized he sounded as if he were already giving his Conway's presentation.

She perked up. "Wow. Interesting. I've thought a lot about that myself. I'd love to talk to you about it sometime."

"We'll have to do that," he said, slightly surprised that she had any kind of life of the mind. He had imagined she spent all her time color-coordinating pot holders and drying herbs. "But now, I'm afraid I have to get right back to it. I'm up against a real time crunch." He glanced down at the cake. "Thanks again."

"It needs to be refrigerated," she said. "There's whipped cream between the layers."

David felt a sudden flicker of interest. He loved whipped cream. He stood up to take the cake and see Sue out.

"I'll put it away," she said, gesturing him back to work with a casual wave. "Don't let me disturb you. I know the way, because we have the same floor plan, right?"

"Right. Thanks."

"Oh, I almost forgot." She fished in the big square pocket of the flowery garment David associated with nursery school teachers of another era—he seemed to remember they were called smocks—and pulled out what he recognized as Sylvie's Brownie sash. "I promised her I'd sew these on for her."

David was a little confused. Presumably she was referring to the merit badges. "Did they come loose or something?" he asked.

"They were safety-pinned on," said Sue. She picked up the cake and headed toward the stairs leading to the kitchen. "I'll get out of your hair now," she said. "I just wanted to do something nice since you seemed upset about the hedge."

"You've done more than enough." He watched her pick her way through the girls' messy piles of stuff all over the play-room, and hollered after her, "You can let yourself out the kitchen door, if you want."

He sat down and slipped the headphones back on, blot-ting out Sue's footsteps overhead with the Rolling Stones.

"HONEY, I'M HOME," ANITA SAID IN THE PAR-ody style that had been their private joke when he'd first quit his job. A rather grim joke, she thought now; another way she'd tried to mask all her resentment.

"I'm in the kitchen," he said. "How come you're so late?" He was sitting at the table, holding a glass of red wine.

"I called," she said, feeling defensive. "I left a message." The message had been purposely vague. In fact, she had met Frank, with the intention of telling him in person, as gently as possible, that she couldn't sleep with him, she was sorry, she just couldn't, it would just tear her apart with guilt.

Now, she toyed with the idea of telling David she'd had a drink with some women at work to celebrate a birthday. She hoped everyone had eaten by now.

"I had the headphones on most of the day," David enthused. "I did ten pages of notes—just ideas, mostly, but good stuff. Strong stuff. What do you want to do about dinner?"

Sylvie rushed into the room in her flighty way, hugged and kissed her mother, and ran back down to the playroom, answering Anita's "How was school?" with the usual "Fine."

Anita opened the refrigerator. "Oh," she said happily, "you cleaned the fridge. That horrible lake of dried ketchup is gone." She turned and smiled at him. "You're a sweetheart."

He got up from the table and came over to her side. "Was there ketchup there?"

"Don't tell me the girls cleaned it up!" said Anita, turning back to see if she'd imagined it. "And where did this cake come from?"

"Sue Heffernan. Our new neighbor. My God, I guess she cleaned up the ketchup, too."

"What was she doing here—prowling around the house?"

David shrugged. "Just the kitchen, I guess. She brought the cake because she said she was sorry about the hedge. I was working, so she said she'd put the cake in here."

Anita looked more closely. She distinctly remembered plastic bags of vegetables in various stages of freshness stuffed on the shelves. She slid open the vegetable drawer, where they were all neatly filed. "Look at this," she said. "She organized everything. See? The milk and juice are all in a neat row in the door." She examined them more closely. "With the use-by dates in order."

"Maybe she alphabetized the spices, too," said David.

"Too bad she didn't leave something in here we could eat for dinner," said Anita bitterly. Suddenly she felt very tired.

"Hey! I was on a roll," said David. "You can't program creativity. We can always order a pizza, but I can't order up a revolutionary ad campaign just like that." He snapped his fingers.

Lily walked into the kitchen.

"Hi, darling," said Anita, summoning up a smile.

"Pizza? We had pizza yesterday," whined Lily.

"There are some eggs. We could have scrambled eggs," suggested Anita brightly. She looked over at Lily. "We both had a hard day. Do you want to make them?"

"Too much homework," was the brusque reply. Lily left the kitchen and clomped upstairs, yelling, "Call me when dinner's ready!" over the banister.

Exasperated, Anita decided they could all fend for themselves. "Well, I'm not particularly hungry," she said mildly. "I think I'll sit in the living room, drink this glass of wine, and go to bed."

From the top step, Lily yelled, "Mom it's only eight o'clock."

Anita ignored her and went into the dark living room. She turned on a lamp. The room was a mess. Homework was strewn around, there were toys and crayons on the floor. On the sofa lay a half-crumpled tortilla chip bag surrounded by yellow crumbs. Some of the chips had fallen onto the floor and been ground into the rug. Sitting on the coffee table was a plastic bucket. She looked up to see a soggy blotch in the ceiling. "What's this?" she shrieked.

"A leak," said David. "I put the bucket there."

"Brilliant," said Anita sarcastically. "Did you call a plumber by any chance?"

"I was too busy," he snapped. "I'll do it tomorrow."

Anita peered into the bucket. A collection of soggy plaster triangles lay half submerged in the dirty-looking water. "Great! By tomorrow half the ceiling could have fallen down."

"You worry too much about this household stuff," he said. "Sit down. Relax. Let me tell you about my day."

A drip fell noisily into the bucket.

"How can I sit down and relax while the place is falling apart?" she demanded. "It's always a complete disaster. You never make dinner. The kids are all whiny and tense, probably because they live in chaos. I work hard all day at a job I don't particularly enjoy, and I don't deserve this!" She stopped to get her breath. "The least you could have done was call a plumber."

"Anita," he declared solemnly, "this is a crucial time for me. Can't you ever just be supportive?"

She let out a big sigh, and looked away. David responded, in a voice that sounded incredibly pompous to her, "Do you think that on some level you're threatened by my creativity?"

"Oh, for God's sake, David!" Anita took a sip of wine and put her head on the back of the sofa with her eyes closed so she wouldn't have to see the ceiling. "You sound like some talk radio shrink!"

"You haven't even asked about my ideas. I would think you'd be interested. It's our future." Now David sounded petulant.

"I will be glad to take a look at anything that is actually

done," she said, enunciating carefully to show she was angry. "Frankly, I've invested too much optimism in projects that you never carried through on."

She'd never said anything like this to him before. He didn't answer, and her words hung there in the silence. She thought about opening her eyes to see his reaction, but kept them steadfastly closed. If he was looking hurt, she'd feel pressured to back off, and then comfort him.

Finally, she said slowly, "After I take my bath, we should turn off the water at the main, so it won't drip all night. And tomorrow, you'd better call a plumber. It will only get worse."

The bath was a good idea in more ways than one. She was worried that the wonderful, musky smell of Frank's skin still clung to hers.

A NITA LAY IN THE HOT WATER AND LOOKED
at her body appreciatively. It really was as Frank had described it, she thought. "Delicate but voluptuous," he'd said,
his green eyes glowing with admiration. "Small and perfectly
proportioned." She felt sure he wasn't just admiring her in a
superficial way, though. He loved the way she looked because of the way he felt about her.

Anita knew this was true because of the way she felt about
him. Frank wasn't conventionally handsome—certainly nowhere near as good-looking as David. But now she found
everything about him beautiful.

Had it only been a few hours ago that Frank greeted her
outside the restaurant? A clean-cut young pianist was playing
some Jerome Kern tune, and the bar was buzzy and festive
with low-pitched conversation.

"Thank you for coming," he had said gravely. He had a thrilling voice.

"Well, it's just for a little while." She was embarrassed by his intensity. It had seemed only decent to tell him in person that she couldn't sleep with him. But in the end, of course, it had also been impossible.

She had been a nervous wreck on the way to his apartment, but as soon as she arrived there, she felt that everything would be all right. Instead of the flashy, slick, bachelor pad she expected, it was an old-fashioned apartment in a brick building on Capitol Hill, arranged around a courtyard. There were lots of pictures of his daughter Phoebe around, and some slightly worn, old-fashioned furniture his mother had given him when she'd moved into a condominium and he'd been divorced. "My ex got everything," he explained, "and I can't stand the thought of shopping for furniture." There was also a fabulous Oriental carpet, tall bookshelves, an expensive stereo system, and a charming fireplace. The bedroom was spare with a geometrically-patterned comforter on the bed, a plain bureau, and a television. The kitchen was a little sad. There was nothing much in the fridge but a jar of mayonnaise and some ketchup. The apartment was a quiet, peaceful place, but reflected Frank's loneliness, too, making him all the more attractive.

She washed herself slowly in Ivory soap, and smiled. Just a little fling. That's all she asked. Something to take the edge off, someplace where she could run and hide. That's probably all Frank wanted. He didn't know it—he acted as if he were in love with her—but it probably wouldn't last. Then, she'd be a good sport about it and fade back out of his life.

It wasn't until the water began to cool that she dragged herself out of the tub, wrapped herself in a terry robe, and crept quietly into the bedroom, hoping not to be heard.

There were raised, unhappy voices coming from below.

She could foresee a delegation trooping up the stairs to get her to settle some argument. Lately, Lily had taken to flatly refusing to do what David told her to, then appealing to Anita to take her side. And the girls were arguing constantly.

The bedroom was in half-darkness, but it didn't look the way it usually did. The light angling through the blinds was different. Again, Anita had the dreamlike sensation of the familiar mutating in some disturbing way. She went to the window and looked outside.

The change in the light pattern, she realized, was because all the shades were up and all the rooms brightly lit in the new neighbors' house. The facelike surface, for so many years a blank, now looked like a Halloween jack-o'-lantern. She closed the blinds firmly, kicked off her shoes, and lay down on the bed.

Maybe she had overreacted to that plumbing leak. It was because she'd had to walk in pretending everything was normal.

Her time with Frank had been short and intense and she'd left while she was all keyed up. She'd come straight home when she was still reeling, and here everything was a mess and there was no dinner and parts of the ceiling were in a bucket. And then, on top of all that, David had wanted her to be "supportive" about the account he was pitching.

From downstairs she heard the girls start up with their squabbling, then David's sharp, ineffectual snapping. He sounded, she decided with newfound cruelty, like one of those little dogs, bred down to a pointless size but still feisty, scrabbling on the other side of the door when you ring the doorbell.

She put her head under the pillow and thought about calling her mother and telling her how she felt right now. Not about Frank. God forbid. But about how tired she was all the time and how much she didn't like coming home anymore. She knew what her mother would say—what her mother always said in her blunt, tactless way: "I think David should get a job."

How Anita had once sneered at her mother. "Money isn't the main ingredient in a relationship," Anita had replied, implying that her own generation was a better and more idealistic one than her mother's.

She tossed a little in the bed and cataloged all the things in her mind that David should be taking care of and wasn't. She wanted to tell him: "You have to do a better job around here. You have to make dinner and pick up the living room. You should cart those boxes of your aunt Martha's crap to the Salvation Army or something. They've been sitting there for months. You're supposed to make sure we don't run out of milk and bread and clean towels. You have to handle the girls' fighting better, and you should call a plumber. If you don't, I'll be miserable. We'll all be miserable. I'm exhausted when I come home from work." But she realized she wouldn't say any of these things to him. What was the point? David would never change. Nothing would ever change.

She stopped thinking and fell into a dozy, beaten-down stupor, then, with an angry start she remembered again what David had said down there in the living room. "I need you to be supportive."

Supportive! She'd been supporting him and the children for years. Ever since he'd flounced out of the advertising agency. Sure, there'd been a period when they lived on his retirement fund, paid in a lump sum after he'd resigned "on principle."

He had managed to get one small client, a SAAB dealer, to go with him, and everything looked okay for a while, but when the dealership was sold to a competitor, the business went to the new owner's agency.

Anita had had to go back to Lawson's, selling on the floor.

This time, though, she took night courses in retail management and worked her butt off to make buyer. Now, she had
to make sure she kept that job. Her younger boss had done
some ruthless firing last year, replacing older buyers with
younger ones. Everyone dreaded another round. There were
always rumors the store was for sale, too, in which case they
could all be gone.

Thinking about it now, Anita admitted to herself for the
very first time that she'd been a first-class sucker. They were
one job away from losing everything—health insurance,
maybe the house. If David didn't get the Conway's account,
she'd absolutely insist he look for a job. Maybe he could
teach advertising at a community college or something. That
would be a state job with benefits and a pension.

From the other side of the bedroom door she heard
Sylvie's voice. "Mo-om?"

Anita sighed. "What is it?" she said.

"You have to help me with my homework." Sylvie rushed
in, carrying a book and a folder with a clutch of papers
sticking out of it. She jumped onto the bed next to Anita
with a big squeak of bedsprings. "See? It says so, right here."

Anita struggled into a sitting position, flicked on the light,
and read the mint-green sheet Sylvie was flapping at her.
"Your homework is to read to a parent for twenty minutes
and discuss what you read. Answer the questions on the back
of this paper."

"Okay," she said, trying to look happy. Sylvie's teacher
was constantly sending home projects for the parents to do
with the children. Anita resented it, but not as much as
David, who announced that when he was a kid he did his
own homework, and seeing as he was with the girls all day,
Anita could at least take care of all the stuff that came home
from school.

The materials that arrived weekly in the Wednesday folder

seemed based on the idea that first and foremost children needed quality time with their parents, mandated by the school authorities, and that secondly parents would benefit from instruction from the children in correct living. Anita had already traipsed through the house with Sylvie looking for fire hazards, leading her away from outlets overburdened with plugs. She had also been subjected to a water conservation checklist during which she found herself apologizing for how many gallons of water the toilet used and for letting the water run when she brushed her teeth and taking baths that were too deep, like the one she'd just had.

Sometimes, Lily also had homework requiring parental participation. "Talk to your parents about drug abuse," or some questionnaire about "teens and peer pressure" or "anger management." Anita wondered what drug-addicted parents, or the Cambodian immigrants who didn't speak English, made of all this, or how those old-fashioned families she remembered from her own childhood, with five children, could possibly cover all the bases when this stuff arrived home. And didn't they realize a lot of women had to work all day, for heaven's sake?

"Got your book? Good. Tuck in with me, sweetie," she said, folding back the covers. "Take off your shoes, first."

She closed her eyes and tried to pay attention to a story about some children who rode around Manhattan on the backs of dinosaurs, then waited while Sylvie got up three times to find first a pencil, then a pencil sharpener, and finally an eraser. Anita watched her daughter laboriously fill in the answers to "Who was the main person in the story?" "Did that person have a problem?" "How did they solve the problem?" "Did you like the story?"

When they finished, Sylvie said, "Here's some other stuff for you," and began handing more paperwork to Anita in the manner of an executive secretary.

"Do we have to do this now?" said Anita wearily.

"Yes!" said Sylvie. "I have to return all this stuff in my Wednesday folder with your signature on it! It's part of my homework. I don't want a bad grade!"

Anita plowed through the aquarium field trip consent form, feeling her habitual shame as she checked the "No, I cannot drive for this field trip," and skimmed the announcement of the annual parent-teacher-student barbecue and the science fair, both requiring her to say whether or not she could volunteer, as well as an alarming memo from the school nurse about head lice and a flier advertising a workshop on developing your child's self-esteem. Finally, all the papers were refiled in the folder, and Anita kissed Sylvie. "Now, darling, I need a nap, okay?"

"I wish you could come to the aquarium," Sylvie said plaintively, snuggling down under the comforter. "Shannon's mom comes to all the field trips."

"I'm sorry, darling, but my boss won't let me," said Anita.

"What about the barbecue?" said Sylvie, squirming to a sitting position. "It's at lunchtime. Can't you come at lunchtime?"

"We'll see," said Anita. "Maybe." She'd have to take the car downtown in order to make it there and back in time.

Sylvie sighed, and her little shoulders slumped. Anita embraced her and said in an urgent voice, "I wish I could do more things at school, but I just can't, sweetie. I have to work, and my boss, Pam, doesn't have any kids of her own and she doesn't seem to understand how mothers want to spend more time with their children."

"Really?" said Sylvie, clearly astonished at this lack of insight.

Anita was grateful for a way to deflect the conversation from her own parental shortcomings. "Yes. It's kind of sad, isn't it?" she said. "I feel sorry for Pam."

"She sounds mean to me," was Sylvie's verdict.

Downstairs, the doorbell rang. "Did Daddy order pizza after all?" asked Anita in an encouraging voice.

"Oh, boy," said Sylvie, scampering away, leaving the hated folder on the bed. Anita flung the loathsome object with its guilt-producing contents on the floor and fell back on the pillows with relief.

She'd stay right here. She was hungry, but she was afraid that if she went downstairs she might start fighting with David in front of the girls. She knew she was too ragged to control herself right now.

Ten minutes later, David came into the room and flicked on the light. He carried a tray. She propped herself up on her elbows and stared at him, her eyes adjusting to the glare.

"I've brought you some dinner," he said in a conciliatory tone.

"Pizza?"

"No, we had pizza yesterday. We sent out for Chinese."

"Thank you," she said wearily. "But I can come downstairs. I just needed a rest."

"I'm sorry about the leak," he said. "I can see you've had a rough day. I'll call the plumber first thing tomorrow. I even put a Post-it note with 'plumber' written on it on the bathroom mirror to remind myself."

She felt weak and exhausted and confused. She began to cry.

"Anita!" he said, putting down the tray on the bureau and coming to her side. "You poor thing. You're a wreck, aren't you?" He put his arms around her and she put her face on his shoulder and wept into his shirt.

"I love you," he said, patting her gently on the back.

"I love you, too," she said tearfully, wishing it were true.

As HE DROVE THE GIRLS TO SCHOOL THE NEXT day, David thought Anita seemed more stressed out than usual. Sometimes she was more fragile than he realized. He'd get those plumbers on the job. And he'd try to get a little more organized around the house. Having dinner ready when she got home, that would be a nice touch.

The last thing he needed, now that he was finally working on something in earnest, was to have Anita fall apart on him. He remembered that when he'd worked at the ad agency, he'd sometimes come home all wired from work and find things in a big mess with Anita all wrung out and the baby, Lily, crying. He'd really resented it, but he'd hung in there, and he hadn't lost it like she had yesterday evening. Maybe her job drained her more than he realized. He'd try and do a better job around the house.

"Look," cried Sylvie from the backseat. "It's Sue."

David saw his neighbor walking her children to school. The two boys were trudging along, bent over under backpacks like a couple of midgets going on a long hike. Sue was walking between them and talking, holding her hands out rather gracefully.

"Who's Sue?" asked Lily.

"Our new neighbor," answered David, thinking how wholesome and healthy it was to be walking the kids to school instead of driving them. Of course, Sue had nothing better to do. David was always in a rush. In fact, today, he had left with a raincoat over his red-and-white-checked pajamas, and slippers on his feet.

Sylvie was waving enthusiastically at Sue and her boys. This made David slightly uncomfortable. Was he supposed to stop and offer them a ride? He put his foot down on the gas and zoomed away.

But on the way home, after delivering Sylvie and then Lily, he saw Sue again, walking home alone. She had her hands in the pockets of a beige cardigan, and there was a pleasant, alert expression on her face. He pulled over, feeling guilty about passing her earlier.

"Want a ride?" he said, leaning over to the passenger side window.

"Hi!" she said with a big smile. "That'd be great."

He opened the door and she slid in, fastening her seat belt. She turned her face toward him and said without a moment's hesitation, "It was so interesting learning a little about your work yesterday. I'm really intrigued with the idea that working at home has made you more sensitive to family issues. It seems like no one appreciates what people who work at home do. You know, that 'I'm just a housewife' thing."

"No one should underestimate the value of running a home properly," said David solemnly. "When people hear I'm a househusband, they get very weird. They can't handle the idea of a man running a house, no matter how politically correct they pretend to be."

"But you have your other work, too," said Sue.

"It's taken a real backseat to looking after the kids," said David. "I've learned that there are more important things than money." At tax time, he'd been humiliated to see that his annual billings had amounted to three thousand dollars.

"I think that's a very healthy attitude," said Sue admiringly. "And so rare."

"Thanks," he said, turning for just an instant with a smile, before looking back at the road.

"Roger could learn a lot from you. You seem to have given these ideas some real thought."

"Well, writing, even advertising writing, means you have to think about things that are important to people."

"Roger isn't always in touch with his feelings. It can be hard on everyone," Sue said solemnly. She lowered her voice and said in an even more serious tone, "I think getting to know you could help him."

The conversation had taken such an intimate tone so quickly. He hardly knew these people. David was alarmed by the prospect of buddying around with Roger, and providing him with sensitivity training. Neither did he relish the idea of further revelations about his neighbors. The last thing he needed was to get sucked in to their family dramas.

They pulled up to a stop sign, and David glanced over at the car in the lane next to him, a shiny white Lexus. As he often did, he felt rather shabby in the old Volvo wagon he was driving. They'd bought it new, years ago when Lily was a baby. Now, it was pretty much beat up inside and out, but it kept chugging steadfastly along, and they couldn't really afford a new car. He supposed they were stuck with it forever.

"I think men who are in touch with their feelings are pretty rare," said Sue.

David gave a grunt of agreement, and looked at the man in the Lexus. He had one tan hand draped casually over the steering wheel, a glint of gold watch showing beneath an immaculate starched white cuff. The other hand held a cellular phone to his ear. His head was tilted back and he was laughing, revealing perfect white teeth. He was so happy that his eyes were little slits. David knew he was talking to some hot babe. Someone he'd just spent the night screwing up one side and down the other while she begged for more.

"Gosh," said Sue, looking down at David's knee. The raincoat had parted, revealing his vivid red and white checks. "You're wearing pajamas."

David snapped his raincoat back over the offending red and white checks. He hated these pajamas, which Anita had bought at some rock bottom price at the store. He could see her now, picking through a bin of rejects in the bargain basement. With her discount they probably set her back three bucks. The son of the bitch in the Lexus, if he wore pajamas at all, probably wore white silk ones, presented to him by a grateful lover.

"Yeah, I'm in a hurry in the mornings sometimes," David said. He thought about giving her a big smile to show he was a reckless, crazy kind of guy, but he was too depressed.

The man in the Lexus had stopped laughing. Now, he seemed to be crooning into the phone. David had been right. He was talking to a woman. Now he was probably telling her all the exciting things he would do to her when they met again. With his eyes unscrunched, the guy looked vaguely familiar.

Sue peered down around the gearshift. "And slippers, too," she said with a start of delight, as if this were the most unusual, wild, bohemian thing she'd ever seen.

"Mmmm," David said, now completely transfixed with the man in the Lexus. It wasn't just that he represented everything David wasn't. He realized suddenly that he was looking at Skip MacDougal, his assistant back at the ad agency, years ago. He'd hired Skip right out of the University of Washington School of Communications, and Skip had followed him around the office like a puppy.

David remembered the day he'd quit, and Skip had come to him and said, "I really admire you, David. You've really got balls. And talent. I wish I could quit, too, but I'm just getting started. I have to hang in here."

David tried to remember his real name, and wondered if he was still calling himself Skip these days. From the haircut to the expensive-looking suit to the light tan, he oozed prosperity and confidence. David stared some more, dimly aware that Sue was chattering at him about something.

Skip, still on the phone, turned toward the old Volvo. Feeling like an animal caught in the headlights, David slid down behind the wheel and ran his fingers through his hair in an attempt to obscure his face. The last thing David wanted was for Skip to see him schlepping some housewife neighbor around in an old beater. And in his pajamas, for Christ's sake!

"Take our decision on a home," Sue went on. "I've never lived in an older home before. Roger's always insisted we live in the suburbs, but this time I thought charm would be kind of neat. It took me a long time to convince him that home is my work, as important to me as his career is to him." She gave David a little pat on his arm. "Hey, the light's green now."

Skip MacDougal had pulled away while David had been sliding down toward the pedals. He straightened up, yanked the car into gear, and the Volvo rabbitted into the intersection half a block behind the Lexus.

"These older houses can be a headache," said David, trying to sound self-possessed. "I've got to deal with the plumbing today. There's a leak in the living room ceiling."

"Oh, no!" said Sue sympathetically.

David shook his head sadly. "And just when I was getting a leg up on my new campaign. Now I've got to hassle with that all day." Of course, Skip MacDougal wouldn't have to hassle with anything. He probably lived in some stunning penthouse where a team of technicians made sure everything ran like clockwork—a place with a fabulous view of Puget Sound and good art on the walls.

As they pulled up in front of her house, Sue lowered her eyelids and asked, "How was the cake?"

"The cake! It was fabulous. I should have said so." She looked relieved. Evidently, failing to mention the cake had been a major gaffe.

"What with the leak and my work and all, I forgot to thank you. It was terrific." It had in fact been an excellent cake, moist and fluffy, and the whipped cream had a slight almond flavor he liked.

Sue sat there in the front seat smiling at him for a second before she thanked him and got out. He felt as if he were dropping a girl off after a high school date.

Back in the house, David called a plumber he found in the Yellow Pages. A woman told him someone would be out later. He made coffee and took it down to his work area, reviewing the work he'd done the day before on the computer screen. It looked pretty damn good. Despite Anita's lack of interest, he was making real progress.

He thought about his conversation with Sue in the car earlier, when she'd said her home was her career. This was the old fifties take that everyone had sneered at for so long. But Sue didn't seem like some June Cleaver fifties mom whipping up meat loaves and Jell-O surprises. There was obviously some sophisticated taste behind all her domestic efforts. It showed in her house. Maybe it was time to re-evaluate a few attitudes before he got into his campaign.

David sensed that Sue might be helpful to him there. Here was someone who took both home and garden seriously, saw their connection to the family, clearly relished domestic life. And still managed to exude a pleasant serenity. Serenity. That was what was lacking in most modern families. David sensed that on some visceral level, Sue could provide some insights. She could even serve as a one-person focus group to bounce ideas off of.

SHE CAME BY A COUPLE OF HOURS LATER, RAP-ping lightly on the kitchen door. David had been upstairs in the living room with the plumber, a grizzled man with black horn-rimmed glasses. The plumber was up on a ladder pulling away plaster from the ceiling with a ruthlessness David found unsettling.

This time, Sue was carrying a big round glass dish just like one he and Anita owned. For a moment, he thought it was theirs. "I accidentally made too much of this," she said apologetically, "and I thought, since you were working on that plumbing all day, maybe I could help you out. It's real easy to heat up." She held it out for his inspection. Under Saran Wrap he had a brief impression of pasta and very finely grated Parmesan or Romano.

"Wow! That's really thoughtful. Come on in," he said. "Actually, I ended up calling a plumber. I don't have time to do the work myself."

Still holding the casserole, she followed David into the living room. The plumber had torn away a whole chunk of ceiling, leaving a black hole with a dirty-looking metal pipe running across it. He gestured at it with a flashlight. "This pipe just gave out," he said. "It happens. Take a look at that hole. Just rusted through." He started down the ladder.

"I know you aren't going to want to hear this," he continued with the mournful but resigned air of someone who habitually delivered bad news, "but these old galvanized pipes don't last forever. We can open up the ceiling and replace that section, but I can't guarantee that you won't get a leak somewhere else. You might want to consider replumbing the whole thing with copper."

"Good idea," said Sue. "Besides, modern plumbing minimizes the dangers of lead in the water supply."

"She's right," said the plumber, nodding gravely. "Lead in old pipes, that can cause brain damage in children." He went on in the deceptively matter-of-fact tones of the fanatic. "It's my opinion that outdated plumbing is why we have so many people on welfare and in prisons in this country." He shook his head sadly and got back to business. "Like I say, we can just do that one section if you want. But I might be back here a week later and have to tear into everything again. After you've had the ceiling put back together."

"Can't you do that?" said David.

"Sorry. We're plumbers."

"How much will it cost to replumb everything?" asked David, alarmed.

The plumber frowned up at the ceiling. "About three thousand dollars. I'll write you up an estimate. We can bring it all up to code."

"And how much if you just do that one leak?" David asked.

He shrugged. "About a hundred and fifty. This time."

David's impulse was to hire the guy to fix the part that was broken, but Sue, squinting up at the big wound in the ceiling, said, "That pipe looks like it's rusted all through. I bet you'll have more problems later if you don't get new copper pipe in here."

What was she, a shill for the plumber?

"I'm afraid your wife's right," said the plumber. Addressing Sue directly, he said, "It depends how much you value peace of mind."

"I'm just a neighbor," said Sue, flustered.

"We're married, but not to each other," said David jokily. Sue giggled.

"Oh," said the plumber, turning back to David with an air of condescension. "If you can't afford it, we'll just do the one section."

"I can afford it," said David stiffly. "Go ahead, write up an estimate."

The plumber went down to the basement to make some more investigations. "You're doing the right thing," said Sue, "but I'd get another estimate. We had some work done after we moved in. The people we had were great. I'll call them for you. And don't forget to include the cost of replastering and repainting in your budget. Get this guy to tell you just where he'll have to open up the walls and ceilings." She seemed terribly competent and self-assured. David felt once again that he'd underestimated her.

"I hate all this stuff," he said plaintively.

To his surprise, she laughed. A nice friendly laugh. It was as if she found his resistance to home repairs endearing, somehow. "Really?" she said. "I just love this stuff. I'm a great little organizer. Let me make a few phone calls for you."

"Really?" said David. "But I can't impose anymore." He looked down at the casserole. "You even made dinner." He took it from her awkwardly.

"Let me tell you a little secret," she said playfully, lowering her voice and her lashes. "I have way too much energy for one person. I love to help out. I get such a kick out of it. Roger says that if General Motors was in the business of running homes, I'd be chairman of the board." She glanced down at the big glass dish. "Just cook it for half an hour at three fifty," she told him. With a look of concern, she added, "You guys aren't vegetarians or anything, are you? There's ham in it."

"No, we're not," he said, laughing.

"Well, that's good to know," she said. "Anyway, kids love this, but so do adults. It's got a basic macaroni and cheese feel, but the ingredients are just a little more subtle, for the grown-ups."

After she left, David thought about her for quite a while. He hadn't met anyone like Sue Heffernan before. Boy, there was one happy homemaker. She absolutely relished domestic life. She was clearly thrilled with her own homey skills. How often did you hear a housewife say, "God, I'm good!"

That evening when Anita came home, she went into the living room and looked up at the ceiling. "Oh, no! It looks a lot worse!" she said.

"The plumber had to tear away more plaster to see what was wrong," David replied icily. "He can't get to it right away. Besides, we have a decision to make. These old pipes are just giving out. He says we should replumb the whole house."

"Of course he does," said Anita. "Can't he just fix that part?"

"These old galvanized pipes don't last forever. I think we should get it all squared away and up to code."

"How much will that cost?" she demanded in an exasperated tone.

"About three thousand," he said.

"Three thousand! We don't have three thousand dollars."

David shrugged. "We can borrow it. You make a good salary. Anyway, I have a hunch I'll get that Conway's account and we can pay it all back then."

Anita started to say that they couldn't count on any of his theoretical future earnings. But what was the point in undermining him just as he was showing some initiative? She should try not to be so negative.

"Just relax," he said, stroking her shoulder.

"Something smells fabulous," she said, feeling more cheerful all of a sudden. She turned to him, and her tense expression vanished. "Oh, sweetheart, you made dinner. I'm so happy. It smells like those casseroles my mom used to make." She put her arms around him and said in a grateful voice, "You remembered how stressed out I was last night and made a point of having dinner ready, didn't you?"

David patted her on the back. "Yes, sweetheart. And don't worry about the plumbing, either. I'll take care of everything. Just trust me."

5

SYLVIE AND MATT WERE COLORING IN THE Heffernans' downstairs playroom. Sylvie liked it that they had a little table and chairs down here, just like the kindergarten kids had. There was a little kid-sized sofa, too. Chris was getting a little too big for the kid sofa, though. He was slouched there with his legs and one arm sprawled over the edges. His other hand held the controller, which he pointed at the screen while he played Nintendo.

The game went "boing boing boing," and when Chris killed someone or got killed, it made a big crashing sound and he'd draw in his breath sharply, or yell, "Oh, man!"

At first, Sylvie had thought Chris was scary because he was a fourth grader and a boy and so big and loud, and he got so mad when he played his video game, but she was getting used to him.

Sylvie was drawing a house. Lots of times, Sylvie didn't know what to draw and then she always made a house with a pointed roof just like her house and the Heffernans' house. It always had two windows on top with crosses on the windows to make the panes, and a chimney with big curly smoke coming out, and a door and another window below. Next to the house, she usually drew a tree with apples on it. She was doing the apples now, making little circles with the red crayon. Today she'd do a pony next to the house, with a little fence around him. Ponies were hard, though.

She put down the red crayon and looked for a gray one. She wanted the pony to have gray spots. The crayons here were never broken. It was wonderful. And once, when the yellow-green one did break, Sue Scotch-taped the paper wrapping back together and it really worked. Sue seemed to know what kids liked.

Sylvie glanced over at Matt's picture. He was drawing a robot, as he often did. He always used the black crayon and made complicated robots with all the little screws drawn on and stiff arms that had wrenches and grenades in them. Sometimes he made the eyes red or yellow, with matching lights on the big, square head.

Suddenly, Sue came to the top of the stairs. "Chris!" she called down. "Video game time is over!"

"But I'm not dead yet!" he said.

"Chris!" Sue said in a firm, but sweet voice. She had strict rules about video games. Chris could play them for one half hour after school, and another half hour after his homework was done.

"Yeah, yeah, yeah," he said, switching off the controller and flinging it away. The room was suddenly quiet. He fell back on the sofa, and stared at the ceiling. "Hey, Matt," he said. "There's a spider up there. For the spider zoo."

Sylvie looked up and saw the spider. They had them in

the basement at home, too. Spiders and basements just seemed to go together. She didn't like them much, but on the ceiling, they were okay. "What's the spider zoo?" she asked after concentrating for a moment on the pony's head.

Matt cleared his throat and kept on coloring. "We collect spiders," he said. "We've got twenty-three of them in a box."

Sylvie was simultaneously repelled and fascinated. "Can I see them?" she said.

"If we show you, you have to touch them," said Chris. "But you're probably afraid of spiders."

"No, I'm not." Sylvie didn't really want to touch one, though.

"Don't tell Mom about the spiders, okay?" said Matt.

"Okay," said Sylvie. Maybe she could touch one just with the tip of her finger. "I'll do it. Can I see them?"

Chris came over to the table and grinned down at her. "We have races with them, and when they lose, we tear off one leg. You're going to have to tear one off if you want to see them."

"That's mean!" said Sylvie. "You guys are sick."

Matt, working on a troublesome bit of detail in his robot picture, had the tip of his tongue between his teeth.

"Do you really tear off their legs?" Sylvie asked Matt.

Matt waited a long time, then he smiled and said, "No."

Chris laughed. "He pretends to be a real goody-goody, but he's the one that invented the game. He's really sick." Chris contorted his face to look like some kind of a drooling monster.

She wished they'd drop the subject. After Sue was finished waxing the floor, she was going to teach Sylvie how to make fudge. You needed a candy thermometer, and it sounded kind of neat. Sue had all kinds of neat things in her kitchen, like candy thermometers and melon scoops and a little china blackbird for pie juice to bubble up in. It almost made it okay to play with Matt and Chris, because she got to do fun stuff with Sue.

Chris sat down in one of the tiny chairs at the table and pulled it right next to Sylvie's. He put his face really close to hers and said, "Matt is such a weirdo, he wanted to pull all the legs off one of the spiders so it would just be a little round blob, and then it would starve to death."

Sylvie started to shake. "I'm telling your mom!" she said, flinging down the crayon.

Chris grabbed her wrist. "You better not," he said. "My brother's a vampire. He'll come and suck all the blood out of you at night!"

"Shut up!" said Sylvie. Chris was hurting her wrist and she was afraid he might hit her or something if she told.

She pulled her wrist away in a snaky little motion and, feeling braver, she said, "Anyway, Matt's nicer. If anyone's a vampire, it's you."

"Wrong!" said Chris. "Vampires act all sweet and innocent, and then!" He jumped up and made his hands into claws a few inches from her face.

"You have to invite them in, though," said Matt, still coloring. "They can't come in your house unless you invite them in. That's the rule."

"Who'd invite a vampire into their house?" scoffed Sylvie.

"You don't know they're vampires until later, dummy."

"I know a joke about vampires," said Chris.

"What is it?" said Sylvie. A joke about vampires sounded safer. She remembered the Count from *Sesame Street*. He was a joke vampire with muppet bats.

"What does a vampire pack in his lunch?" said Chris.

"I don't know," said Sylvie.

"A Kotex sandwich," said Chris.

Sylvie looked bemused.

"I guess you don't even know what Kotex is," sneered Chris. "It's a thing for periods."

"Stop it!" said Sylvie. She got up and pushed the crayons away. "You are so gross."

Sylvie knew about periods, and had found the subject disturbing ever since she saw a big bloodstain once on Lily's sheet, and Lily told her it was her period that came sooner than she thought. But Mom had explained that it was perfectly natural, and it meant you were growing up and it wasn't a gross thing at all, and really it was a good thing because it meant you could have darling little babies someday, but it was a private, woman thing. Which was why Chris shouldn't be talking about it at all.

Sue came back to the top of the stairs. "Sylvie!" she called out. "Ready to make fudge?"

With a surge of relief, Sylvie started to scramble away, but before she did, Chris hissed at her, "Don't tell Mom about the spiders or you'll be really sorry."

"Come on, sweetie," said Sue.

Matt pushed his glasses up. "Can I help?" he yelled plaintively up the stairs.

"No, honey. You boys stay down there. I'm going to spend some time just with Sylvie."

Good! That served them right. Even Matt, who was never really mean, was kind of creepy. His robot pictures were unpleasant and he just sat there while Chris said all those gross things like it was no big deal. Maybe he really did torture spiders.

Once in the safety of the kitchen, Sylvie felt kind of wobbly. She didn't have to act strong now. There were even tears in the corners of her eyes.

"What's the matter, honey?" said Sue, kneeling down in front of her and putting her hands on Sylvie's shoulders.

"Sometimes the boys are mean," she said.

"Don't pay any attention to them," Sue said. She gave Sylvie a hug. "Boys aren't like little girls. They can't help it."

Sylvie collapsed into the hug against Sue's soft shoulder. She felt safer now. She was glad Sue didn't ask what the boys had said. She didn't want to tell on them, because then Chris might hurt her.

"I'll tell you a secret, Sylvie," Sue whispered into her ear. "I love my boys, but I always wanted a little girl. That's why, as soon as I saw you, I knew I wanted to be with you and we could do special things together. I don't know if your mom and dad wanted you to be a girl, but I'm sure glad you are."

Sylvie pondered this last remark as Sue tied an apron on her and got the step stool for her to stand on next to the stove. Once, when she and Lily had a really bad fight, Lily screamed, "Mom and Dad didn't even plan you. And then, you were a girl and they already had one."

When Sylvie had run downstairs to ask Dad about it, he'd kissed her and said, "Of course we wanted you, pumpkin," only to be followed by Lily, who had stomped into the room and yelled, "Dad said you were a big surprise! I heard him!"

Dad had given Lily a really dirty look, and said, "A wonderful surprise."

Did Sue know something about all this? Sylvie guessed her parents wanted her now that she was here.

"Did you want Matt to be a girl?" Sylvie asked Sue as she watched squares of chocolate melting in the double boiler.

"I always wanted a daughter," said Sue. "A little girl just like you."

IT HAD BEEN ABOUT A MONTH SINCE SUE HEF-fernan had cut a hole in the hedge, and now she seemed to have trimmed it again. Anita noticed it from the kitchen window when she and David and the girls were sitting down to a big dinner of lasagne and salad.

"Looks like old Sue's been wielding the hedge clippers again," she said in a kidding · way. "The opening is all neatened up and she seems to have lopped another six inches off the top. I assume she got your okay, David."

He'd been so nasty about it at the time, but now he seemed incredibly chummy with their new neighbor. He'd even conned her into walking Sylvie to school with her boys every morning.

David looked out the window. "She's been talking about putting a little gate there," he said. "She showed me a picture of one in an English garden in some magazine. I think it will look very attractive."

"That sounds nice," said Anita. "Aren't you glad I went over there with you and saved you from making a complete idiot of yourself that first night?" David didn't reply, and Anita persisted. "After all, now that Sue is walking Sylvie to school every day and Lily's taking the bus, you get to sleep in." She smiled as if she were just teasing him, but she knew she was being bitchy. She couldn't seem to help herself. She didn't understand why the more David got his act together, the more she seemed to resent him. For the past month or so, ever since she'd collapsed in bed and told him he had to do a better job, everything seemed suddenly cleaner, and more organized and restful.

Nowadays it wasn't coming home to the breakfast dishes that brought on these sudden jabs of frustrated anger. It was David himself.

David laid down his fork. "Sue only offered to walk Sylvie to school because she walks her boys there every day anyway," he said with petulant dignity. "And she knows I'm pushing hard on the campaign. I'm not using that time to sleep in. I'm working."

"I was just kidding!" said Anita lightly. He had surprised her by sounding hurt instead of irritated. She didn't like him to sound hurt. It put her in the wrong and gave him a moral victory. The girls ate in watchful silence, like judges on the sideline in a tennis match, but she was pretty sure they couldn't sense the depth of hostility beneath her banal remarks.

Just in case, she decided she had better try to be pleasant. "This is a great dinner, David," she said warmly. But then she heard herself adding with a little smile, "I'm glad you've thrown yourself into this campaign about domestic happiness. It seems to have made you a better househusband."

Lily gave her mother a wary, sidelong glance.

Anita, feeling a heavy burden of carrying the entire family's conversation, turned to Sylvie. "How's school?" she said. "Do you like walking?"

"It's cool," said Sylvie. "Sue tells us stories on the way."

"That's nice," said Anita, reaching over and stroking Sylvie's hair possessively. Did Sue, chirping away telling stories to her child every morning, hold her hand, too?

"The Heffernans are having lasagne tonight, too," announced Sylvie.

"Sue creeps me out," interjected Lily. "When I get home from school, she's always hanging around here, dropping stuff off or just snooping. I can't stand her."

"She's nice," protested Sylvie.

"Oh, God!" snapped Lily. "That shows how much you know."

"Jesus," snarled David. "I'm sick of all this fighting. No more talk about the Heffernans." Anita flinched a little at the surprising outburst.

Sylvie looked surprised and hurt. "How come?"

"Oh, I'm just sick of talking about them." He helped himself to more salad. "Let's talk about something else."

"Now that we have these organized meals and all," said Lily, "I guess we're going to have to learn how to talk like those TV families that eat real dinners. Everyone saying what happened at school and stuff."

"I think it's very pleasant to have a meal every night at the same time," replied Anita, pleased to be able to say something positive. "I didn't realize it, but we had sort of turned into a family of grazers."

"Yes, we had," said David forcefully. "That kind of casualness creeps up on you. You have to make a conscious effort to make family life a priority. Lots of course correction. Real analysis of the problems."

"What problems?" said Sylvie.

"We don't have any problems, darling," said Anita. "Daddy meant other people and their problems."

There was a little silence, during which Anita felt an oppressive sadness lingering over them all. Lily pleased her by saying in an uncharacteristically cheerful voice, "Hey, Mom, if I set my alarm for when you get up, will you French braid my hair?"

"Of course, darling. Your hair is perfect for it." Anita gave her daughter a big smile.

Later that evening, Anita sat on Sylvie's bed in the semidark and tucked her in. Sylvie smiled sleepily at her mother, and Anita remembered how as babies the girls had that same lovely, goofy, heavy-lidded look right after she'd nursed them. Milky little roundheaded babies falling asleep, smooth blank faces radiating blissful peace.

"Does Sue tell fun stories?" asked Anita. "What are they about?"

"They're dumb stories," said Sylvie. "About squirrels and bunnies and stuff. But it's kind of neat, anyway."

"Sylvie," said Anita, trying to sound casual, "how did you know the Heffernans were having lasagne? Just like us?"

"I helped!" said Sylvie, opening her eyes back up and look-ing surprised that Anita didn't know. "We made two. One for them and one for us. I grated the cheese."

"You and Daddy?" Anita had tensed up.

Sylvie put a hand on her mother's shoulder. "Me and Sue." She looked worried. "Sue said her mom had to work and didn't have time to teach her to cook, just like you, so she wants to teach me. That's okay, isn't it?"

Anita kissed her daughter's forehead and tried not to let on that she was upset. Sue was well-meaning, but she had no business undermining Anita like that. There was, however, no reason Sylvie should be made to feel disloyal. "Of course, darling," she said. "Don't worry about it. I wish I could be with you more, but I just can't. You understand that, don't you?"

"Yeah." Sylvie reached up with both hands and fingered Anita's gold earrings. "I love these," she said. "They're so smooth."

"Maybe when you're big I'll give them to you," she said, smiling.

"Oh, boy!"

"And darling, I put your Wednesday folder by the door so you won't forget it." Anita realized how pathetic it was that she was proud of having remembered this detail of Sylvie's life.

"It's okay, Mom. Sue always reminds me. Oh, and Sue is making cupcakes with lemon frosting for the barbecue, and I get to frost them," she said happily.

Anita's feeling of defeat was replaced by a sharp jolt of energy. "Darling," she said decisively, "I'm coming to your barbecue, okay? I'll just be brave and stand up to Pam."

"Wow! Promise!"

"Promise," said Anita.

In the morning she went into Lily's room. She sat behind her daughter on the bed while she braided her hair, deftly gathering up the sections of shiny dark strands, looking down fondly at the back of Lily's bent neck above the lace edge of her flannel nightgown, where softer, fuzzier hairs grew.

"Can I get out of Spanish?" said Lily. "I don't see why I have to take Spanish in eighth grade. Can't I do that stuff in high school?"

"What's wrong with Spanish?" said Anita.

"I hate Mrs. Contreras," said Lily.

"I want you to have a head start, so when you get to high school you'll already be ahead of the people who didn't take a language," said Anita.

"Okay, but I'm getting a C," said Lily stubbornly.

"I think you can do better than that," said Anita, but in a gentle way. She really didn't want to start in with Lily about her grades now. It was so peaceful here, just the two of them, the early morning light coming in at the window.

Last night she'd been slightly agitated about the idea of Sylvie, perhaps out of neglect, getting so close to their new neighbor, and she'd decided to make a point of giving her more time and attention. Now, Anita reminded herself that she needed to make sure Lily didn't feel shut out in the process.

"What's the big deal about grades, anyway? It doesn't count for college until high school," said Lily. "I don't get it."

"Lily, I want you to do well now so you get in the habit of getting good grades by the time you're in high school. Mothers want their daughters to have better lives, it's just natural. I know it's sometimes hard to see the point of it all, but I wish I'd done a lot better."

"Mom!" Lily sounded surprised. "I'd love to be just like

you. You're so pretty and you have that great job and every-thing. You even know how to French braid my hair. You're definitely one of the coolest moms."

Anita sighed. "I don't want to just pass on grooming tips, sweetie. I want you to have lots of choices, so you can have any kind of job you want. And so you can go to an interest-ing college and meet interesting people and get an interest-ing job."

"You didn't finish college 'cause you fell in love with Dad and got married, but you did okay," said Lily. "You have a great life, don't you?"

"Yes, of course I do, darling," said Anita. "But I'm very sorry I didn't finish college. I ended up doing work I wasn't that interested in because I didn't finish college."

"But working at Lawson's is so cool."

Anita smiled. "Well, it's all right, but it isn't what I origi-nally wanted to do. I majored in art history and I kind of hoped to work in a museum some day. A lot of people don't get to do the kind of work they want to, but the better education you have, the less you have to compromise."

She doubted Lily would get it. She wanted to tell her, "I'm sorry I got dragged down by your father because I got car-ried away by love." Maybe there would be another time when she could make her point somehow, when Lily was older. She slid the rubber band from her wrist to the stiff, shiny end of Lily's braid. "There. I'm finished." She bent down and kissed Lily's exposed neck.

THE NEXT AFTERNOON, ANITA LAY IN BED NEXT to Frank Shaw, kissed his shoulder, and gazed blissfully at his profile. "I feel wonderful," she sighed. "How can anything that feels so good be bad?"

He turned toward her and stroked her cheek. "Are you

feeling guilty? Oh, Anita! I'm sorry to put you through all this. But I can't help it, I want as much of you as I can have. I'm completely single minded about you, and I don't care what's right or wrong."

She kissed his mouth. "It doesn't seem to matter," she said. "You're so wonderful that I'm willing to pay the price."

"I don't have to lie or sneak around," he said. "You do. But I have to wait. I want to be able to reach out for you whenever I feel like it."

"I'm sorry," said Anita weakly.

"I know this makes you nervous. God, the way you jumped when that guy looked at you in the restaurant!" They'd had a quick lunch earlier. Frank had just kissed her and was stroking her cheek when Anita noticed someone staring at her. He had glasses and was sitting at a table full of businessmen some distance away. Frank had told her she was paranoid and that the man was just admiring her.

"It's my fault," Frank said now. "I kept after you. I couldn't help it. I wanted you so much. I just want to be with you all the time." He sounded so intense, it frightened her.

"When?" she said girlishly, trying to lighten the tone. "When did you decide you wanted me?"

He laughed. "I'd seen you at Phoebe's softball games, of course, but you were just another attractive woman. I didn't notice you that much. But then I saw you at Julie's party. You looked so beautiful and so sad."

She propped herself up on one arm.

"Sad?"

He nodded, drawing his finger down the bridge of her nose and tapping the tip of it. She found the gesture a little condescending. "I asked Julie about you. I didn't tell her that I'd seen you before at Phoebe's games but now I really saw you for the first time. I just said, 'Who's that beautiful, sad woman?' "

"I don't know how to take that," said Anita, lying on her back and staring at the ceiling. "First of all, I think I'm reasonably attractive, but not beautiful."

"I'll be the judge of that," he said rather smugly.

"Oh, I'm happy to have you be mistaken about it," she said. "But I didn't realize I looked sad." Did she look sad now? She couldn't possibly. Not after what they'd just done together. Every inch of her felt happy now.

"Even then, I wouldn't have come after you like I did," he said. "I could see you were a respectable married woman and all that. But Julie said, 'Oh, that's Anita. She's been unhappily married for years to a real flake.' I have to say it emboldened me."

"Julie said that?" Anita flipped over on her stomach and buried her face in the pillow. Julie had always seemed so friendly and nice about David. "I hope you and your charming husband can come to our party," she'd said. Julie had flirted with David a little, treated him like an interesting, good-looking man. Anita hadn't minded. It meant that she had a husband with something going for him. Anita had thought people were impressed by David. He was good-looking, and always acted confident. Anita knew he was kind of a flake, but she thought she'd managed to cover for him. "I had no idea I was an object of pity. How awful."

"An object of admiration, too," Frank added quickly, stroking her hair. "She said you were really brave and never complained. I thought that was classy. My ex-wife used to complain about me every chance she got. I'm sure she complained about me to strangers on airplanes."

Anita emerged from the pillow. How could anyone have any complaints about Frank? His wife must have been out of her mind.

"I didn't even know I was that unhappy," said Anita. "There were bad times, but then good times, too."

"How did you meet?" asked Frank.

"I sold him a tie," said Anita.

For years, Anita had made this a meet-cute story. Now, she didn't want to make it cute. Frank looked too interested. She shrugged. "I was an art history major at the University of Washington, working part-time at Lawson's in men's furnishings. He came in and bought a tie."

"And picked you up?" said Frank, sounding superficially light but perhaps a little edgy underneath.

"Well, he mentioned that he'd never had to wear a tie. That was a kind of badge of honor back then. He wore jeans and turtlenecks. He worked at an ad agency. In fact, it was the ad agency the store used, so he had a discount."

"So why was he buying a tie? A funeral or something?"

"He was nominated for an award from the Ad Club. It was a pretty big deal. He told me all about it and I acted impressed. Well, to be honest, I *was* impressed. He invited me along and it seemed really big time, so I said yes."

"Did he win?"

"Yes."

Anita had been so thrilled, sitting at the table with big executives from the store, and having these glamorous young women from the agency, all hot for David, check her out and wonder what the deal was.

That evening, it later transpired, had been the high point of his career. The Lawson's spring catalog had been an award winner, but a sales disaster. It was all very pretty and fuzzy and artsy—David had been influenced by the Swedish film *Elvira Madigan*—but the customers just got a mood, a feel. They didn't get a yearning for specific items. David had been called on the carpet and told to tone down the artsy stuff next time out. He'd kept his job, but his career seemed to stall. Eventually, he'd quit in a huff.

"So you worked yourself up from the sales floor," said Frank appreciatively.

"That happened later. I went back to work when the kids were eight and two, after David's freelancing fell apart. But I was a lot older and smarter. I'd never particularly wanted a career in retail, but I got ambitious. We needed the money."

"You poor darling. It sounds tough."

"I missed the girls, of course. At first I thought it would just be temporary. I thought he was so talented that something would come along and I could relax. But it never did. The hard part was the way he made my job sound so crass all the time."

Frank gave an angry snort. "Crass! It paid the bills. And since when was advertising so pure and holy?"

"I suppose I thought he was morally superior because he was creative. But lately I can't seem to stop myself from picking on him. For so long I tried to make myself still love him even though he just sat around the house and let things fall apart. Now, things seem to have been pulled together. And he's trying to get his career back on track."

Frank lifted a skeptical eyebrow. "Yeah, right. When does he make that presentation, anyway?"

"Not for two weeks." Anita sighed. "Who knows, maybe it will work out. I should hope it will, but the awful thing is, I feel ambivalent. If he bombs, then I feel justified in writing him off as a loser." She was horrified at how cold she sounded. She hoped Frank didn't think she was hard-hearted.

"I understand," said Frank. "If he succeeds, it will be a lot tougher to disengage. You'll be losing part of your justification for leaving."

Anita was sorry she'd told him last time they met that once in a while she thought about leaving David. She'd made it clear it was just an errant thought, not a serious thing at all. Now he was talking as if everything were leading up to some inevitable bust-up.

"You make compromises," said Anita. "But after I blew up a while ago and told him he'd have to do a better job around the place, he actually heard me and did something about it. The house is clean and nice and we have regular meals and the laundry gets done. It's amazing."

"He must be terrified of losing you," said Frank. "After all, where would he go? What would he do?"

Anita hadn't let herself think too much about that. "I don't know," she said. "I suppose he'd have to get a job." That's what her mother was always carrying on about. "But the horrible thing is, the better things are, the more he irritates me. The other day, watching him chew his dinner, I realized I've always hated the way he ate."

But had she? Maybe there'd once been a time she'd found that childlike, heavy-jawed chewing endearing. She couldn't remember. She couldn't remember a lot of things, lately, or rather, she remembered them differently.

Like going back to work years ago. She'd completely blocked out the pain she'd felt spending all day away from her daughters. Sylvie had been so little. But lately it had all come rushing back and seemed even more tragic than when she'd first experienced it. She remembered going off that first day with a horrible feeling in her stomach—like the first day of school. Most of all, she remembered this terrible sense of having failed, somehow, leaving the girls for hours and hours every day. But tons of mothers went back to work. She'd been ashamed of feeling that she should somehow be exempt. Maybe that's why she'd blocked all her ambivalence. Shame.

What else was she denying? And how strange that she was being more honest with herself just as she had turned into a liar to her family.

She turned to Frank. "I can't leave him because I hate the way he chews, can I? It wouldn't be fair." She rubbed her face on his chest.

"Fairness has nothing to do with it," said Frank, stroking the back of her neck. "Believe me, I've been there. Eventually, you get to the point where you know you can't go back."

She turned her head sideways on his chest so she could talk and listen to his heart beating at the same time. "I don't know if I believe unhappiness is a good enough reason to bust up a marriage," she said. "I might have believed that before I had children. Now I think maybe our parents were right and we don't have a right to expect to be happy all the time. Just sometimes. Like now."

"Still," said Frank. "He must be scared."

"Scared? I doubt it. David has no idea I've ever thought of bailing out."

"You've never even discussed it?" Frank sounded disappointed with her.

"Oh, Frank!" said Anita, raising her head and looking into his face.

"Do I seem like a vulture circling a dying marriage?" he said, frowning. "I'm sorry. I want what's best for you, of course." He sighed. "I'm not going to declare myself all over again. You know how I feel." He gave her a brave, crooked smile. "And I wish you'd help me pick out a tie. I hate buying ties."

Anita propped herself up on one elbow and smiled. "I was very good at it. There's a whole technique. You flip the tie around your fingers and show how it looks knotted." She twirled her hand in the air.

Frank seized her fingers and kissed them.

"Actually, with your green eyes, you should go for something more in olive and gold tones."

"I adore you," he said. "I think about you all the time. I want you with me all the time."

"You do?" she said, trying not to sound eager. "All the time?"

He looked angry for a second. Once in a while she saw a flicker of anger in him and it scared her. "Look, Anita, let's not discuss it, all right? There's only so much I can take."

"I'm sorry," she said, trying not to sound delighted. He loved her! He did! She kissed him just above one eye and on one cheekbone, and then on the mouth until he yielded and kissed her back and wrapped his arm around her narrow back and pulled her toward him.

She wanted the conversation to end, to hurtle back to the world populated by just the two of them. The idea of David and the girls lurking somehow in the corner of the room was threatening and wearying at the same time.

Frank sighed. After a moment of silence, he finally said, "It isn't easy," and then he jerked suddenly away and drew the sheet up to his chin. "Knowing you sleep in the same bed with him every night."

His physical withdrawal was painful, leaving her with a terrible, panicky longing for reassurance. "There's something I haven't told you," she said in a serious voice, offering her confidence in tones indicating how precious it was. "I think David is lying to me. I don't believe he really is pulling his own weight. I think he's somehow suckered our new neighbor into taking over his duties." She'd been ashamed to tell him, ashamed of David, ashamed of her own odd household.

Now he looked interested. "Really?" he said.

Anita told him how Sue walked the children to school, and made dinners that David had tried to palm off as his own. "Sylvie confirmed my suspicions about last night's lasagne," she explained.

"So he lied to you?" said Frank, clearly fascinated. "About lasagne?"

"It's pathetic, isn't it?" said Anita. She was relieved. Frank wasn't blaming her for David and his shabby subterfuge. For years now, she'd felt like some conspirator in whatever David did. At first she had basked in the glow of his triumphs, later she had taken on the shame of his weakness and tried to cover for him. But maybe she had really been covering for herself.

"So what's in it for Sue?" said Frank.

"Beats me. David can be quite charming when he wants to be. And Sue's kind of an overfriendly supermom type with too much energy. She even cleaned our refrigerator once."

"Maybe she's making a play for him. With her lasagne." Frank clearly liked this scenario.

"She's hardly his type," Anita countered.

"They have plenty of opportunity," said Frank. "Hanging around the house all day."

Anita had a brief, disgusting vision of David and Sue grunting and thrashing around in her very own bed, the bed where her children had been conceived. Then, she laughed at the absurdity of it. "If you'd met Sue, you'd realize she's not exactly the type to get carried away by grand passion. Not if it meant giving up a Cub Scout troop meeting or a cookie-baking session."

Frank smiled. "You're cute when you're patronizing."

"Did I sound smug?"

He pulled her toward him. "If anyone has the right to be smug about her capacity for passion, sweetheart, it is you."

"I thought that part of my life was over," said Anita seriously. "It seems astonishing now."

"It certainly does," he said, burying his face between her breasts.

"My God, Frank," she said suddenly, shaking him off. "I

just figured out who that guy was in the restaurant. It was Sue's husband! I'd only seen him once before, just for a few minutes, and I couldn't place him. But that's who it was. I'm sure of it. He saw you stroking my face like that. And you kissed me at the table, too."

"He probably didn't recognize you, either," said Frank. "You just remembered now because you were thinking about his wife. Besides, so what? Maybe I kissed you and maybe he saw that. It's not like he has video of us in flagrante delicto." Frank wrapped his hands around her shoulders and leaned over, pushing her down onto the bed. "Your nerves are shot. Let me help you relax."

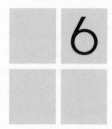

6

"**O**UR HOUSE IS KIND OF MESSY," SAID
Lily, leading her new friend Amy in the front door.

Amy looked around, taking in the tidy blue-carpeted living room, with its large, slightly dingy beige sofa, two teal blue chairs, and a coffee table with a row of magazines overlapping neatly, like in a dentist's office. The rug bore the marks of recent vacuuming like neat furrows on a flat Midwestern field.

"Wow. This isn't messy," she said.

Lily shrugged. "I guess that's what I always say. It used to be messy around here, but lately it's like a totally different house." Both girls flung their coats and backpacks on the sofa. "My room's still pretty messy, though," said Lily. She liked that. There was still some space the way it used to be.

Her own space. She liked her room messy, and Dad didn't seem to care. Mom got upset, but she really didn't have time to push. "I'm waiting to clean it up when my grandma comes. She always sleeps in my room."

Lily was so happy that Amy was here. Lily's best friend, Claire, had moved away in March, and Lily knew that Amy's best friend, Samantha, had ditched her to get in with the disgusting preppie girls' posse led by Kirsten Knutsen, who socially terrorized the eighth grade.

When Sue had started walking Sylvie to school, she had suggested Lily walk with them part of the way, then turn off for the middle school, but Lily had decided to take the bus. Not only didn't she want to be seen walking every day with a bunch of little kids and a mom, she actually got kind of creeped out by Sue. Sue was just like those preppie girls, pretending to be really sweet, but mean underneath.

It was on the bus that she started being friends with Amy. Maybe they could even be best friends. Amy had endeared herself to Lily by leaning over in social studies when they were studying the Struggle for African-American Freedom unit and calling the preppie girls the KKK, which she explained stood for Kirsten Knutsen's Klan.

Lily led Amy into the kitchen in search of food. In the kitchen, the two girls encountered Sue, wringing out the sponge mop in the sink. "Oh, don't come in," she said sharply. "The floor's still wet and you might slip."

"No, we won't," said Lily, striding over to the fridge and opening it. Amy hung back at the door.

"Aren't you going to introduce me to your friend?" said Sue pointedly.

"This is Amy. This is Sue," said Lily through clenched teeth. "We're going to do our homework and watch some MTV downstairs."

"Oh, but your father's down there working," said Sue, coming over and standing by Lily and looking into the fridge with her. "There are some oranges if you want a snack."

"I'll figure something out." Lily grabbed a couple of Cokes. "I guess we'll have to go up to my room," she said over her shoulder to Amy, and moved on to the cupboard where she corralled some tortilla chips and a jar of salsa and a bag of marshmallows.

"I'm so glad you've brought a friend home, Lily," said Sue as the girls started toward the stairs. Lily turned around and gave her a steely glance. Why didn't she just go ahead and tell Amy that Lily didn't have any friends, that she was a total loser? She meant it to be mean, Lily was sure of it.

"How come you're mopping our floor?" she said belligerently.

"Oh, I just noticed it could use a quick once-over," Sue answered, hanging the mop back up in the broom closet. "And your dad's so busy."

"Come on, Amy," said Lily.

The girls went into Lily's room and arranged themselves on Lily's unmade bed with their snacks.

"Is Sue your stepmother?" asked Amy.

"No, she's just a totally demented neighbor who comes over here and acts like she owns the place," said Lily. "Plus she hates me. Did you hear what she said?" Lily made a face and imitated Sue's voice. " 'I'm so glad you have a friend.' "

"I really like your room," said Amy, popping a Coke. "It's cool." She admired the collages Lily had made from magazines and taped to the walls. "You can tell this is a really creative person's room."

"I can't believe she's in here mopping our floor," said Lily.

"Is she like here to look after your little sister or something?" said Amy.

"My dad supposedly works at home. Basically, he's kind of a slacker and he lets Sue hang out because she's like a crazy homemaker type who loves to clean and cook and stuff. But he's very creative and talented," Lily added defensively. "That's where I get it from."

"Maybe they'll get married," said Amy. "And she'll be your wicked stepmother. I live with my mom, thank God. I only have to deal with the evil Marcia every other weekend."

"My parents are still together. They would never split up," said Lily.

"Oh, yeah? Does your mom work?"

"At Lawson's. We get a fifteen percent discount on everything," said Lily with quiet pride.

"Cool." Amy opened the marshmallow bag and popped one into her mouth. "This sometimes gets stuck in my braces, but I don't care. How does your mom like this Sue person being around?"

"By the time Mom comes home, she's gone."

"Weird," said Amy.

Lily could tell Amy thought Sue was interesting, so she went on. "At first, she just came over to drop off my little sister. She walks her to school with her own kids. Then she started hanging out here. Kind of organizing stuff and shit. My dad just stays down in the basement, working. I think he thinks she's weird, too."

"Is she like friends with your mom?" asked Amy.

"No. The thing is, she actually does make the house cleaner. And makes dinner sometimes. Well, most of the time. That makes Mom happy when she comes home from work. My mom and dad used to fight all the time about cleaning the house and dinner and stuff. Now they don't fight anymore."

"She doesn't know it's Sue?"

Lily shrugged. "Sort of. I don't know. We don't talk about it a lot." Mom was happier. That was the most important thing.

Amy lowered her voice and said fervently, "I think she's a major bitch. I already know you and I'm your friend. But say I was like someone totally new. Like someone you were assigned to do a joint language arts project with, or something, and I walked in and she said that to me like she did? You would be totally embarrassed."

Lily touched Amy's hand. "I'm so glad you get it. But you're right. Around the wrong person, Sue could be totally embarrassing."

"I'd tell your mom. It's too weird having someone come in your house and scrub your floor."

"Maybe I'll just tell my dad I don't want that psycho around," said Lily. "What do you think?"

The door opened and Sue stood there, holding a tray with two glasses of milk and a plate of cookies. "I thought you girls might like some of these," she said. "I baked some extra ones, so I just went home and got them."

Lily raced toward the door to take the tray. She had a sudden fear that Sue had heard every word, or worse, that she would come in and sit down with them. Sue put her head slightly to one side and smiled. "And I brought milk because cookies are better with milk than with Coke, right?"

"Okay," said Lily. Why didn't she even knock? God, she couldn't even have a quiet talk with Amy without Sue in her face. She took the tray, mumbled, "Thanks," and held her ground, blocking the entry until Sue turned and went away, then Lily slammed the door after her and pressed down the lock button in the center of the knob.

"Ohmigod," said Amy, wide-eyed and clearly thrilled. "I bet she heard you call her a psycho. I can't believe it!"

Both girls began giggling hysterically, then muffled their

laughter in the pillows on the bed. After a wonderful, giddy five minutes, during which Lily thought her heart would burst, they came up for air.

"I can't believe it," repeated Amy. "Milk and homemade cookies on a tray. She's totally RoboMom."

Lily waved her hands up and down. "Maybe she put drugs in the cookies," she said. "Maybe she's some total weirdo who knocks people out, then cleans out their closets and does all the laundry and irons and shit."

The girls embraced each other and indulged in more hysterical laughter.

Amy's face took on the look of a demented zombie with unseeing eyes. In a creepy, robot-like voice she chanted, "Must clean. Must clean this house. Nothing will stop me."

"That's it!" said Lily. "She's an android. And something got messed up in the programming, so she's overpumped and comes over here and does our house, not just her own."

Amy bit into a cookie, chewed, swallowed, then clutched her throat and pretended to be dying, waving a rigid hand in the air as she slid off the bed with an impressive death rattle.

In a bizarre way, Lily was glad Sue had been here today. Laughing at her weirdness was making it easy to bond with Amy. Amy would be a very satisfactory best friend, and Lily needed one very badly.

DAVID CAME UPSTAIRS AND WANDERED INTO THE living room. He frowned at the row of neatly overlapping magazines and messed them up a little. It looked too neat somehow. Besides, Anita wouldn't believe he'd done that.

He sat down heavily on the sofa and let his head fall back so that he was staring up at the beige ceiling. The plasterers and painters had really done a good job. They hadn't had much choice, with Sue watching them like a hawk as she brought them coffee. Anita had wanted to do some of the work herself. She really could be awfully cheap sometimes, but he'd talked her into hiring it out, at Sue's suggestion. Then, good old Sue had managed to get the bids out and arrange everything, so he could work. It was wonderful, really, to be spared all that. David found workmen threatening. They were always trying to make you feel like an idiot because you weren't skilled in their stupid trade.

Sue really was a remarkable woman. Helping with Sylvie and the plumbers, bringing those casseroles over, casually wiping the counters while they talked and had coffee in the kitchen. She was so quietly efficient that he didn't notice the way she'd just bustle through the place and get it all straightened out in no time. It was when she produced a stack of neatly folded laundry from a basket that had sat on the stairs for a couple of days that he realized how helpful she had become.

"Hi!" said a voice behind him.

David started. He hadn't known Sue was still in the house. She was usually gone by now. "I just noticed that the kitchen floor could use a quick once-over, and then I went home to get some cookies for Lily and her friend. They're upstairs."

Sue came around to the front of the sofa and sat in the little blue chair next to it, sitting forward as if about to spring back out.

"Oh, that was nice."

"You look worried," she said, suddenly crinkling her forehead sympathetically. "Is everything all right? Is the work going well?"

He smiled at her. There was something so touching about her concern. "I'm having the materials printed up and produced now. There's just a little fine-tuning left. I think it's a pretty damn good presentation."

"I'm sure it is," she said.

"You know, Sue," he continued, "I'm not sure I could have done it without you. You've been such a good friend these last weeks."

Her face took on an expression he hadn't seen before. She looked pleased, but also very serene. "I'm glad you think so," she said with a little smile.

"And that's not all," he said. "By your example, I've learned a lot about the satisfactions of running a home properly. About its almost spiritual quality. I've put that into the campaign."

Now she looked quite breathless. Her eyes were shiny and there were two bright pink spots in her cheeks. Was she blushing at his praise? The change in her face was like something from a Victorian novel where the heroine emotes through her complexion.

"Anyway," he said, suddenly embarrassed, "you've been a big help." He rose. "Well, I guess I should get back to it." Actually, he'd already packed it in for the day, but he was anxious for her to leave. He'd pretend he was still working, then sneak back up and read the evening paper.

"Before you do," Sue said, her old sensible self again, "I thought I should mention to you that Lily seems unhappy. You don't think she resents me or anything, do you? She was kind of snippy with me."

"Lily?" said David vaguely. He hated this kind of conversation, where he was expected to discuss hurt feelings.

Sue seemed to sense his mood. "It's not important," she said.

"Lily can be pretty irritating sometimes," said David, fearing he'd been too abrupt. "Teenage girls can be really sulky and sarcastic. My sister used to be like that. To be honest, I find myself just tuning Lily out a lot of the time."

"She doesn't spend much time with her mother," said Sue sympathetically. "Just when she needs her most."

Now David was beginning to feel irritated. Sue seldom mentioned Anita. It was another part of the unspoken pact. Like clearing out after the kids got home. "Anita works hard all day," he said. "Sometimes she's pretty ragged when she gets home. But so are a lot of mothers these days."

"It's a shame, isn't it?" said Sue.

David pointedly refrained from asking just what snippy thing Lily had said, because he didn't want to get into a blow by blow of a catfight. "Maybe it's kind of a female territorial thing. It might be helpful if you let her have the run of house in the afternoons. You're usually gone when she comes home from school."

"Oh, I don't think it's that," said Sue with confidence. "It's men who are territorial. Women are nurturant."

"Anyway, Anita's mother is coming out from Denver on Mother's Day weekend and staying for a while," David went on. "Lily is crazy about her grandmother. Maybe that will settle her down." He was suddenly worried that Sue would be hanging around and fussing with household chores in front of Anita's mother. He could just imagine how that would go over. His mother-in-law was always lying in wait for signs of his inadequacies. And she was so uptight and conventional, she'd think it was odd Sue was helping so much around here. Maybe it *was* a little odd. Anyway, he had to keep Sue at bay for that week.

"You're lucky to have a nice family Mother's Day," said Sue.

David hated the whole idea of Mother's Day, believing that it was a nefarious invention of florists and greeting card companies. He shrugged. "We never make a big deal about it."

Sue looked slightly shocked at this. David reflected that even reasonable women tended to buy into all that corny holiday stuff. He added lightly, "After all, isn't every day Mother's Day?"

Sue smiled sadly. "I get a little depressed at the thought of our first holiday away from our extended family."

"We don't have any extended family here, either," said David breezily, hoping to prevent her from getting maudlin. "Anita's an only child, and her father died a few years ago, and I'm not that close to my family, I'm afraid." In fact, recently David was feuding openly with his mother and sister. He felt they had screwed him over royally when it came to dividing up Aunt Martha's estate, dumping a lot of old kitchenware and blankets on him while creaming off the good stuff. His dad had taken his mother's side, of course, just to avoid trouble. To be honest, David didn't really miss any of them.

"Hey, I've got an idea!" said Sue, brightening up. "Why don't you all come to our place for Mother's Day dinner? It would cheer me up so much to have some guests."

"That's very nice of you," said David with a smile. He hated the idea. He wanted to keep Anita and her mother away from Sue, who would probably let slip that she was doing so much over here during the day. That would just upset them. But how could he turn down any request from Sue when she'd been so kind? "Let me see what Anita has in mind," he said lamely. He'd figure out a way to get out of it later.

"I hope she'll want to come," said Sue. She leaned over the coffee table and restored the magazines to their overlapping row.

7

A FEW DAYS LATER, DAVID STOOD IN THE living room surrounded by big pieces of black cardboard with cartoon versions of his TV ads in his proposed campaign. Mark's storyboards made the spots look lively and fun. David had run up a huge graphics bill for this presentation, but he was pretty sure the investment would pay off.

And Sue had turned out to be a lifesaver. Not only had her take on domestic life served as real inspiration, she'd actually provided him with the slogan for the whole campaign. He'd been completely stumped at the time, and he'd shown her the material. "It's wonderful, David," she'd said. "It kind of says, 'From our family to yours.'" It was exactly what he'd been looking for.

David had taken the campaign much further along than

he'd needed to. He'd gone right ahead and written a slew of fabulous TV spots, with radio reinforcement.

It was great stuff, and, when he got the account, he would have a huge leg up on the creative. He could go right into production, get those spots running by midsummer, and start collecting some terrific media commissions.

The people down at the copy place had done an excellent job putting all the explanatory materials together into a thick booklet in classy red glossy covers with black plastic spiral bindings. The three Conway siblings could take their time going over David's creative rationale and his description of the underlying philosophy. Of course, the real key was David's own presentation. This was what would make it or break it. Because the Conways had been so receptive in their initial meeting, David felt sure he could easily get them onboard.

He'd been a little worried about his skimpy portfolio, but the whole family concept provided him with the perfect explanation for the fact that most of his past work was pretty old, and his recent stuff was small, low-budget print. But if the Conways mentioned that, he was ready.

"I was home with my children, regrouping and getting in touch with the next phase." Pause for a little chuckle. "You know, my kids don't know it, bless their little hearts, but the whole time I was teaching them to tie their shoes and look both ways before they crossed the street, they were teaching me plenty. About life. About families. About values." At this point, he'd zap the Conway sister, Sandy, with some sincere eye contact. Her desk was full of kid pictures.

In fact, he was pretty sure that Sandy was the key decision maker here. The two brothers had seemed to view advertising as a burdensome ancillary expense, complaining about the printing bills for their dreary newspaper inserts. Bob, a

CPA, had said he disliked advertising because he didn't feel there was any adequate way to measure the return on investment.

Sandy had more of an understanding of the creative aspects. "We definitely need something new and fresh—something that will tell people that Conway's, although it's an old family business, is moving with the times," she had said earnestly. That suited David just fine. He was always confident in his ability to turn on the charm with women.

As he stacked up his materials, David realized that he had a little flutter in his stomach when he thought about the actual pitch. He mustn't panic now. He had to stay confident and relaxed, the way he'd been at that initial meeting. There were just twelve more days until his appointment. He'd better not lose his nerve between now and then. A good presentation was like staying afloat. You had to let yourself be buoyed up. As soon as you thought about it, you'd sink.

He wandered into the kitchen and looked out the window into the garden. Spring was definitely turning into summer. All the new green shoots were darkening up, and the shrubs were taking on a lazy, blowsier look, bobbing heavily in a light breeze. The sky was cloudless and a solid blue, none of that tentative spring pallor, white at the horizon. The sun lit everything in a uniform, steady light. He stepped outside to take it in more deeply.

It all seemed to fit in with his own mood. His creative spurt was over. Now he could settle down and bask in the summery atmosphere of getting the account and look forward to reaping the fruits of his efforts.

He had just convinced himself that his concept was terrific and that he shouldn't worry when Sue came through the hedge. She was wearing a wide-brimmed straw hat and a floaty cotton dress, and she carried a sturdy-looking wooden-handled trowel.

"Hi, David," she said.

"You look nice and summery," he said, walking across the lawn toward her.

"I'm thinning out a shade bed full of violets and ferns," she said rather breathlessly. "I was wondering if you guys wanted some. Want to have a look?"

David had absolutely no interest in gardening beyond admiring the general effects of the light on the foliage of the anonymous shrubs that lined his own yard, but he welcomed the distraction. He really should try to forget about the presentation, so he wouldn't make himself nervous.

He followed her through the hedge, and was startled to see that she had strung up a clothesline across the garden. A couple of massive white sheets were billowing like sails in the gentle breeze. He hadn't seen laundry hanging on the line since his childhood. His mother had had some kind of square arrangement of clotheslines in rows around a pole set in concrete. He remembered flapping around among the sheets imagining that he was in some Arabian Nights tent.

Sue led him to an area near the side of the house. "What do you think?" she said, pointing with her trowel at a small patch of garden in the shade of the eaves of the house.

"Okay, I guess," he said vaguely. "I'm not sure where we'd put them."

"I know just the spot. Right by the door leading to the basement. That's kind of a neglected area. I've been dying to make something of it."

"All right."

"I'll bring them over. It's not the best time to transplant, obviously, but what the heck, they'll probably take if we just keep them watered."

David, bored with plants, and figuring they would be Anita's responsibility in any case, turned and looked at the sheets flapping prettily. "Is your dryer broken?" he asked.

Sue gave him a superior smile, and he realized his mistake. Of course it wasn't. Nothing in Sue's house was ever broken. "The sheets just smell so fabulous when you dry them outside," she said. To demonstrate, she went over and picked up a corner of one of them and buried her face in it. David remembered the way his children, as sleepy babies, used to bury their little faces in a favorite blanket. "See," she said, handing it to him.

Rather self-consciously, he placed his own face against the fabric and inhaled. She was right. It smelled fabulous—like summer and fresh air. He remembered that smell now from his own childhood. "Wow," he said. Sue smiled at him. She had lovely rosy glints on her skin. The sunlight illuminated the slightly snubby tip of her nose and the swell of her cheeks like a woman in some old Flemish painting. Her face had a spattering of pale gold freckles he'd never noticed before, and he caught a whiff of lavender cologne, another clean, summery smell.

David suddenly realized they were standing side by side, both still clutching the fragrant sheet as if they were about to climb underneath it into bed together. He hastily dropped his corner. He flashed back on her face just before she'd mushed it into that sheet with all the glee of a born sensualist. Her narrow eyes were closed and her lips had opened just slightly, in anticipation of pleasure.

He heard a telephone ring. He was pretty sure it was coming from the neighbor on the other side, but he said, "The phone!" and took off at a canter through the hedge and up his back steps.

When he got back to the kitchen, he let out a sigh. That was all he needed, Sue coming on to him! He'd have to make sure it didn't happen again. Apart from anything else, it was simply too inconvenient, seeing as they saw so much of each other. He'd keep his manner more distant from now on.

Just then, his phone actually did ring.

It was Sandy Conway.

"Hi, Sandy," he said, trying to sound as if he was sitting calmly at a desk in a cunningly designed and ultrachic home office, rather than bracing himself on the sink over a bunch of dirty dishes, still panting from his sprint across the yard.

"Hi," she said. "It's about the presentation on Thursday."

"Right. I'm looking forward to it. I think you'll all agree I've got a great concept that will give you that updated look and feel you wanted."

"Yes, well, we were wondering if you could put it off for a while," she said, sounding just a little apologetic and whiny. "We're just not ready to deal with this yet." David didn't reply, and she went on. "My brothers and I had a long talk about the overhead last night, and we're going to have to go slow here in terms of developing any new financial commitments." She took a long breath. "And something else has come up. You see, Sam's daughter, Jennifer, is a communications major at Washington State over in Pullman. She'll be graduating in June, and we thought we might bring her into the loop here. Bob thinks it would really be helpful to have her attend the presentations. She's the only one in the family with any real expertise in advertising."

By now, David had recovered from the initial shock. He got the picture only too clearly. First of all, they were cheaping out. David sensed the hand of Bob, the CPA, behind this. He was tempted to snap, "Never let the bookkeeper run the business." But squeezing out a decent budget was do-able, over time. The more alarming development was the prospect of having to grovel before yet another Conway, some stupid sorority girl named Jennifer.

"Well, Sandy," he said as pleasantly as he could, "bear in mind that as far as budget goes, a one-man creative shop like me can afford to tailor any campaign to strict budgetary requirements. That's because my own overhead is so low. Something to think about."

"Sure," said Sandy vaguely.

"And of course I'd be happy to have Jennifer there. It'll be fun to see the take a kid fresh out of school has on this. So when do you want to reschedule?"

"She graduates the fifteenth of June, and then she'll be in Europe with her boyfriend for six weeks."

Terrific. The boyfriend will probably be part of the decision-making process, too, David thought. He imagined a surly, downy-lipped ag major whose conceptual range consisted of "Excellent!" and "Sucks!" contributing his inarticulate, knee-jerk thoughts to the proceedings.

"I see," he replied, trying to sound calm.

"How about if we call you?"

"Sure thing," said David, taking a kindly avuncular tone. "But I've gotta tell you, Sandy, I've got some hot ideas for Conway's. I'd hate to see you waste too much more time before you get that advertising of yours smoothed out and updated."

"Well it's worked pretty well for thirty years," said Sandy defensively. "I guess we can stagger on through the summer."

"Of course, of course."

When he hung up the phone, he realized he was shaking. He looked out the window into the garden and its dumb, still, heartless beauty.

He dreaded telling Anita about the postponement. She would just use it to undermine him, as if it were somehow his fault. She'd been so negative recently. She was turning out just like her mother, lying in wait for him to screw up, like some predator stalking the deer herd on the lookout for the slightest limp or falter.

Oh, hell, he thought. Sue came up the porch steps. He didn't want to see anyone just now. Especially not Sue.

He opened the door, suppressing the desire to snap, "What is it now?"

"Hi!" she said cheerfully. "I put those plants in. Want to take a look?"

David wasn't interested in the ferns and violets. In fact, he felt like going back to bed and pulling the blankets over his head. Nevertheless, he took the path of least resistance, traipsing after Sue down the porch steps and around to a little patch of ground by the basement door.

"This is a nice shady patch," she said, "but with poor soil. "I enriched it with peat moss, and I put in some baby's tears, which should fill out soon."

David stared down at the little outcroppings of green, dripping with water. The space they now occupied had been bare, rocky ground, with the dryer vent sprouting from the house the only focal point.

"The violets will bloom in the spring, and we can put some lily of the valley here, too," Sue went on enthusiastically.

David managed a grunt. She looked at him with what he took as a hurt expression.

"It's really nice, Sue. I'm sorry I don't sound as interested as I should. It's just that I've had some bad news."

"Oh, no!" she said, her worried expression creating a characteristic series of ridges in her smooth forehead.

"It's my presentation. The Conway's Home and Garden Center account. They sound like they're waffling. They've got some niece involved, some college kid. I'm afraid the whole thing's going to peter out. After all the hard work I put in to the campaign."

Sue gave him an incredibly intent gaze with her still blue eyes. "I'm not worried, David," she said in a low, calm voice. "I believe in your ideas, your sensitivity, your ability. When they see what you've come up with, they'll go for it like a shot."

The force of her confidence startled and thrilled him. After a moment, he said, "Maybe you're right." He felt very grateful to her. She really believed in him, and in so doing made it possible for him to believe, too. "I really appreciate your saying that, Sue. You're a true friend."

That was it. She was a friend. He'd just imagined that little erotic frisson a while ago. Probably because he hardly ever got laid these days. And how long had it been since he'd had a real friend?

Sue bent down and patted the dirt around the ferns. "About Mother's Day—" she said.

"We'd love to come," he replied impulsively. "We're all really looking forward to it."

"WHAT!" SAID ANITA AT THE DINNER TABLE that night. "How could you possibly do that without consulting me?"

"I thought it was sweet of them to invite us over on a family holiday. They're kind of homesick, I think."

"And since when do we make a big deal about Mother's Day?" said Anita. She gave Lily and Sylvie a tight smile. "All I want is some of those cute homemade cards you girls make." In the past, Anita used to have to nag David to remind him to take the girls shopping for a gift for her, which all seemed too depressing. She'd worried that he'd procrastinate or forget and the girls would be embarrassed not to have a gift for her. One year she announced that the homemade cards that usually accompanied the gifts were the most important thing and all she wanted from now on.

"But, Mom, I want to go to Sue's!" said Sylvie.

Anita gave her a thoughtful look, then turned her attention back to David. "You accepted without consulting me.

You'll have to get us out of it." It really was insufferable of him to have said yes. She wasn't going to put up with it.

"Grandma's going to be here," said Lily emphatically. "She won't want to go over to the Heffernans'. I want it just to be our family." Anita felt grateful for her backup.

"I thought you'd be pleased," said David to Anita. "Sue will put together a great meal, and all we have to do is show up with a bottle of wine. And like I said, they're lonely."

"I don't see why we have to cheer them up! I didn't realize you were so fond of the Heffernans."

"They're nice," said Sylvie.

"They're nerds," said Lily. "And Sue is a psycho. Pass the potatoes, please."

"I want to go," said Sylvie stubbornly.

Anita handed Lily the dish of scalloped potatoes. "What do you mean Sue is a psycho?" she asked.

Lily glanced at her father, then back at her mother. "I don't know," she said, and shrugged.

"All right. Question number two. Who made these scalloped potatoes?" Anita pointed accusingly at the dish and its rows of perfect circles, glossy with cheese and dotted with bacon bits and chives.

Three pairs of eyes stared back at her, but no one answered.

"Was it Sue?" asked Anita.

"Yes, as a matter of fact, it was," said David pleasantly. "She's just incredibly neighborly."

"Maybe she can just cater for us on Mother's Day," said Anita sarcastically. "That way we don't have to actually socialize with them."

Lily snickered, and David gave her a dirty look. "I wish you wouldn't sneer at people, Anita. No wonder Lily is so cynical."

Lily looked defiantly at her father. "I think it's just too weird having Sue cleaning up after us and stuff," she said. "I'd rather have it messy than have her here all the time."

David put down his fork. He said sharply, "You're exaggerating, Lily. Sue isn't over here all the time." He glanced over at Anita. "Anyway, it's a big help what with my workload and Mom working late so much."

"I like Sue," said Sylvie plaintively.

"Just how much is she here?" demanded Anita.

"Every day," said Lily. "She acts like she's our mom."

Anita turned to David. "Are you encouraging this woman? I don't like the idea of her taking over my home."

"She's superenergetic and very kind," said David. "She kind of keeps everything running on an even keel."

"That's your job!" said Anita, trying not to shout. "But if you can't handle it, I'd rather you just let things slide instead of having her hanging around over here all the time."

"It's good for children to have an orderly home," David told Anita in what sounded to her like an incredibly prissy tone. Was he quoting Sue?

"When did this revelation come to you?" she snapped.

"To be honest, it's something I'd kind of forgotten until I saw Sue in action. She's really inspiring." He leaned over the table and said in a kind of gloating way, "You probably think she's just a dumb housewife, but she has some interesting ideas I've used for the Conway's campaign."

"Oh, really?" Anita pushed her plate away. "Like what? How to make appliances shine, or keep the shower curtains from mildewing!"

"No!" said David. "High-concept stuff. You wouldn't get it, because you're so wrapped up in your job. Sue happens to have some real insights into what makes families work."

"Don't you lecture me about families," said Anita angrily.

"If you had a real job, I wouldn't have to spend so much time hanging on to mine."

"Are you fighting?" said Sylvie in a scared voice.

"Of course not," said Anita, reaching over and patting her hand. "I'm just crabby because I get tired at work. I'm sorry."

"So what's the deal?" demanded Lily. "Do we have to go to the Heffernans' for dinner on Mother's Day?"

David and Anita answered simultaneously. She said, "No," and he said, "Yes."

8

"DAVID ABSOLUTELY INSISTED. I COULDN'T tell him why I just can't face Sue's husband. Then, the girls were getting alarmed because I was starting to yell, so finally I caved in." Anita was whispering into her office phone. Thank God for her daily call with Frank from the office. She really needed to ventilate about this.

Frank said, "Hmm," in a neutral way. She wanted him to say something like, "Oh, you poor thing."

"Maybe you were right and Roger Heffernan didn't recognize me that day in the restaurant," Anita went on, keeping her voice low. She was always afraid someone would hear through the paper-thin walls of her office, or that Pam was looming outside her door, waiting to burst in with new horrible details of her humiliating incentive scheme to jack up sales and reduce markdowns. "But if he did, he'll be sitting there, gloating, in front of David and the girls. And my mother. Then he'll tell his wife, if he hasn't already."

Anita had a vision of Sue acting polite and correct, but all the time thinking what a slut Anita was and feeling sorry for David and the girls for being saddled with her.

"Why don't you tell David about us yourself?" suggested Frank with maddening calmness. "Then he'll know. And as for the kids and your mother, well it isn't really any of their business, is it?"

"I just can't imagine how David would react."

"He won't like it, that's for sure, but there's nothing he can do." Frank sounded calm, logical, and lawyer-like. Anita found his competence sexy but a little cold. "You have all the cards, Anita. You're supporting the whole thing. I suppose if he decided to leave, he could come after you for some maintenance, but most men would be too proud. Just don't move out yourself, because he'll have a good shot at getting the house."

And the girls, too, thought Anita in a panic. What if he got custody? She'd keep knocking herself out at Lawson's sending them a support check every month, while he lolled around waiting for Sue to bring over supper. The girls would think she had abandoned them. But she didn't want to talk to Frank about the girls.

"I think I'll say I'm sick," she said. "At the last minute."

"Okay. Then come around to my place. I'll pick up a bottle of champagne and we'll celebrate our own way."

"It sounds wonderful," she said, laughing. "But you know I can't."

"When can we?" he said. "Tomorrow? Another long lunch? Just come straight to my place."

"Yes," she said, opening her desk drawer and looking fondly at the key that lay there among pens and pencils and Post-it notes. "At twelve. I can probably get away for two hours at least. Two of your precious billable hours." Then she remembered. "Oh, hell, I forgot. I promised Sylvie I'd come to the school barbecue."

"Surely you can get out of that!"

"I never go to any of her school things. I'm sorry, darling."

"I understand you have your priorities," said Frank stiffly.

"How about the day after tomorrow?" said Anita desperately. "I love you, you know that. Please don't be angry. I'm doing my best."

He sighed. "This is hell. I want to be with you whenever I want. I want to spend the whole night with you. I want to wake up with you, and then we can make love again in the morning." Now he sounded sweet and vulnerable, which Anita found very exciting coming from someone who could be strong and competent.

"I love you," she said again.

THE NEXT DAY IT RAINED. AT LUNCHTIME, ANITA reported to Sylvie's classroom and stood at the back with other parents waving shyly at their children who turned around ignoring Miss Carr and stared at the parents while the teacher went over the change in plans in a booming voice. The barbecue grills had been moved from the big grassy field where the event was originally to have taken place to a sheltered area lined with bicycle racks off the gym. Children would be escorted through the food lines by parents, then everyone would report back to the classroom to eat the meal indoors.

Anita was assigned to take Sylvie and a little boy with a runny nose named Carlos through the smoky line for hamburgers and canned baked beans, carrot sticks, and cupcakes. She noticed Sue behind one of the serving tables, a pink construction paper name tag pinned to her blue-and-white-striped chef's apron. Sue was beaming at all the children in her line and ladling out beans, chatting easily with all the parents as if she knew them all.

Anita nudged Sylvie and the snuffling, silent Carlos, who clung to her hand with a damp little grasp, into another line. She didn't want to deal directly with Sue's Mother's Day invitation. Let David get them out of that.

Sylvie yanked her other hand, pulling down Anita's ear to the level of her mouth. "I'm glad you came, so everyone can see how pretty you are," she whispered to her mother.

All young children thought their mothers were beautiful, Anita knew. But did Sylvie really just want her there to show her off? A trophy mom? Maybe the main thing was to show that your mother cared enough to come. Just like the residents of old people's homes who wanted their children to visit so they could brag about it to the other old people. Frank didn't care about any of that, about what people thought. He just wanted her all for himself.

"I CLEANED IT ALL UP FOR YOU." LILY SAT ON the bed while her grandmother unpacked her suitcase and put her things in the drawer Lily had cleared out for her. "I'm so happy you're here."

Evelyn Reynolds looked around the room. "You've changed things here. You've got pictures of good-looking guys around!" She smiled at her granddaughter. "You'll be breaking hearts before you know it."

Lily smiled and looked down at her lap. "I don't think so," she said.

"No one ever thinks they will," said Evelyn. "Your mother was very shy when she was a teenager. But pretty soon boys were phoning up and she was picking and choosing."

"And she chose Dad," said Lily.

Lily caught just a hint of a compressed lip, then Grandma turned to her and said, "Thank goodness, or you wouldn't be here!" and bent and kissed her.

Lily hugged her. Grandma had very soft skin and she smelled of roses and had nice soft gray hair, too, very fine and fluffy.

"So I understand we'll be having dinner at the neighbors' tomorrow," said Evelyn. "Are they nice?"

Lily wrinkled up her nose. "The lady is weird. She's over here all the time, butting in and cleaning up and stuff."

"Really?"

"It's okay, I guess," said Lily, sensing her grandmother's disapproval. "It's nicer for Mom to come home to a clean house. Dad's been really busy with his work and stuff. It's sort of like having a housekeeper."

"Does your mother pay her?"

"No. She just does it. Anyway, she's mostly not here when I come home from school." Lily wanted to tell Grandma all about it but at the same time she didn't want her to think they were a weird family, letting some wacko come in and take over. "But she even does the laundry sometimes. I know, because I was borrowing one of Dad's handkerchiefs and I looked in his drawer and saw that all his socks are rolled in these weird little balls. Mom just turns over the cuffs like you do, and Dad always stuffs them all in the drawer without sorting them."

Evelyn, who had been folding her nightgown, paused. Her eyebrows rose.

"And she makes two dinners a lot of the time. One for her family and one for ours, and then brings ours over here."

"Maybe she's just very nice and doesn't think your father can cope," said Evelyn, resuming her folding.

"She pretends to be nice, but I kind of wonder," said Lily,

swinging her legs against the side of the bed. "Dad says I'm too cynical."

"You're not too cynical," said Evelyn loyally. Lily had noticed Grandma liked to contradict Dad, but she was pleased with the compliment. "You're sensible, Lily. I've always known that. You get it from me. Your mother isn't cynical enough, sometimes." She clicked her tongue. "I'll have to check out this Sue."

"Oh, I don't want to upset Mom," said Lily. "I think she'd be a lot more stressed out if the house was messy like before." Lily wasn't sure she should have complained. She had a sense of having unleashed something. Grandma loved her so fiercely. That fierceness, she sensed, could come out in other ways that might be unsettling. "Don't make a big deal of it, okay? Promise?"

"All right, honey," said her grandmother with a sweet smile. "Tell me about school. Tell me about the new best friend you wrote me about."

ANITA FIGURED THAT IF SHE ANNOUNCED IN front of her mother she was too sick to go to the Heffernans', David couldn't make a scene by accusing her of malingering. She had worked on a gradual, two-day buildup, referring to vague muscle pain and a feeling of general weakness, and occasionally placing two fingers on her temple and wincing, the way people did in painkiller commercials.

She had orchestrated a brief rally that morning, and given her mother the blouse she'd bought for her for Mother's Day. Then, she'd reclined on the sofa, reading the paper while the girls trashed the kitchen making a big breakfast of waffles in her honor. At breakfast, she admired the cards they'd made. Lily's was a collage of fashion models snipped out of *Vogue* and *Elle*, with the inscription, "I love you, Mom. You're totally the best. Have a super day. XOXOXO. With this card you are entitled to one free Saturday afternoon. (I will take Sylvie to a movie on the bus!) Love, Lily."

Sylvie's card, on green construction paper, had a pasted-on drawing of a smiling face that was presumably Anita, with a halo over it. Inside, it read, "You are my angel Mom. I love love love love love you. Do you love me? Love, Sylvie."

"Of course I love you, sweetheart," said Anita, grabbing her playfully. "How can you even ask that?" She kissed Sylvie's neck and blew on it, as she had when Sylvie was a baby. Sylvie giggled and squirmed.

Later that afternoon, while David was reading the paper and her mother was sitting between the girls on the sofa showing them how to do cross-stitch embroidery, Anita came into the living room to make her announcement. "I'm afraid if I don't feel better soon, I won't be able to go. I'm afraid what I've got is this bug that's going around the office."

"You look fine," said her mother sharply over the half-glasses she wore when she did needlework. "Let me feel your forehead." Anita dutifully presented her forehead to her mother.

"You don't have a temperature," Evelyn announced.

"Mother, it's not that I'm trying to skip school or something," said Anita with a brave little smile. "I really don't feel well. I need rest." She turned to David, who seemed to have been half listening to her. "You'll have to give them my excuses," she said. "In fact, I think I'll tuck in right now."

"You're not coming with us?" he said.

"Can we bring you anything, dear?" said her mother. "Tea or something?"

Before she had a chance to answer, David said, "I'm sure if you just have a nap, you can make it. We're not due there for an hour."

"I'm not up to it," Anita replied with finality.

An hour later, before they all left to troop through the hedge, David came upstairs. "I really wish you'd come," he said to Anita in a whiny voice. "Sue will be so disappointed."

"I just can't," Anita said feebly. She fell back onto the pillows. "Have a good time, and tell them I'm sorry."

"All right. By the way, the Conway's presentation has been postponed. They're on vacation or something. See you later."

Anita knew there was more to it than that. She could tell by that pinched, cowardly look he always got when he lied. And, by the fact that he'd brought this up just when her mother was here so she couldn't nag him about pursuing another account or grill him about what had really gone wrong, or point out to him sarcastically that the plumbing work they'd put on Visa with his assurance they could pay it off right away was revolving around at 18 percent every month. But she didn't care. She was so relieved she'd got out of going to Sue's.

As soon as they had all left, and the house was blissfully quiet, she picked up the bedside phone and called Frank. "They're gone," she said. "I'm all alone. It's wonderful."

At the Heffernans' front door, David explained that Anita was ill and very sorry she couldn't come.

"She's sick? What a shame!" Sue exclaimed with that sweet, wrinkly-browed expression of concern. "It's not her stomach or anything, is it?"

"No," David reassured her. "Seems to be kind of a bug. Her muscles ache."

She stepped back and he looked down, startled at Sue's outfit. She was wearing what appeared to be a dancer's leotard, a tight spandex top revealing the shape of her breasts and the outline of her nipples, and a flowing skirt in flowered chiffon that looked like a big scarf tied around her hips. Usually she wore jeans with those odd smocks over them, or long denim jumpers that resembled maternity dresses, worn with cozy wool socks and chic but sensible shoes.

In the past, David had, as was his habit, tried to figure out what Sue looked like under her smocks and jumpers, but he realized now he'd got it wrong. Dressed like this it was clear she did have a waist after all, and an old-fashioned, voluptuous hourglass figure. Oh, well, if the evening dragged on a bit, at least he'd be able to ogle Sue discreetly. Did she know what she looked like? He doubted it.

He introduced Evelyn, who said, "It's so nice of you to have us. Poor Anita is overworked, I think." Evelyn gave Sue's impressive chest a startled glance. Sue led them all into the living room. "My daughter puts in long hours at that job of hers," Evelyn went on. "She never complains, but I know it's stressful."

Another dig, thought David. She may just as well have been wearing a sign with an arrow pointing to him and saying, "This bum should get a job and support my daughter."

Roger wore a loud pink-and-green madras shirt, the type favored by the country club fun guy, and a pair of navy blue Dockers, the portly, middle-aged guy's best friend. He rattled ice cubes over a big copper tray full of bottles, and turned and nodded as his wife introduced Evelyn, then gave David a hearty handshake. He said, "Catch any of that game today?" while Evelyn said, "What a nice room. So homey."

David took in the details—the orange cast to the wooden floors, the gauzy cotton curtains, the fireplace mantel decorated with glass bowls, the big sofa full of embroidered pillows. He remembered that he and Anita had thought the whole place looked just a little too much like a magazine layout the first time they saw it. Now he decided it was more than tastefully chic. It reflected Sue's traditional personality and her devotion to home. It was such a female room, thought David. Anita spent so much time at the store figuring out what was fashionable and hard-edged that she'd lost touch with this kind of old-fashioned honest coziness.

The only jarring note was a big bouquet of long-stemmed red roses, glossy and too vivid for the pastel room. They were arranged stiffly in a big, cut-glass vase. Sue noticed David looking at them, and said, "For me, from Roger. For Mother's Day."

"Lovely," said Evelyn, clearly thinking it was too bad her daughter was married to a jerk who didn't get her flowers. But Anita wasn't his mother.

"Yes, they're gorgeous," said Sue. David felt she was just trying to be kind. Those tight, ovoid, red roses were all wrong for Sue. She should have white or pale yellow, big and blowsy. Besides, what kind of a husband gave his wife flowers on Mother's Day? Someone who thought of her not as a lover, but as the mother of his children, that's who.

Roger got everybody drinks, while Sue passed around almonds with some kind of caramelized glaze, and something white wrapped in grape leaves. Lily sat with a Coke next to her grandmother on the sofa. Sylvie was encouraged to play downstairs with the boys, but decided to sit on the other side of Evelyn and nuzzle into her. The sounds of video games could be heard from the basement.

Sue and Evelyn made polite small talk while Roger, after dispensing drinks to the guests, sat there with a pleasant expression and sipped his bourbon, ignoring them completely. David studied him. Roger seemed to be about his own age, but he looked like a man from another generation. His dark thinning hair, combed over in a pathetic attempt to hide a bald spot, gleamed with the kind of hair oil David's own father had worn, and he had the complacent, authoritarian look David associated with bosses or cops.

"I thought it would be hard for the boys, changing schools and all," Sue was saying, "but they've adjusted so well. And we're lucky to have such nice neighbors. Right, Rog?"

Roger looked at her and smiled. It was clear he hadn't heard a word she said. His mind had flickered in on his name, like a dog. His gaze drifted over to David. "I understand you had to replumb over there," he said with a chuckle. What was so funny about plumbing? "These old houses are a pain, aren't they?"

"People like them for their charm," said David.

Roger barked out another little laugh. "Sue had her heart set on this place. Said she always wanted an old-fashioned house." He shrugged. "I stuck the sellers with a lot of improvements. New plumbing, wiring. Made them pay to convert the old oil furnace to gas. Say, do you have gas heat or oil?"

"Gas," said David, wondering why Roger cared.

There was a burst of activity from the other side of the room as Matt and Chris emerged, wearing matching pressed khakis and dark green crewneck sweaters. After they were introduced to Evelyn, they sat down politely on the sofa with soft drinks. Roger gazed briefly at his sons and resumed his conversation with David. "Sue got the old-fashioned house she wanted, but I made sure it was practical, too." He leaned over confidentially. "I'd made out like a bandit on our old house in Milwaukee, and my company gave me a terrific relocation allowance. Enough to upgrade this old place plenty. It was a firetrap and a sitting duck for intruders, if you ask me." He shook his head. "Flimsy latches on all the windows. I had 'em all replaced and we put in a complete home security system. Then we replaced an old fuse box with circuit breakers. What kind of shape is your wiring in?"

David shrugged. "Beats me." Actually, he knew that the

wiring was terrible. The circuit breakers were always trip-
ping, sending them groping their way to the basement to flip
them. Anita was always bitching about it.

"I guess in the insurance business you think about all these
things more," said David. "About what can go wrong, I mean.
I don't give it much thought. I just like a place with some
sense of history, good lines, honest architecture."

What an oaf this guy was! His whole definition of a home
was based on the physical plant, while his wife knocked
herself out making it warm and comfortable and welcoming.
All her efforts were probably lost on Roger.

And earlier the big jerk had completely tuned out the
women's conversation, ignoring his wife when she graciously
tried to get him involved. Now, they were supposed to talk
to each other about wiring and plumbing, just because they
were both guys.

Sue came over with a tray of some kind of white cheese
with little blue and yellow flower petals on the top. With her
ankles together, she bent over from the waist, giving David a
long, heady view of her breasts, suspended in spandex and
swelling over the scoop neck of the leotard, as if they were
trying to escape. David took a cracker. "Great outfit, Sue," he
blurted out in what he realized immediately was a misguided
attempt to cover his excitement.

"Why, thank you," she said sweetly. Clearly, she had no
idea how hot she looked.

"She thinks that getup is artistic-looking," said Roger
boorishly. Jesus! Couldn't he see his wife's nipples sticking
out like that? Sue didn't seem to notice she'd been insulted.
Maybe his put-downs were so ingrained in their marriage,
she'd become immune.

As Sue drifted off toward the female half of the room, her
skirt swaying, setting off the delightful curve of her hips

flaring from that little waist, Roger turned back to David. "Sorry your wife's sick," he said with an odd smirk. "I thought she might not join us."

What was Roger talking about? thought David. How could he possibly have known Anita wouldn't come? The guy probably didn't even realize he wasn't making sense. David decided to get into the women's conversation and exclude Roger.

Evelyn was saying to Sue in her sharp voice, "It's wonderful that you're able to be home with your kids. Of course, when my daughter was first married, David was working. Anita stayed home with the girls when they were little."

Sue stood up. "I have to pop in and glaze the chicken," she said. "Sylvie, I'm afraid you might get spattered. Lily, do you want to help me?"

Lily scowled, and said nothing.

"I'll help you, Sue," said David. Their exit now would stop his mother-in-law from going on anymore about his shortcomings to Sue. Plus it would show Roger how a classy, supportive guy behaved. He was pleased that Roger looked startled as David followed Sue into the kitchen.

"I'm sorry about Anita," Sue said, opening the oven and peering inside it. She fussed with a pastry brush and a glass bowl with some amber liquid.

David looked out the kitchen window up to the room where Anita lay. He could see her outline against the partially opened blinds. She seemed to be on the phone.

"If there's nothing wrong with her stomach, we should at least bring her over a plate of food," continued Sue.

"Oh, she'll be okay." David turned away from the window. "Want me to finish that?" He took over with the pastry brush while Sue inverted a big copper mold over a platter. A quivering reddish, aspicky mass slid out.

"Roger just told me he had thought Anita wouldn't come," he said. "What did he mean by that?"

"Oh, nothing," said Sue quickly, looking solemn and horrified.

"What is it?" David demanded. Did Sue know that Anita resented her?

Sue scuttled out from behind her aspic, breasts bouncing. She came to his side and whispered, "Maybe I shouldn't tell you this, but when I told Roger I invited you guys, he said Anita would never show up because she knows he saw her having lunch with a man downtown."

"So?" said David. "She's a businesswoman. She has male friends and acquaintances. I don't see—"

Sue seemed to hesitate a moment. "The guy was kissing her, Roger said. He just knew she was having an affair with the guy." Sue looked away. "It's terrible. I'm so sorry."

David turned to face the window of his bedroom.

"I'm sure he was mistaken," he said smoothly. "Anita does business with a lot of fashion people. They're all gushy and kissy. Like actors. It doesn't mean a thing." He turned back and smiled at Sue, who was watching him intently.

"I'm sure you're right," she said, taking hold of his arm. "I thought it must be a mistake." Looking embarrassed and distracted, she began to garnish the edge of the aspic with some kind of veiny wild leaves. "I couldn't imagine someone married to you ever wanting to have an affair," she said.

"Do you realize we've been talking for almost an hour?" said Anita, snuggling deeper into the pillows. "I haven't done that since I was a teenager."

She was lolling luxuriously in the middle of the bed instead of huddling to her side trying not to touch David. Her

white lace nightgown looked very pretty. She was sorry
Frank couldn't admire her in it.

What was so refreshing was that they hadn't talked about
David or her marriage at all. Instead, they'd talked about
what they'd been like as children, and what countries they'd
like to visit, and how much they loved each other. At times,
they just purred happily into the phone. "Your voice is so
sexy," she said. "Just listening to it is like having part of you
here. This is so much better than making small talk with
those boring neighbors."

The stairs creaked. Anita let out a little gasp. She listened
hard. All was quiet.

"What is it?" said Frank, sounding very alarmed.

"Nothing." She giggled. "I thought I heard something
downstairs. I'm feeling guilty, I guess."

"I should be there to take care of you, Anita. Check out
funny noises for you. I don't think you've ever been properly
taken care of. I mean, you're perfectly capable, I know that,
it's just that there's something fragile and vulnerable . . ."

"Oh, Frank," she said. "I love you so much!"

A discreet but insistent knock sounded at the bedroom
door. Anita let out a little cry and instinctively pulled the
covers up to cover her décolletage. Who could it be? David
would never knock. The children would rush in, and her
mother always barked, "Anita?" and pushed the door open.

The door opened and Sue stood there smiling and holding
a plate. "I've brought you some Mother's Day dinner," she
said, coming over to the bedside. "We're all having such a
good time, I felt sorry for you here all alone. This is a Poly-
nesian chicken with a ginger and papaya glaze and a kind of
summery tomato aspic salad I invented, with a vegetable
stock, pureed carrots, parsley, and cilantro. I hope you like
it."

Anita felt she was at one of those restaurants where the

servers rattle on about the composition of all the dishes, an impression reinforced when Sue laid the tray on the bed and said, "Well, enjoy!"

Anita found herself shrinking away. She gradually became aware of Frank's frantic, tiny voice coming from the receiver she was still holding. She lifted it and said shortly, "My neighbor's just dropped by. I'll call you back," and pushed down the disconnect button with her thumb. "You frightened me," she said to Sue.

"Gosh, I'm sorry," said Sue breezily. "I'm in and out of here all the time. I guess I got in the habit of just walking in. And I didn't want you to get out of bed if you were sick." She put her fingers over her face and looked out at Anita, the way she had when they'd confronted her about cutting a hole in the hedge.

"It's okay," said Anita.

"Do you have a temperature?" asked Sue solicitously.

Anita had a horrible vision of Sue sitting down on the edge of the bed and watching her eat. "Oh, I'll be fine," she said. "Please don't bother about me anymore."

"I didn't mean to bother you," said Sue, looking even more apologetic and embarrassed.

"No, no," said Anita. "I said please don't bother *about* me. Your own family must be missing you."

"Yes. They're waiting for me," said Sue. "Your family, too. We're all having a great time."

"I'm sorry I couldn't be there," said Anita, who suddenly wanted to leap out of bed and throw Sue physically out of the house.

Sue smiled and looked relieved, as if she felt forgiven. "Happy Mother's Day, Anita!" she said.

9

THE NEXT MORNING, ANITA CREPT DOWNSTAIRS quietly so as not to wake her mother, or the girls. They didn't have to get ready for school for another hour, and she was looking forward to creeping out of the place without running into anyone.

To her surprise, her mother was already up, sitting at the kitchen table in her yellow quilted bathrobe, drinking coffee and looking out across to the Heffernans'.

"Mom! What are you doing up?" said Anita. She didn't want to talk to anyone. Maybe not even Frank.

"I couldn't sleep," said her mother. "I'm so worried about you."

"Oh, I'm feeling much better," said Anita, turning away from her mother's concerned face.

"Is David having an affair with that Sue person?" asked her mother bluntly.

"David?" said Anita, amazed. "Of course not. What makes you ask that?"

"I heard you two fighting last night. Lily was asleep, thank God."

"Please, Mom," said Anita, sitting down across from her at the table. "It's too painful."

"I sort of imagined you were confronting him about it," said her mother. She narrowed her eyes. "I think it hasn't started yet, but there's something going on. The time to do something is now, before it gets off the ground. That woman has to be stopped."

"Really, Mom, don't you think you're being a little dramatic?" Anita tried not to smile. The idea of David and Sue—it was absurd.

"There's something not quite right about her. I can tell," her mother said in a very serious voice.

"Sue is a little odd," agreed Anita. "I have to admit she scared me coming into the house last night with that plate of food. But she seems well-meaning."

"Anita, you can be so gullible," said her mother in the decisive way that always made Anita tense up. "She stared at David all night, and completely ignored her husband. Who didn't seem to notice, incidentally, or maybe just doesn't care that she was wearing a painted-on top that left nothing to the imagination. And Lily tells me she's over here practically running your house!"

"Well, what am I supposed to do?" Anita demanded. "Tell David she can't come over here?"

"Why not? I don't like the way she's pushed her way in and sucked up to your girls. Sylvie seems to be completely under her sway. And I'm pretty sure she's lusting after your husband. Men are such suckers for that kind of thing, and he's home all day with nothing better to do."

"I can't stay here and keep tabs on him," Anita protested. "I have to go to work, or we'll all starve."

Her mother sat up a little straighter and gave Anita an alert, pleased smile. It was the first time Anita had even hinted that she resented supporting the family all by herself.

"All the more reason for you to lay down the law," retorted her mother.

"I tried to do that last night," admitted Anita. "That's what our fight was about. I told him I didn't want her here so much. She really upset me, marching in like that."

"What did he say?" demanded her mother eagerly.

Anita sighed. "Oh, it's all so pathetic," she began.

Her mother sighed, too. "If I wasn't in Denver it would be easier. I'd know how you were because I'd see you day in and day out. These visits are difficult for both of us. I end up asking you all these questions at once. I worry so much. I can't stand not knowing how things are with you." Her voice sounded weak and a little frightened. "I'm sorry, honey. I just feel strongly that things aren't good. It feels tense here."

"It *is* tense, Mom," said Anita, looking down at her mother's hand splayed out on the table as Evelyn leaned forward, a supplicant for her daughter's confidences. Someday, that's what my hand will look like, Anita thought, staring at the raised veins and little flecks of brown. She covered her mother's hand with her own. Her mother clutched back at her, and Anita said, "I love you, Mom. Try not to worry."

"I wish I had more confidence in David," her mother said. "You've been a saint all these years, you really have. You never complain about him. Most women would have. . . ."

Anita began to cry.

"Honey!" Her mother rose and came around to the table

and embraced her. Anita turned in her chair, let herself collapse onto her mother's soft chest, and wept. Her mother patted her back. "Oh, Anita, honey, what is it?"

Anita pulled her head off her mother's bosom. "I'm not a saint," she sobbed. "I'm in love with another man. I can't help it. I hate being here with David and I don't know what to do."

Her mother grabbed Anita by the shoulders and pushed her back, still holding on so she could scrutinize her daughter's face.

"Is he married too?" she asked.

Anita, startled that this should be her mother's first reaction, shook her head silently and sniffed.

"That's good."

"Mom! Aren't you shocked?"

"Is he a good person?"

Anita nodded. "I think so. Yes, he is. I know he is."

"Oh, honey!" Her mother embraced her again. "I'm so sorry. You're going through hell, aren't you? Do you think you'll leave David?"

"I can't imagine that. It seems so drastic."

Evelyn began to rock Anita gently. "Does David know?"

"I didn't think he did," said Anita. "But last night, when I started to complain about Sue, he turned on me. Asked me if there was someone else." Anita didn't mention the fact that he'd pointed to a reddish mark Frank had left on her shoulder when he'd clutched her as he climaxed. "That sure looks like a thumbprint, Anita," he'd said unpleasantly. "And I know I didn't leave it there."

"Let me know if I can do anything to help," her mother said. "Do you want me to take the girls while you figure all this out?"

"I don't know how to figure anything out," said Anita.

Evelyn bit her lower lip. "Maybe I should change that flight tomorrow. Stay here longer. I hate to have you alone at a time like this."

But I'm not alone, thought Anita. I have Frank.

"Aren't you shocked, Mom? I am." She was flabbergasted at how calm her mother was that her daughter was an adulteress.

"I'm surprised it hasn't happened sooner. You're so charming and attractive. And you've been carrying David for years. It's bound to have undermined your respect for him."

"But the children—" began Anita.

"Ah, the children," said her mother. "That's always it. If it weren't for children, everything would be so simple, wouldn't it?" She shrugged. "A note on the fridge and you'd be gone, right?"

"I'm sorry to burden you with all this," said Anita.

"Sweetheart, don't you see? I feel much better. I'm sorry for you, of course, but it was not knowing what was going on that was so hard. I can stand trouble. Not knowing, that's something else again."

"Oh, Mom!" said Anita, hugging her mother again. "I love you."

"This other fellow," said her mother intently. "What does he do for a living?"

"He's a lawyer."

Anita's mother looked slightly nervous. "Is he with a good firm?"

"Mo-om," said Anita, smiling a little despite herself.

"Well, is he?"

"He's a partner in one of the best firms in town."

"Good! I wouldn't want him to be some penniless public defender or anything. There are too many lawyers around these days. A lot of them are starving."

Anita was stunned. Mom didn't care about right or wrong.

All she cared about was her child. All she wanted was for someone to take care of her child as she had once done. As she still tried to do, but wouldn't be able to do for much longer.

She herself felt as fiercely about Lily and Sylvie. She wanted to make sure they were safe and protected. Even if it meant protecting them from their own mother's crazy passion for Frank, and what it could do to their world.

LATER, AFTER ANITA HAD LEFT, THE GIRLS WOKE up and came downstairs. Evelyn made French toast for them. David still hadn't emerged from the bedroom. Lily had left for the bus, and Evelyn was loading the dishwasher when Sue appeared at the back door, holding a jar of mayonnaise.

Evelyn opened the door. "Thank you again for last night," she said without enthusiasm.

"Wasn't it great!" said Sue. "Is Sylvie ready?"

"For what?"

Sylvie left the table and scampered to the door. "Sue always walks me to school," she said.

"Oh, but honeybunch," said Evelyn, "I was hoping I could do that today. Mrs. Heffernan is so nice, but we mustn't impose."

"It's not an imposition at all," said Sue stiffly. "You don't understand."

"Thanks, anyway," said Evelyn in a the-subject-is-now-closed way. For good measure, she added, "And I'll pick her up, too, if it's somehow too much for David." To Sylvie she said, "Run along and get your homework and all that, dear."

"Okay, Grandma." Sylvie tripped away in her usual cheerful way, apparently completely unaware two adult women had been fighting over her.

"Where's David?" demanded Sue.

"He's still asleep," Evelyn replied curtly.

"I can't get this open," said Sue, holding up the jar. "I thought maybe David could help."

"Why don't you ask your own husband?" said Evelyn pointedly.

"He's at work. I'm sorry to bother you."

"Let me give it a try," said Evelyn. She grabbed the jar and wrenched. "It feels like someone put it on there with a vise," she commented, handing back the jar.

"Can you ask David to come over and open it later?" said Sue, tilting her face up a little defiantly.

"I'll pass on the message," said Evelyn.

"And maybe you could send Sylvie over after school," Sue added.

"The girls will be busy all day," said Evelyn. She turned away and got on with the dishes to indicate the conversation was over.

"There's a trick to that dishwasher," said Sue. "Let me show you. See? The lid to the soap dispenser won't release in the second cycle unless you make sure this little catch here is in the right position."

"Where?" said Evelyn, bending over and peering in.

"Here," said Sue. She put down the jar of mayonnaise and took Evelyn's hand, guiding it down by the silverware section. "You have to kind of lift it on one side when you close it. The hinge is a little tired."

Evelyn was aware of a strange jabbing sensation. She looked down to see her hand stuck on the point of a paring knife. With a cry of pain, she pulled her hand back. There was a gash across the knuckle of her thumb. Blood was oozing out in a straight line.

"Oh, no," said Sue, stepping back. "You should never put a sharp knife in there with the blade going up. I've told David, but he always forgets." She peered into the machine herself and clicked her tongue.

Evelyn turned on the faucet and ran cold water over the cut. She felt suddenly weak and willed herself not to faint. The water made rusty pink circles as it ran into the garbage disposal.

"Does it hurt?" asked Sue. "Let me get you a paper towel."

"Just go, all right?" boomed Evelyn. "I'll handle it. You've done enough."

"You don't think I did it on purpose, do you?" said Sue, her eyes widening.

Evelyn turned and looked at her. She hadn't thought that until Sue mentioned it, but now she wondered.

Sue swallowed and, looking embarrassed, backed out the door, saying, "I'm sorry."

Feeling a huge sense of relief, Evelyn went to get a paper towel. She sat down heavily in a chair and mashed the wad of paper against the cut, watching it turn swiftly red.

At least, Evelyn thought with grim satisfaction, she'd managed to get Sue to leave. With people like that, you had to be forceful. Give them an inch and they'd take a mile.

It was an hour later, after Evelyn returned from walking Sylvie to school, when David finally emerged, unshaven and dressed in jeans, sweatshirt, and his bedroom slippers. An indignant Evelyn was waiting for him in the kitchen, a huge bandage of gauze and white adhesive tape tied around her thumb.

"I think that woman's nuts," she said after she'd told him the story. "She deliberately pushed my hand onto that knife because I wouldn't turn over Sylvie, because she knows I see through her."

"Oh, come on, Evelyn," said David wearily. "I can't believe she did it on purpose."

He looked over at the mayonnaise jar. "This is the jar she left?"

"That's right. She tightened it up good and hard to give her an excuse to come over here and bother you."

David sighed. "I'll go over there and see if I can sort this out."

David marched across the lawn and through the hedge. Terrific. Just as he'd suspected, his mother-in-law had managed to mix it up with Sue. He'd tell Sue that the old bitch was senile and to keep clear until tomorrow when she flew back to Denver and things would be back to normal.

Or as normal as they could be when you were wondering if your wife was cheating on you. Last night, scrutinizing that mark on Anita's shoulder, he'd been ready to believe it. By the light of day, though, it seemed less likely. Anita didn't have time to be fooling around, did she? But just the idea that she might be was upsetting enough.

What he really hoped was that if Anita was having an affair, it would all blow over without his needing to know about it. Above all, he didn't want Sue to know that her husband had been right. That would be just too humiliating.

Sue was waiting for him in the kitchen.

"Is your mother-in-law all right?" she said, looking pathetic and remorseful.

"Of course she is," said David. "But, listen, Sue, she's a little high-strung. Like Anita. Maybe you'd better stay out of the way today. She's flying out tomorrow."

"Of course," said Sue. "I feel so awful. I really didn't know the knife was there. I was just showing her—"

"Never mind," said David, patting her shoulder.

She fell silent and smiled. "I'm glad you liked that outfit I had on last night," she said. "Roger said I looked like a beatnik."

"It was great," he said. "Very simple." He could hardly say, "It sure showed off those breasts to advantage."

He grimaced as he gave the lid of the jar a turn. Finally it popped open. "Here's your mayo."

"Wow! Thanks!" Changing her tone, she said gravely, "David, I wanted to talk to you about last night. I'm sorry I told you what Roger saw in that restaurant. I've been feeling so guilty. I wouldn't want to come between a husband and wife. I'm so sorry."

"Hey, that's okay."

"It's just that I think of you as a friend."

"Listen, Sue, I appreciate it." He gave her a perfunctory hug. "Anita and I have some things to work out. We've been talking about going into counseling," he lied. Turning problems over to professionals seemed to make them all less sordid somehow. "I'll be in touch."

He headed for the door, and Sue gave him a friendly little wave good-bye. Back in his own kitchen he announced to Evelyn that he'd picked up that twenty-four-hour bug Anita had had and was going to spend the day in bed. Let her run things around here today. She seemed to like to be in charge.

LOGICALLY, ANITA TOLD HERSELF, SHE PROBABLY got the cold from that runny-nosed Carlos in Sylvie's class, but because she had lied about being ill on Mother's Day, she felt that she was being justly punished. She felt the first inklings two days later driving back from taking her mother to the airport—a sneezy itch in her nose and an ache in her throat that promised to get worse before it got better.

She took two aspirin before she went to work, and tried to pretend that the whole thing would just go away, but by eleven, she felt hot and flushed, and had raided the office cupboard for a large box of Kleenex. What she needed, she decided, was some kind of cold pill that would dry up her sinuses and keep her temperature down. She'd get some at lunchtime. That way, she could keep going.

Pam Gates, her boss, came into the office, took one look at Anita snuffling noisily into a tissue, stepped backward, and said, "You're sick. Go home!"

"No, I'll be okay if I get some Contac or Sudafed or something," said Anita.

"Forget it," said Pam. "I don't want to catch anything." She scuttled out of the office, the errand that had brought her there in the first place apparently forgotten.

Pam's hypochondria around the office was legendary. Not only did she habitually regale everyone with all the ghastly details of her own symptoms, which usually seemed to involve her gastrointestinal system, she was also terrified of catching anything from anyone else.

Everyone in the department had learned that you could get a day off by coughing a little, and saying bravely that you felt a little bit lousy but wanted to tough it out. "Go home!" Pam would bark, jumping out of germ range, and the slacker would say in a weak, fake reluctant voice, "Maybe you're right, Pam," and hack away some more on the way to the door.

The trouble was, Anita didn't want to go home. Last time she'd been sick, she had lain there listening feverishly to David squabbling with the girls from downstairs, feeling as if she should get up and serve as umpire, but it had been okay during the hours when they were at school.

Now, though, with things so tense between them, the prospect of being alone with David in the house filled her with a bleak dread. What if he seized the opportunity to grill her about Frank? She'd be too weak to keep stonewalling.

She wasn't even sure she wanted to anymore, anyway. She imagined dragging herself downstairs to make herself a cup of tea and then being cornered by him in the kitchen with fresh accusations, then bursting into tears.

Besides, if she were home, she couldn't talk to Frank on the phone, couldn't meet him after work as they had planned.

Reluctantly, she picked up the phone and called Frank, feeling the usual butterflies as she spoke to his secretary, Lorna. Lorna always sounded completely businesslike. Anita imagined her gossiping all over the firm about the frequency of her calls.

"I seem to have a cold," she said when he came on the line.

"Poor Anita," he said, melting her heart with his tenderness. "What are your symptoms?"

"Sore throat, fever. And an extremely runny nose. Pam is sending me home. Oh, Frank, I wanted to see you so much. I'm sorry." She realized how anguished she sounded.

"Don't apologize! You can't help it," he said. "But I'll miss you."

"Isn't this awful," she said. "I would never have thought that my getting a little cold and not being able to see you would seem like such a huge tragedy!"

"Did you take anything for it?"

"Just a couple of aspirin. If it weren't for Pam insisting I go home, I'd take some Contac or something and soldier on, then I could see you tonight."

"Don't take that stuff," he said. "It just masks the symptoms. You need to rest. This is probably the result of all the stress you've been through."

"I don't know. I thought I was being punished because I lied on Mother's Day and said I was sick, and now I am. Oh Frank, I don't want to go home and lie there in that house with just David there. I'll be so miserable."

"Don't go home. I'll come and get you and take you to my place and take care of you all afternoon. I've only got one appointment, and I'll cancel it."

"Oh, Frank! I can't ask you to do that. Besides, I'm so unattractive right now," she said. "My eyes feel like they're all red, and I'm going through the Kleenex at an amazing rate. It's better that you don't see me like this."

"You're always beautiful," he said. "Besides, I've never seen you with a cold. I want to know what you're like all the time. In sickness as well as in health. Wait for me at the loading zone on the Pine Street side of the store. I'll be there in five minutes."

She shivered there on the street, in her thin summer dress, feeling the ineffectual sun on her arms, looking anxiously in the direction his car would come from. When he did arrive, she slid gratefully into the seat beside him and let her head collapse against his shoulder. "I'm being too dramatic," she said. "It's just a cold."

"I'll take care of you," he said, placing his hand on her forehead. "Yes, you've definitely got a temperature." He kissed her gently on the mouth, and she said anxiously, "but you'll get my cold."

"I don't care," he said.

Back at his apartment, he led her by the hand to his bed and told her to lie down, then he undressed her and brought her one of his T-shirts, big and soft and light gray, and pulled it over her head.

"There," he said, sitting on the side of the bed and smiling down at her as if pleased with his handiwork. He caressed her breast through the T-shirt. He kissed her forehead and stood up. "Kindly Dr. Shaw is going to make you a nice hot toddy and then tuck you in."

"Oh, darling, you're so sweet," she said. "I really am pathetic, aren't I?"

"I think you've never been as adorable as you are now, wearing my T-shirt and snuffling into my handkerchief."

"Oh, Frank," she said, "I mustn't get used to you taking care of me. I don't deserve it. It's all based on my lying to everyone." She fell back on the pillow and began to weep.

"Rest," he said. "You need to rest." He stroked her forehead and she lay there feeling weak and guilty, dreading the time this evening when she'd have to tear herself away from this warm, quiet place and go back home.

THAT NIGHT, ANITA AWOKE QUITE SUDDENLY, with a feeling of dread. She looked over at the clock. It was four-fifteen in the morning. She fumbled for Kleenex and blew her nose as quietly as possible so as not to wake David.

For some time now, Anita had been waking up around four, and even the exhaustion she felt from this cold didn't spare her. It was almost as if there were some biological process at work. She masked her anxieties during the day, but they returned to haunt her in the middle of the night when her guard was down.

Fright was what seemed to actually wake her, and then it took her a few moments to realize what was scaring her. The fear would then be replaced by a feeling of hopelessness, and her mind would begin to race.

Over and over again, she imagined David confronting her with her adultery, even though he hadn't brought it up since Mother's Day, when he'd asked her about the reddish mark on her shoulder. In her imagination, she confessed the whole thing. Sometimes it went well and he seemed to understand. Other times he became violent and yelled and the girls overheard him.

She also imagined Frank demanding that she leave David, and threatening to end it if she didn't. Or, in another version, telling her that having just a part of her was enough, that he understood she had to keep her family together. Sometimes she even imagined Frank meeting someone else—someone single and available, and younger. This scenario got her physically, right in the gut, and she'd curl up, cramped with jealousy and anger.

Sometimes she imagined getting David to leave. But where would he go? She couldn't afford to support him, even in some cheap apartment. Anyway, that would be too pathetic. And who would take care of the girls during the day? Lily was old enough to be home by herself, but Sylvie wasn't.

She also imagined fleeing to Frank's apartment. Which she couldn't do, of course, because of the girls. There was no room for children there.

Her worst imaginings concerned the girls. She tried to find ways to explain to them how she felt about Frank, but she knew it couldn't be done. They hadn't experienced anything remotely like passionate love. Children only knew about the love that meant they were safe and cared for and loved themselves. They would see her love for Frank as undermining that. Anita herself hadn't understood how strong her feelings could be. If anyone had told her, even after it first started, she wouldn't have believed it. The girls would never understand. They wouldn't forgive her, certainly not for years to come, maybe not ever.

Maybe she should get some sleeping pills. She was afraid, though, that if she did, she would pay for it somehow. These insomniac interludes, horrible as they were, were probably the safest way for her to panic. This way, she could spend her hour or so every night mulling over all the possibilities, weighing the pain of each one in solitude, without worrying the girls or losing it in front of David.

She wouldn't want Frank to see her this way, either. She was shocked that she could be going through such turmoil and yet be so completely happy and calm when she was with him. She wished he were here now, so she could reach for him. She imagined him alone in his apartment—his clean, organized, homey apartment—sleeping peacefully. She had never seen him really asleep, only collapsed after making love, exhausted and blissful.

Suddenly, she heard a cry. It had come from Sylvie's room. Anita swung out of bed and rushed down the hall.

Sylvie was asleep, on her back, her head lolling to and fro, her face contorted. "No, no!" she was shouting.

Anita stroked her forehead, then kissed it. "Wake up, darling," she said. "You're having a nightmare."

Sylvie tossed some more and spoke in her sleep, but Anita couldn't make out the words. The child was trembling, clearly terrified.

Anita shook her and said more loudly, "Wake up, Sylvie! It's all right. Everything's all right."

Sylvie's eyes opened. "Scary. It's so scary. Vampires. They suck your blood." Her eyes looked glazed over as if she were still asleep. "You have to invite them in."

"There aren't any vampires here, darling," said Anita. "And if there were, we wouldn't invite them in."

"You don't know they're bad," said Sylvie. She looked less strange, but still half-asleep. "They seem nice."

Anita pulled her up and wrapped her arms around her and began to rock her back and forth. "It's all right," she said, holding the warm little body against her, patting her back. "I'm here."

Sylvie struggled in her arms. "I'm scared," she said. "I want Sue. Sue!"

It was after five by the time Anita had settled Sylvie back down. She lay next to her on top of the covers on the narrow bed and waited until her daughter's breathing indicated she was asleep and calm. Then she walked back down the hall to her own bedroom, went over to David's side of the bed, and shook him roughly.

When he woke, looking up at her fuzzily, she stood over him and said in a firm, level voice, "Sue has got to go. She is not going to come over here anymore. If you won't get Sylvie to school, I will. But I want Sue completely out of our lives. Got that?"

David looked frightened. He glanced over at the green digits on the clock. "Jesus," he said, "it's five-twelve. What the hell is the matter with you?"

"Sylvie had a nightmare. I went in there." Anita angrily grabbed the Kleenex box, yanked one out, and blew her nose violently. "She asked for Sue."

"And you're waking me up to tell me this?"

"I'm her mother, not Sue!" said Anita.

"Of course you are. She was probably just half-asleep and confused, that's all. Anyway, let's talk about it in the morning."

"There's nothing to talk about," said Anita. "Just get rid of her."

10

David sat Sue down at his kitchen table when she arrived the next day with the lunch she had just made—peanut butter sandwiches on sourdough bread, and nectarine slices dusted with cinnamon.

"It's hard to tell you this," he said, "but I think while my marriage is in such rocky shape, it might be better if you were here less. Anita is very high-strung and for some reason she seems to resent your presence here."

Sue looked mortified. She put her hand on the side of her face and crinkled up her brow in the way David had come to find so touching. "Oh, no!" she said. "Why on earth does she feel that way? I'm only trying to help."

"Who knows?" said David, letting out a dramatic sigh. "Maybe she's threatened by you. She's kind of screwed up and she knows your core is solid and that you're a wonderful mother. It's her own lack of self-esteem."

"I don't understand," said Sue. "I've tried to be nice to her."

"You're always nice," said David. "But things are rough right now around here. . . ."

"Did you tell her what I said about the guy in the restaurant?" Sue asked urgently. "If she thinks I told you about that, then maybe that's why . . ."

David seized on this suggestion. "That must be it. Anyway, I guess it would be better if I take Sylvie to school for a while." He wondered whether he should offer to take Matt and Chris, too. It only seemed fair, but he really didn't want to. In fact, he didn't want to take Sylvie, either. David was never at his best in the mornings. It really was very unreasonable of Anita to be so obsessed by this, just when he needed to redouble his work efforts and perhaps start canvassing for some new clients.

"I think you should stand up to her," said Sue, looking stubborn. "I don't think she's in any position to tell you who should take Sylvie to school. After all, you're the primary caretaker."

"Well, yes, I think that's part of the problem. Last night, Sylvie had a nightmare. Anita went in there and Sylvie called out for you."

Sue's face blossomed into a big smile. "She did?"

"Anyway, let's just cool it for a while, okay?" Her smile had made him nervous for some reason.

"All right," said Sue.

"Thanks for being so understanding." He really was relieved. Maybe Anita actually had a point, not that he'd ever admit it to her. Sue had been over here a lot.

"I suppose I can still come over and straighten up a little while they're in school. And leave before they come home. Anita won't even know I've been here." Sue giggled and looked just a tiny bit flirtatious. David was mostly just relieved she wasn't going to fall apart on him. "But I'll miss the girls. Especially Sylvie. She'll miss me, too." His relief had been premature. Now her eyes seemed to be misting up.

David hoped to God she wouldn't cry. He had felt from an early age that dealing with hurt women was a treacherous undertaking.

"I'm sorry, Sue," he said.

She turned back to him, her eyes glittery with tears. "Why are you giving in so easily? Stand up to her! Don't be so weak." There was a shrillness in her voice he'd never heard before, and the word "weak" sliced into him like a knife. How dare she call him that?

"Excuse me, Sue, but I'm trying to save my marriage. Maybe things are a little weird around here. Maybe you do spend too much time here and maybe it is strange that you're cleaning the house and feeding us. You do have your own family, after all."

"But, David, I've bonded with yours, too." She took his hands in hers and said in a rather desperate, low voice, "This house just cried out for me. I really believe it's fate that I moved in here when I did. Just when Anita deserts you emotionally, when maybe, and I hope it's not true, she's cheating on you, I turn up. To take care of you and the girls. I think it's all meant to be."

David felt a sudden panicky urge to muscle her out of the house and back through her hedge across the property line. Shaking a little, he pulled away and said, "I think things are a little out of hand, Sue. Maybe you're getting too emotionally involved."

"But, David, the girls need me, and I love them."

The phone rang. He rose to get it, grateful for the distraction, but Sue stood up and blocked his path. "Let the machine get it," she said. "This is important. What do you mean 'too emotionally involved'? Is that such a terrible thing?" Her voice softened. "Feelings are important. I can't talk about anything with Roger. It's so wonderful to be able to open up to you. You have so much sensitivity. I feel you really understand me."

The phone stopped ringing. "This is a hard time for me to deal with these issues right now," he said, pushing away his plate and glass.

She picked them up. "I know," she said calmly, carrying them to the sink. He watched her from behind. Her prim, freshly ironed white blouse tucked into khaki trousers showed off the sway of her hips as she walked. Sue rinsed off the dishes and began loading them into the dishwasher. "But you know, David, when you get that Conway's account, things will be different. You'll be able to stand up to Anita then, won't you?" She turned and faced him. "Until then, I understand how you feel. I don't want to do anything that will make things hard for you."

"Thanks, Sue," he said solemnly. "You're very understanding." His panic receded. Her little outburst had passed and she was sounding like practical, thoughtful Sue again. Women all got gushy once in a while. They couldn't help it, especially when they adored someone the way he felt Sue adored him. She was gazing at him with a completely open, vulnerable face. It suddenly struck him that if he wanted to, he bet he could fuck her right now.

Maybe that would calm her down. David had already speculated about the Heffernans' sex life. Roger hardly struck him as a demon in the sack. Looking at Sue leaning on the counter with her head at that girlish little angle, and that feminine body with its heavy breasts and wide, curvy hips, and that wide-open, come-on-in look, he decided that Sue was probably a very passionate woman and a great lay. In fact, he realized he'd been thinking that for quite a while.

Well, he thought, suddenly getting excited, why the hell not? True, she might reject him, run back to her house, never come by again. And he could tell Anita that he'd made sure she wouldn't bother them again. That would solve the whole thing rather neatly.

On the other hand, she might respond. Then he could bury his face in those soft breasts and push inside her and give her what she really needed, what she'd really appreciate. After all, Anita might be getting some. Why should he deny himself?

He pushed away the kitchen chair and moved toward her. It had been so long since he'd made a pass at someone. He'd forgotten how exciting it was, the risk of rejection and the thrill of conquest. Was he really doing this? He felt a terrific charge as he walked up to her. Should he kiss her on the mouth? Or just touch her hair and gaze into her eyes. Maybe he should make it seem like a sensitive, friendship kind of thing, and see if it took on an erotic tinge.

She stood there, watching him come toward her. He couldn't tell what she was thinking.

He put his hands on her shoulders and said, "Sue," in a soft voice.

She didn't move, just stared up at him with her mouth slightly open. "Oh, David," she said.

"You've meant so much to me," he said, and lowered his head, grazing her forehead with his lips.

She wrapped her arms around his neck and pulled his face to hers. He felt her lips on his, felt her tongue in his mouth, a fat tongue, he thought, tasting of peanut butter. He felt her knee sliding up his leg, felt the unfamiliar body smashed up against his, warm and fleshy and wide, without any sense of bone or structure to it.

He yanked himself away, horrified by her intensity. "I'm sorry," he began. "I don't know what came over me."

"It's all right," she said. "I understand. Men have needs. Women, too. And when they're not being met . . ." She patted her hair self-consciously.

After a long pause, she said in a sad little voice, "I led an extremely sheltered life when I was a teenager. I was pretty young when I got married. I've only slept with Roger. I don't know what other people are like. But I'm sure with you, with someone sensitive and caring like you, it would be different." Then she burst into tears and said, "I feel like such a fool." She buried her face in her hands.

"Oh, Sue," he said. He peeled the hands away from her face. "You're so sweet." He kissed her very lightly on the mouth and then on her cheeks, which tasted salty from her tears, and then on her little upturned nose. This time, she didn't cling to him. She snuffled a little and giggled. Then she started giving him identical, light little kisses.

He kissed her closed eyes and she let out a little sigh of happiness. She put her head on his shoulder and he felt her whole body relax.

So while everyone else David had known was screwing everything in sight during the reckless days of his youth with the sexual revolution raging, poor Sue was saving herself for that geek Roger. She was practically a virgin. But she was all grown up and mature and smart enough to know she was missing something. It would only be a kindness to show her how it could be with someone who knew what they were doing. Sex with him would be, in the phrase of game show announcers, a lovely parting gift, something she would cherish forever in a bittersweet way as she went on like the old-fashioned, good sport she was, caring for Roger and the boys.

He stroked her back and kissed the top of her head. But where? That was the question. Not in his bed. For one thing, it wasn't made, and it might seem tacky to her to usurp the marriage bed. The children's beds were out. Their rooms were disaster areas. And he might have to clean the sheets or something afterward. There was a sofa bed down in the basement that the girls opened up when they had slumber parties, but unfolding it was a terrible job. Besides, it squeaked, and last time he'd looked at it, it seemed to be full of popcorn. Anyway, it would seem too premeditated and cold-blooded, not to mention ridiculously unsexy, to leave Sue standing by while he wrestled with the thing.

That left, by default, the living room sofa. He could lead her in there fairly casually from the kitchen. He'd just have to make sure the curtains were drawn so the mailman didn't catch them.

They were necking on the sofa like a couple of hot, sweaty teenagers when the phone rang again. He started to peel himself off her, but she yanked him down with the crook of her elbow and said, "Not now," before plunging that fat tongue back into his mouth and reaching down to feel his hardening cock through his jeans. She seemed to be checking on it, the way she might check on the progress of a leg of lamb cooking in the oven. She seemed satisfied that he was coming along nicely, gave a throaty little moan, and patted him in a way that was so motherly, he was afraid he'd lose his developing erection.

He didn't want that to happen. He reached desperately under her blouse and pushed it up, encountering a white lace cotton bra. He grabbed her breasts through the stiff material. A second later she was arched up toward him with her hands behind her back, concentrating as she unhooked what seemed like a huge row of fasteners before falling back down on the sofa cushions.

He slid the straps off her shoulders—she had strong,

swimmer's shoulders he saw now, and her big soft breasts with small, purplish nipples tumbled out. He put a hand on each one and squeezed and buried his face between them.

Suddenly, she cleared her throat. "Don't worry about my getting pregnant," she said.

David hadn't given it a thought, but suddenly he panicked.

"But maybe you've had a vasectomy or something," she went on. "Roger had one," she said, stroking his face.

"No, I didn't," said David, suddenly panicking. "Maybe—"

Then she giggled. "Don't worry. It's all right. I'm completely safe myself." She laughed again, and her narrow eyes looked incredibly feline. She arched up toward him and kissed him. He saw those fine, blond downy hairs on her face and smelled her skin. She snaked a hand around, pulling him down to her by the small of his back.

He rubbed his face against hers, marveling that she could have scared him like that, teased him. But then he forgot all about it as she plunged that plump tongue into his ear.

ANITA CAME BACK LATE FROM LUNCH, TRYING not to meet the receptionist's eye as she picked up her phone messages. "Oh, damn," she said. One of them was from the nurse at Sylvie's school.

Sylvie, it appeared, had a temperature. "There's a spring cold going around," the nurse said in a cheery voice.

"Someone will be by to pick her up," said Anita. She immediately called home, only to get the machine. Where the hell was David? She had an important meeting this afternoon, and hated to explain she had to deal with a kid. Everyone would act sympathetic, but the childless ones secretly sneered, she knew, especially Pam, whose desk featured lots of snapshots of her cats in silver frames.

She took a cab to the school and asked the driver to wait while she went in and got Sylvie, who was lying on a little cot in the nurse's office, damp and pink and feverish. The nurse told Anita that she just needed rest, liquids, and something to get her fever down.

In the back of the cab, Sylvie leaned on her mother and sniffed and held on to her the way she had as a baby. Anita smoothed back her hair and kissed her hot little face. "We'll take you home and put on your pajamas and tuck you right in," she said. Sylvie smiled and just said, "Mommy," and Anita suddenly felt that worrying about that stupid meeting was silly.

DAVID WONDERED HOW LONG HE WOULD BE EX-pected to lie there before getting up and pulling his jeans back on and checking the two phone messages. To his consternation, Sue wasn't showing any signs of pulling herself together. She lay back with her arm behind her head, a slight haze of sweat on her face, her eyes closed, her damp lips parted. She was partly covered by her blouse, which lay twisted on her chest like some bit of drapery in a classical painting. Her white cotton underwear and her khaki trousers were somewhere in the gully between the sofa and the coffee table.

She looked incredibly naked. Perhaps it was the whiteness of her skin, or the fleshy mass of her, so unlike Anita's compact little body. Or maybe it was the fact she still wore her fuzzy white socks, or that she was splayed out like that in the living room.

He bent over and kissed her forehead in a friendly way. God, he sure hoped she wasn't falling asleep. Her narrow eyes opened. "Oh, David," she said. "That was beautiful."

"Boy, it sure was," he said, wishing she'd get up, get

dressed, and go home. He slid into his jeans—he'd kept his shirt on throughout their coupling—to provide a good example. "Fabulous."

Sue shifted on the sofa, raising one knee a little and sliding one shiny calf languorously against the other. Her eyes closed again.

"I'll make us some coffee," he said cheerily. "Don't you think you'd better get dressed?"

"Mmm," she said dreamily. He knew she wanted him to lie there with her for hours, cradling her head in his arms and whispering to her how great it had been. Damn.

David dashed into the kitchen and filled the coffee machine with water, congratulating himself on this maneuver. Making coffee seemed a decently thoughtful thing to do après sex, and it also would wake her up. Just rushing to the phone to get the messages might seem a little insensitive. He felt physically good, satisfied and tingly, but mentally overwhelmed and slightly panicky. It had all happened so fast. Maybe it had been a pretty stupid thing to do. God, he wanted her out of there.

He glanced at her through the doorway as he passed to the phone. She was sitting up and searching around her feet for her clothes. Good.

There were two messages. The first, from the school nurse, said Sylvie had a temperature of 101 and should be picked up. The nurse ended the message with, "I'll call your work number, too."

The second message was an irritable Anita. "Where are you? The school nurse called. Now I'll have to take a cab over to school and pick up Sylvie, and miss our weekly sales meeting."

David's heart started thumping. "Get dressed," he snapped at Sue. "Anita's on her way over here. Sylvie's sick and she's bringing her home."

Sue, sitting on the sofa in sensible cotton underpants, was pouring her breasts into her bra. "She seemed a little warm this morning. We'll take care of her." She bent over and hooked up the back.

"You mustn't be here when they come back!" said David. Jesus! What if Anita walked in now! And hadn't Sue heard what he'd just told her in the kitchen over those peanut butter sandwiches they seemed to have eaten days ago? Anita didn't want her around in any case! He fell to his knees in front of the coffee table and groped around for her shoes while she wriggled into her blouse and pulled on the khakis.

"I'm really sorry," he said. "I didn't mean for this to end so abruptly." He waited impatiently for her to button and zip, then handed her one of the shoes.

"It's all right, David," she said dreamily, gazing at him and extending her hand slowly to accept it. "This is only the first time."

"Please hurry up!" he said, reminded of all the times he'd tried to get the girls to get their shoes on when they were late for something.

Outside, he heard a car pull up. He went to the window and looked out. It was the taxi. Fortunately it always took Anita forever to figure out how much to tip. He'd probably be able to shove Sue out the backdoor just in time.

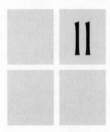

A NITA DIDN'T BOTHER TO COMPUTE THE 15
percent down to the penny, then round up to the nearest
quarter the way she usually did. She wanted to get Sylvie
into bed and make sure she was warm. She thrust a ten and a
five at the driver and said, "Keep the change."

"I was afraid you wouldn't come, Mommy," Sylvie said
groggily on the porch as Anita tried the knob, rapped on the
door, and then, impatient, searched her purse for her key.

"Of course I came, darling," she said. "I'll always take care
of you. Especially when you're sick."

She unlocked the door. She hadn't heard his footsteps
approaching, so she was startled to see David standing there
right inside. He had a panicky look on his face. "I got your
message," he said.

"She's all right," she said. "Just that damn cold I have, the nurse says."

Then Anita heard something from the living room. A throat being cleared. She looked inside. Sue was sitting on the sofa tying the laces of a suede oxford. Its mate was underneath the coffee table. Anita stared at her.

"How's Sylvie?" asked Sue, calmly picking up the second shoe. "Does she have a temperature?" She looked flushed and her usual sleek coiffure was disarranged. David hovered nearby.

Anita gathered Sylvie to her, folding the child's face into her skirt. "Come upstairs, darling," she said shakily, whisking Sylvie away toward the stairs.

"My boys had that, too," Sue shouted after her. "It's going around."

Upstairs, Anita helped Sylvie undress and found her favorite pink pajamas with a picture of a coy, long-lashed pony across the chest. She was startled to see that all the nightgowns and pajamas were folded neatly away in the chest of drawers instead of bunched in the way they used to be. Sue's work, no doubt. Sylvie, sitting on the side of the bed, instinctively put her white little arms straight up as her mother pulled the sleeves over her fists, then rolled gratefully under the covers. Anita went into the bathroom for some Children's Tylenol. From below, she heard the back door in the kitchen close.

When she had settled Sylvie down and stroked her forehead and kissed it and tucked in her blanket, she went slowly downstairs.

David was sitting in the living room drinking a cup of coffee. "Want some?" he said, holding it up inquiringly.

"No," she said coldly. "Listen, David, I need to do a lot of thinking. I want you to know this is all very painful."

"What is there to think about?" he said.

"Whether there's any point in our going on," she said.

"I suppose you're upset about Sue," he said. "I told her. Just like you asked me to. I told her she's not welcome here anymore. We had just finished discussing it."

"Yeah," said Anita. "Right. And then you rubbed her feet."

"Jesus, Anita. She took off her shoes because she had her feet up on the coffee table."

Anita started to say that her mother had warned her, but then David would drag in that red mark on her shoulder again.

"I explained to her very tactfully that she's been around too much. I think she gets the idea," said David. He sounded a tiny bit more confident. "Look, honey, maybe some counseling would be a good idea. It's covered under your health plan, right? We've both been under a lot of pressure." He gave her a big smile.

DAVID COLLAPSED WITH RELIEF WHEN HE WAS FI-nally alone, both women gone. Anita couldn't prove a thing, he told himself. All she'd seen was Sue tying her shoe. If he just brazenly denied that anything had happened, there wasn't anything she could do about it.

Relax, he told himself, stifling a re-emergence of panic. Anita was too conventional to bust up their family. She always said she'd hated all the moving around she'd had to do as a military brat, and that she would do whatever it took to provide the girls with a stable environment.

And besides, she loved him! She'd hero-worshipped him at first. Okay, lately she seemed to have lost faith in his market-ability, but that would all come back when he got his career back on track.

David did want to save his marriage. He simply couldn't

imagine life without Anita. Would she stay here and throw him out? Where would he live? And, more to the point, what would he live on?

Suddenly, he grew indignant. How dare she throw him out when he was the one who looked after the girls? If Anita wanted to do something foolish, she'd have to be the one to move out. He was staying right here. And she'd have to support them, too. He'd insist on it. She wouldn't walk out on the girls, he thought with satisfaction. Everything would be all right. But it would be better if he distanced himself from Sue. He'd have a little chat with her. She'd understand. But not right away. Later, when she'd had a chance to calm down. The poor thing, married to that idiot Roger! Naturally she'd been bowled over by a sexual encounter with someone more sensitive and passionate. He'd give her a few days to come back down to earth.

Sue called him the next morning. She sounded sweet and shy. "Listen," she said, "about yesterday—"

"These things sometimes just happen," said David. "I don't think we should let it get to us. We should forgive ourselves and get on with our lives."

"You're right," said Sue. "We couldn't help it. We got carried away."

David was relieved at her take. He'd feared some big dramatic declaration of love or something. He cleared his throat, and brought up the other thing that had been bothering him. "Remember, remember your asking me if I'd had a vasectomy? And saying Roger had one?"

"Yes, David," she said.

"Well, then you said you were completely 'safe.' What did you mean exactly? That the time of the month . . ." Surely Sue wasn't using any kind of contraception if her husband was shooting blanks. David didn't trust women's cycles. Lily had been okay, he had agreed to that, but Sylvie was certainly a big surprise. He'd made such a big fuss about it that Anita had finally agreed to a tubal ligation right after Sylvie's birth. He always wondered just how accidental that pregnancy was, and imagined that Anita's willingness to have the procedure done was in penance for her deception.

Sue laughed. "You know Roger," she said. "Mr. Insurance. He actually went ahead and had a vasectomy even though my tubes were tied. Talk about suspenders and a belt!"

"Well, that's good," said David in a sensitive voice. "I'd hate for you to have to go through . . . to suffer . . ." he trailed off. Jesus! He must have been out of his mind. That would have been a hell of a note—just when he was trying to patch things up with Anita!

"Listen, Sue, things are very rocky at home right now. Anita and I are probably going into counseling. I'm very upset about it all. She's even hinting about ending the marriage. Listen, Sue, I'm going to need some time to—"

"Oh, David, I never expected this to happen. I don't want anyone to be hurt!"

"No, of course not," said David.

"Especially not the children," said Sue.

"No, no," said David.

"Roger doesn't suspect anything. We're having some people from his company over for a barbecue this weekend. I was thinking if you came, too, it might seem more natural. And maybe it would be reassuring to Anita, too."

"I don't think that's a good idea," said David.

"Why don't I come over and we can talk things out together," she said, sounding sweet and reasonable.

"No! For one thing, Sylvie's still home sick."

"I can bring her some soup."

"No! I promised Anita I wouldn't see you for a while. Sylvie would mention it. We can't drag her into this."

"Well, I don't see why we can't just be friends, like before."

"No! Give me some space, please." He tried to think of some way to get her to back off without hurting her. "If I didn't respect you so much, I wouldn't ask this," he said solemnly. "Let me regroup. Then we can talk about this like good friends."

"Yes, David," she said. "I'll be waiting."

"Space for growth is the nicest gift you can give me right now," he said firmly. "Listen, I've got to go. Sylvie needs me."

He hung up and stood staring at the phone for a minute or so, terrified it would ring again. Then he began pacing nervously around the kitchen. At one point, he drew the blinds facing the Heffernans' house, casting the kitchen into an unnatural dimness. He felt cornered and besieged. He had a feeling that things had all gone horribly wrong, and that it had happened so fast.

"LAST NIGHT WAS THE ABSOLUTE WORST." ANITA was talking to her mother away from her office, on the eighth-floor pay phone outside the ladies' room where she could have some privacy. She couldn't whisper into the phone in her office, as she did when she talked to Frank, because her mother was slightly deaf. "I couldn't even bring myself to talk to him. I went to bed early and lay there in the dark, then pretended to be asleep when he came to bed. Oh, Mom, my own house is feeling like a prison."

"Anita!" her mother said.

"He mentioned going into counseling, but I can't stand the idea of talking about any of this. It would be humiliating."

"Are you still seeing the lawyer?" asked her mother eagerly.

"Yes. Oh, Mom, I think I love him, I really do. He wants

me to go to San Francisco with him this weekend. God, I wish I could. A few days away and I might have some better perspective."

"Why don't you?" demanded Evelyn.

"I can't just run off with another man for the weekend! What would the girls think?" Anita was amazed at her mother.

"Tell them you're coming to see me for the weekend," said Evelyn. "I'll cover for you."

"Mom! You'd do that?"

"Yes, I would," her mother said. "I just want you to be happy."

Out of gratitude, Anita decided to do something she had always resisted—admit that her mother might be right. "Mom, you know what? I think maybe you were right about David and Sue," she said. "I think it's possible they're having an affair."

"I knew it!" said Evelyn triumphantly. "For God's sake, Anita, I didn't tell you not to marry him in the first place, because it wasn't any of my business and you wouldn't have listened, anyway. And I know I shouldn't tell you to leave him now, but I don't see why you put up with him."

"It's not that easy, Mom. There are the children. And besides, there's nowhere for him to go. He doesn't even have a job."

SUE HAD SAID SHE WOULDN'T CALL OR COME over, but David was still nervous about it. Women could get clingy real fast after you fucked them, that much he remembered from his bachelorhood. To be well clear of her, in case she did call or come by, David walked a couple of blocks up to the Honey Bee Bakery and Café and bought a *New York Times* from the box outside. He had told Sylvie, who was feeling better and happily watching cartoons, that he'd be back in a while.

As usual, the Honey Bee was full of young mothers with babies in strollers, people of both sexes who looked like graduate students, and a lot of middle-aged men, mostly unaccompanied, who sat reading or writing in journals or on tiny computers as they ate cinnamon rolls and drank espresso at tables with red-checkered tablecloths.

David hadn't been here for a while. The truth was, he had found himself avoiding the place ever since a *Seattle Times* newspaper column had described the Honey Bee as a middle-aged slacker hangout, full of unambitious househusbands who came on to the younger women who worked there. David thought it was a pretty snotty article. Just because there were people who'd opted out of the rat race, that was no reason to sneer at them and deny them their sexuality. At least they weren't sitting around in smoky bars all afternoon.

He slid into a corner table, pushed aside the "Bus Your Own Table" sign that he found so irritating, seeing as there was also a big tip jar at the cash register, and settled in with his double-tall latte and his almond croissant.

He tried to read his paper but he couldn't concentrate. If only Conway's would see the light. If that would just work out the way it was supposed to, he felt sure Anita would respect him. They'd go into counseling together and get everything back on track. Thank God Sue seemed, so far, anyway, to understand that what happened on the couch was just one of those things. She was sweet and vulnerable and he'd grown fond of her, but he was married to Anita. They had a life together, and children.

It would all be all right. It had to be. God, if it didn't all get back the way it had been, what would become of him? What if Anita managed to kick him out and he ended up in some cheap apartment, working at a 7-Eleven or something?

It was a grim and very real possibility. All those sob stories you read about middle-aged wives being cast out into some run-down trailer park full of felons and their Dobermans by unfeeling husbands—it could happen to him, too. And, he realized bitterly, because he was a man, no one would feel the least bit sorry for him.

David was beginning to feel that he had some mark of the loser on him that everyone could see, that anything he tried, no matter how worthy, was bound to fail. He had become pathetic, without knowing quite how. It was so unfair. And now Anita was restive and hostile. She was probably repulsed by the air of failure that surrounded him, as if he were secreting some noxious substance from his pores that enveloped him in a cloud.

David was suddenly startled by a friendly voice. "Hi, David! Haven't seen you around here lately." It was Ed Margolin, who lived up the street. He'd even been interviewed for the Honey Bee newspaper story, in which it was tactfully made clear that *he* wasn't one of the middle-aged slacker regulars who came on to the young women behind the counter. The article had mentioned that Ed Margolin had once been an electrical engineer. Ed had a grizzled gray beard and was wearing a T-shirt that said, "AIDS 10K Run," faded nylon shorts, and a pair of rubber thongs. He carried a cappuccino and a clipboard.

"Sit down," said David. Ed was boring, with a tendency to maunder on about what he had discovered on the Internet, but right now, David was desperate for distraction. "Hey, Ed, I read about you in the paper."

Ed sat down and chuckled. "Yeah, I had my fifteen minutes of fame, I guess. So where've you been?"

David shrugged. "Oh, working pretty hard. Putting together a big ad campaign. What about you?"

"Well, interestingly, after that column came out, Laura decided she wanted to be a slacker, too." Laura was Ed's wife, a corporate attorney for the phone company. Lily baby-sat their two children occasionally.

"Oh, yeah?"

"Yeah. She quit the phone company and we took her retirement and paid off the mortgage. We got our overhead down to practically nothing, and Laura works part-time at a community college, training paralegals."

"Really?" said David.

"We got involved in this simplified-living movement. Heard about it?"

"Kind of a revolt against the consumer society thing, right?"

"Absolutely." Ed removed a bright yellow flyer from his clipboard and handed it to David. "We have study groups where we pool tips on downsizing and avoiding the stresses and strains of modern life. It's been great. We're growing our own vegetables and Laura's even learned how to can them like her grandmother used to do. We buy our clothes used, and we cut up all the credit cards. It's been fabulous. You know, people used to live simply all the time, but they've forgotten how. Now, all these skills are being revived, and it's a terrific challenge. We think it teaches the kids better values, too."

David cut off Ed's canned-sounding speech. "How are the kids taking it?"

Ed shrugged. "They're bitching and moaning a lot, but they'll get used to it. If they don't get with the program we'll get rid of the TV. We already yanked the cable. TV's one of the biggest sources of dissatisfaction around, if you ask me."

Ed leaned over confidentially. "You know what's the best part about Laura ditching that nine-to-fiver? While the kids are at school, we can screw like minks."

Ed sat back in his chair, knocked back his cappuccino,

then rose. He gave David's shoulder a little fraternal squeeze before he left, presumably to go home and have wild sex with Laura.

Ed had given David a flicker of hope. Maybe it was possible to be happy again. A family meal. The four of them sitting around the dinner table. That would make everything seem more normal and less threatening. On the way out, David bought a loaf of the Honey Bee's dark, dense, healthy-looking bread, and then went over to the grocery store to buy something for dinner, ending up with cobs of corn and pork chops, the kind of meal his mother always cooked.

David had a flash from his childhood of his own family sitting around the dinner table. He realized that probably his parents weren't always happy. He remembered the times when his mother's mouth was set in a mean, defensive line, and his father would storm off to his garage workshop and bang away angrily on some crafts project. Despite those bad times, David's parents had toughed it out and behaved as if everything was okay, and eventually it was. Maybe, if he and Anita just kept acting like everything was the way it should be, this whole thing would blow over.

BACK HOME, SYLVIE WAS DRIFTING AROUND THE kitchen in her pajamas, staring into the fridge, apparently looking for a snack.

"I think you're well enough to eat dinner with us in your robe and slippers," David said. He slathered some barbecue sauce on the pork chops and put them in the fridge, ready to pop under the grill as soon as Anita walked in the door. He wanted all four of them to eat together. Then Anita would understand instinctively what it was all about. She couldn't bust up a family.

Later, as he was setting the table, he heard Anita's heels clicking up the steps. She came into the kitchen and stared at him silently. God, she looked terrible. Her face was sad and pinched, and she seemed smaller and more compact than ever, as if all of her were tightening up, matter being sucked into a black hole.

"Hi!" he called out, sounding as friendly and normal as possible. "Ready to eat in fifteen minutes or so? How was your day?"

Lily walked in. "Hi, Mom!" she said, and kissed her mother. Anita immediately began to fake it for the kid's benefit, David noted. Why couldn't she do that for him? "Oh, all right, I guess," she said in a pleasant, relaxed voice, brushing her hair away from her face and actually smiling a little. "Usual stuff."

"When's dinner?" asked Lily.

"Fifteen minutes or so," said David, turning up the burner under the water for the corn. "Want a glass of wine, Anita?"

"I'll get it," she said, clicking over to the fridge.

"I ran into Ed Margolin today," said David. "We had kind of an interesting talk."

"Oh, yeah?" Anita sounded weary and uninterested.

"Yeah. He and Laura have been getting into this simplified-living movement. She works part-time now, and he's home all day and they live on practically nothing because they've got their overhead cranked down so low. Apparently, they're incredibly happy."

"That's nice," said Anita.

"They cut up all their credit cards, and they're wearing recycled clothes, and they're growing their own vegetables and canning them," said David enthusiastically.

Lily clicked her tongue. "Last time I baby-sat there, there was nothing good to eat in the fridge," she reported. "Just some really depressing bean soup thing they wanted me to heat up for the kids. And no Coke or anything. And they got rid of the cable and there were no magazines to read."

She drifted out of the kitchen, and David looked nervously over at Anita to see if she would change her demeanor and tense back up now that their child witness was gone. He couldn't tell, because she was standing with her back to him, staring out at the backyard, and sipping wine.

"They have some seminar thing Ed's organizing explaining the whole concept of downsizing and I thought maybe this is something we could check into," he went on. "The flyer's on the fridge door."

Anita turned, pulled the yellow flyer out from under the fridge magnet, and scanned it. David went on in a voice he tried to make sound casual. "They're very happy. Ed said they actually make love in the middle of the day when the kids are gone. I was kind of touched." He had been very moved by Ed's contented smile. Surely Anita would remember how passionate they had once been about each other. David thought dreamily of Sundays in bed, before the kids were born, fucking and reading the Sunday paper, then fucking again.

Anita whirled around and gave him a look of horror and fury. "What! You're suggesting I work part-time and we live on beans and wear clothes from the Salvation Army!"

"No, no," he said nervously. This wasn't the reaction he'd imagined. "I know how important your career is. I just thought maybe we've been focusing on the wrong things here. Maybe we've been too caught up in the rat race, and that's why you've grown resentful about my work."

"What work?" said Anita. "You never did level with me about that Conway's thing. I notice we haven't heard a thing about that lately!"

"I think there are spiritual dimensions to my staying at home that you haven't grasped," said David desperately.

"My God!" said Anita. "Spiritual dimensions! I suppose you think Ed Margolin is St. Francis of Assisi leading a holy life right here on our block. Ed Margolin is nothing but a lazy slacker. He's thrilled he's found some justification for sitting around the Honey Bee all day while his wife works her butt off. And now he's got her at home so she can slave away canning vegetables all day while he runs these stupid seminars." She flung the flyer on the counter. "Fine. Maybe they're happy. Maybe it works for them, but don't tell me that you haven't done anything in years because of some spiritual quest." She slammed her wineglass down on the counter.

"Anita!"

She lowered her voice and said in a loud whisper, "And as for sex in the afternoons, it looks to me like you and Sue have already got that little program going just fine." She pointed at the loaf of bread he'd bought earlier. "Who baked that? Sue?"

"No! The Honey Bee! Pull yourself together, Anita. I really resent your insinuations about Sue. There's only so much of this I can take."

"I feel the same way," said Anita. "The idea that I should lower my expectations to meet your lousy performance because Ed Margolin managed to brainwash his wife with this crap! We have a couple of kids to send to college! We have house payments!"

"God, you're so defensive!" said David, pitching corn into boiling water, then jumping back from the hot splashes. "I just thought it might be good for us to get a take on an alternative way of looking at things. It might be good for the kids, too. I mean, do you want them to grow up completely victimized by people getting them to buy shit they don't need!"

"David, I never realized what a total hypocrite you are! How do you think I make our living? By getting people to buy shit they don't need! And if you ever got an advertising account like Conway's, you'd be doing the same thing."

"Well, I'm not suggesting we go live off the land some- where. I'm just saying maybe some of our problems relate to a consumerist—"

"Oh, for God's sake! I can't believe this. It's the most pa- thetic, self-justifying—it's a new low, let me tell you that. And how dumb do you think I am? Do you really think I'm going to sit around the Margolins' living room talking about canning? A pleasant, simple life doing domestic things like that is a luxury I can't afford! You're not an advertised prod- uct that can be repositioned, David. You're not interested in simple living—you're just finally ashamed you don't contrib- ute much around here. In cash or in kind. You're looking for a trendy alibi."

"I guess you think I should get a nine-to-five job," snapped David. "And let the kids fend for themselves."

She hit herself on the forehead with a closed fist, the same gesture the children made when they said, "Duh!" to indicate stupidity. "A job! What a novel idea! Don't you know how scary it is that we have one income? I could get thrown out of Lawson's any day now, if Pam decides she's having a bad day."

"Well, let's see what happens with Conway's," he said ner- vously. "Then let's re-evaluate everything. If you think it would make a difference in our relationship . . ."

"It just might be too late for that now," she said in a cold little voice.

"I could probably still find a job," he said. "Don't worry."

"No," she said. "I meant it might be too late for us. I don't know if I can ever feel about you the way I used to. I'm afraid it's just too late."

"We need some counseling," said David. "Counseling. It'll make a difference."

"I don't have the heart for it," said Anita. All her anger seemed to have fallen away and she sagged, then buried her face in her hands. "Look, I need to think. I need some time away. I've arranged to spend the weekend with my mother. We'll tell the girls she's sick or something. Nothing major, just that she needs me to help out because her back went out."

"You're just flying off to Denver for the weekend?"

"That's right."

"Fine. If you want to run away from your problems, go right ahead. You are planning to come back, I presume?" He was furious with her. Just when he'd come up with some strategies to save their marriage, she'd ridiculed him, and then announced she was bailing out for the weekend.

"Oh, for God's sake! Of course I am. I just want a few days away. Is that so bad?" Anita's voice had taken on a pathetic little victim's tremble that made him even angrier.

"And since when has your mother's been a place to run when things are tough? She'll just spend the weekend telling you what's wrong with me. This is a total cop-out, Anita. You should be in counseling with me, not running to your mother."

"Please stop nagging me," said Anita wearily.

For the first time, David felt she might actually slip away. He went over to her and tried to put his arms around her. "Anita," he said, "how did this happen? I can't stand this. You seem to hate me."

Anita twitched her arms like a frightened animal shaking

him off and burst into tears. "I hate this!" she said. "I didn't want this to happen." Then she pushed him aside and clattered out of the kitchen and up the stairs.

The two girls emerged from the downstairs playroom just in time to hear her pounding feet and her sobs.

"What's the matter with Mom?" said Lily, clearly alarmed.

"She's worried about Grandma," said David calmly, although he was trembling with fury at the way Anita had shaken him off like that. "Her back went out. Mom's going there this weekend to help her out." He couldn't remember Anita ever physically wriggling away from him like he was some loathsome thing. For the first time in his life, he understood completely how men could slam their wives and lovers against walls and knock them down stairs.

12

THE NEXT MORNING, ANITA PACKED FURTIVELY as David slept. At the bottom of her suitcase, underneath the jeans and T-shirts she'd be expected to wear moping around her mother's house, she buried a slinky peach satin nightgown, and something to wear out to dinner in San Francisco, black silk pants and an ivory-colored silk sweater.

When she went into Lily's room to kiss her good-bye, Lily was sitting up in bed looking appealingly disheveled and sleepy. "I'm worried about Grandma. Maybe I should come, too," she said.

"Oh, it'll be okay. I just want to make sure she's comfortable."

Lily rubbed her eyes and blinked hard. "Will you call me and tell me how she is?"

"Of course, darling. But maybe it's better if you don't call

165

me at Grandma's. I might be helping her into the bath or something. Really, it's no big deal. People's backs go out all the time, and I didn't want her to feel alone."

"Is there something you're not telling me?" Lily looked awake now, and suddenly frightened.

"Of course not," Anita said, not daring to ask what Lily thought she was hiding.

"Were you crying like that last night because Grandma is really a lot sicker than you said? Is she going to die or anything? Are you lying about it being just her back?"

"Absolutely not!" Anita gave her daughter a hug. "You must believe me."

"I do," said Lily with relief. "I guess you wouldn't lie."

Sylvie was already up and playing on the floor of her room with some small stuffed animals. Anita felt her daughter's forehead. "Good. You're definitely better. You'll be fine this weekend, just take it kind of easy, okay?"

"Okay."

"Daddy will take good care of you," said Anita, embracing her.

"And maybe Sue," added Sylvie cheerfully, then noticing Anita's involuntary stiffening, she added, "just because you'll be gone."

"I don't think we need to bother Sue," said Anita briskly, giving her daughter some pats on the back. "Listen, sweetie, I'll call you from Grandma's, okay?"

"Okay, Mom." Sylvie turned back to her stuffed animals.

Anita carried her suitcase downstairs where she encountered David, returning from the front porch in his bathrobe with the newspaper in his hand.

"Are you leaving now?" he said, looking surprised. "Don't you want me to drive you to the airport?"

"No, it's such an early flight, I ordered the shuttle." Anita consulted her watch. "I think I'd better go out there and wait on the curb."

"When will you be back?"

"Sunday evening. I'll call the girls."

"I don't like this at all," said David.

"I just need time to think," said Anita. "I just need a little break." She gave him a twisted, pleading little smile. "And David, there's one thing I want you to promise me. Keep Sue away from here while I'm gone, okay? Keep her away from the girls. It's very important to me."

David frowned. "All right. Anyway, I already agreed to that even though I think you're obsessing on this thing. I'm really concerned about you. And us."

Anita sighed and they heard a slight beep from the curb. She picked up her bag and went down to walk to the street where a blue and yellow airport shuttle van was waiting.

She didn't even look back and wave at him, David thought bitterly. He took the paper up to bed and crawled back under the covers. An advertising insert slid out and he began to bat it aside, then he noticed it was the Conway's Home and Garden Center piece. What were they doing in the Saturday paper, anyway? It had the lowest readership of the week.

And the production values! While other chains had glossy four-color stuff, Conway's was using black-and-white newsprint, with some splotches of red. The headline was an uninspired "End of Summer Savings." The whole page was divided into boring little squares with clip-art pictures of items and a price and one line of copy in a type so tiny no one would ever bother to read it. "Gas-Powered Lawn Edger. $170. Powerful 32 cc 2-cycle engine for a picture-perfect lawn." "House and Trim Paints, $18.49 per gal. Resists stains and mildew while providing one-coat coverage for years of lasting beauty."

Disgusted, he flung the thing away. These people should be crawling on their hands and knees begging him to drag their dreary little stores into the modern age with award-winning ads! Instead, they were jerking him around. He decided he'd call Sandy on Monday and ask to have his presentation scheduled for a definite day and time. Surely they didn't want to continue with this shitty-looking advertising for much longer!

Then, feeling humiliated even though he was alone, he turned to the want ads. A brief scan gave him a lurching feeling in his stomach and he flung that section aside in disgust, too. Now, he didn't even want to read the rest of the paper. Everything was all so depressing.

He had just about fallen back asleep when Sylvie came into the room. She was all dressed, and disgustingly bouncy. In some ways it was easier when she was sick.

"Guess what! I was in the backyard and I saw Sue. She's having a party, and we're invited! I told her Mom had to go to Grandma's, so she said this way we could have dinner at their house tonight. It's a barbecue, and she's letting me help her decorate the yard."

He'd told Sue in no uncertain terms that he didn't want to go to face Roger at his company barbecue. And, he'd promised Anita he'd keep Sue away. What was he supposed to do now?

But he hadn't initiated this. Sue wasn't coming over here. She had asked them over there. Anita couldn't feel invaded if they were at her house. And actually, mused David, facing the Heffernans in a crowd like that was probably the best way to get things back on normal footing after what had happened with Sue on the living room sofa two days ago.

Anyway, David had absolutely no idea how to say no. He could come up with some excuse, but then he and the girls would have to huddle inside the house after lying about a previous commitment while raucous party noises drifted over the hedge.

Sylvie, meanwhile, had already dashed away, assuming that of course they would go to Sue's party.

Later, after he got up, Lily announced that she wasn't going to Sue's barbecue because she was going shopping with Amy, then bringing her back home to watch a video and spend the night. Sylvie disappeared through the hedge early on to help Sue prepare for the barbecue.

David was grateful to be rid of the children. With Anita gone to "think things over," he felt like a stunned and battered bird that had hit a plate-glass window head on and collapsed weakly into the garden bed.

He got up late, then spent some time drinking beer and wandering around the house feeling anxious and unhappy. As the day dragged on, he began to dread the barbecue. For one thing it was as hot as hell outside. For another, he was slightly drunk and feeling too sluggish to be social.

But by late afternoon, the sounds of happy party-goers reached him in the kitchen. David had run out of beer, and although going out to get more seemed like a huge effort, he liked the idea of keeping a low buzz going to deaden his anxiety. He was also getting hungry, not having eaten since breakfast. He imagined Sue would have some great food laid on.

He experienced a little flicker of fear as he went through the opening in the hedge. Would Sue be able to handle it? What if she acted all emotional and Roger suspected?

She had, as usual, worked her domestic magic. The garden had been transformed. Japanese lanterns hung from the trees. Pots of ferns and white flowers in the corners of the sunny brick patio made everything seem cool, and a green-and-white-striped awning had been set up to provide shade over part of the lawn.

There was already a crowd standing around nibbling on appetizers and drinking beer, wine, and some kind of tall fruity drink decorated with flowers. Sylvie was dashing around with Matt and Chris, who had been decked out in matching Hawaiian-print shirts for the occasion. To his huge relief, Sue gave him a big natural, neighborly smile, waved, and said, "Hi, David. Glad you could make it!"

David went over to where she was talking to a group of people. "This is our neighbor, David Jamison," she said. He nodded politely and shook hands as she made introductions to a fiftyish couple he found less than prepossessing. Marnie wore rather greasy orange lipstick, and her purple halter top revealed too much over-tanned shoulder and breast. Al had a ravaged face and white sideburns that clashed with his youthful reddish toupee.

Sylvie ran up. "Daddy!" she said happily.

"Hi, sweetheart," he said, tousling her hair.

Marnie looked down at Sylvie, now embracing David's waist. "But, Sue, I thought this was your little girl!" she said in a voice roughened by years of cigarettes and booze.

Al nudged his wife broadly and said, "We better not tell Roger about this!" Sue managed to roll her eyes in a cute way at his stupid joke, and David realized she could handle anything with aplomb.

Relieved, he gazed over at Roger, who was fiddling with a barbecue grill. Roger wore a too-small T-shirt and shorts, revealing flabby white arms and legs. David felt sorry for him and smug at the same time. He'd never find out, poor jerk, that someone else had fucked his wife.

"Sylvie's not my daughter, she's a neighbor, but a very special neighbor," said Sue, beaming down at the child who, still clinging to David, turned her head to smile up at her. "I only have boys, so it's a real treat for me." David glanced over at Matt and Chris, who were now wrestling with each other at the edge of the lawn, their faces all screwed up with aggression, their legs waving in the air.

"What a doll. She's been so helpful," Marnie went on. "Carrying out trays and passing them around. It's real sweet."

"And she helped me put together a lot of the food," put in Sue while Sylvie preened. "Sylvie, tell Daddy he should try some of the Hawaiian hors d'oeuvres we made."

Sue looked very pretty, David thought. She had on a kind of tropical sundress that showed off the tops of her breasts, and she had on more makeup than usual. Her mouth looked pinker and shinier and her eyelashes thicker.

"And I helped hang the lanterns up and stick the cool giant candles in the ground and everything," said Sylvie, jumping up and down.

"Let's go over and check out some of that food you made," said David, taking her hand. He thought maybe it was time to push off. In his slightly tipsy state, he might not be able to conceal the fact that he was leering at his hostess. Even though he wasn't sure it would ever happen again, the fact that he'd had her gave him a proprietary little glow of satisfaction.

"Isn't everything beautiful here?" said Sylvie, leading him by the hand over to a long table filled with plates of delicacies fringed with big green leaves. "Look, Sue put flowers on the table, too." Sure enough, there were pale, orchid-like blossoms scattered artfully between the plates, reminding David of something from a slick food layout. "I wish we could have a cool party like this sometime," Sylvie added wistfully.

He made a noncommittal reply, and got himself a plate, filling it with tasty-looking odds and ends skewered with thin pieces of bamboo, then he looked around for the booze department. There were two big glass punch bowls featuring a flamingo-colored concoction. A little boat made of cut pineapple and maraschino cherries and papaya floated in each one, bearing a paper sail that read, "Spiked," or "Unspiked."

Fortunately, there was also wine and beer. David fished a bottle of Heineken out of a tub of ice and twisted off the cap. He smiled at a lot of people, and reflected that he was completely uninterested in actually meeting any of them. After all, they were all from Roger's office. David knew very little about corporate life, but assumed that most people in it were boring philistines short on taste, like Marge and Al.

Over by the barbecue grill, Sue was smearing something from a plastic bottle all over Roger's pale arms and legs, announcing to the onlookers, "He needs at least thirty or he burns to a crisp and peels." She worked her way efficiently around to the back of his neck. Roger, arms stuck obediently out, stood there looking like a large infant.

Al, whose toupee David thought must be unbearably hot, watched this operation and ogled Sue. "Say, I'm awfully sensitive myself. Roger, you don't mind if she rubs some of that sunblock on me, do you?"

Roger gave a short, unpleasant laugh, and Sue said archly, "Oh, you guys," and then applied some of the stuff to Roger's bald spot in a stagy way that got a big laugh.

Suddenly, somewhere behind him, he heard the sound of a glass breaking, and a woman's slightly drunken laugh. It was sad, really, David thought—this fabulously produced party for these oafish guests. Sue was really wasted on Roger.

She hustled past him toward the sound of the breaking glass, carrying the plastic bottle. He noticed it was children's sunblock, which seemed somehow appropriate. Roger wasn't a lover to her, just another child to take care of.

He gave Sue a wistful smile, but she'd already passed him and was assuring someone that breaking the glass was no big deal. "Leave it there," she said. "I'll get a broom."

He took another pull on his bottle. David decided he was glad he'd come over here. It had been a big boost to his ego to be reminded he'd been able to score with an attractive woman. The beer and his revitalized self-esteem glowed happily within him. Maybe it hadn't been such a big mistake fucking Sue, after all. She was now carrying a dustpan full of shards of glass back up the porch stairs and making the woman who'd broken it feel better. "I just buy these things by the dozen at Costco," she was saying. She really was amazing, taking care of everyone, yet seeming to be having a great time at her own party, too.

A second later, Sue came back out of the house, smiling and carrying a big wooden board full of raw steaks, and David felt even happier. Those cute little hors d'oeuvres had been okay, but the prospect of a juicy steak and some more beer sounded great, a classic summer combination. He just hoped Roger knew something about barbecuing. With an eye to evaluating his neighbor's technique, and overseeing things to make sure his own steak was good and rare, David drifted over to the grill.

"Hi, Roger!" he said in a friendly way.

"Oh, hi, Dave," said Roger.

No one had called him Dave since high school, and it bugged him, but he just smiled. "Great party," he said. "Nice of you to include me."

Roger didn't acknowledge this remark. He was staring over at the board with all the steaks.

"The steaks look great, too," added David.

"Sue!" bellowed Roger. She scurried over and looked back and forth between the two men with a worried expression.

"There are wasps all over the meat," Roger said. You better get something to cover it up." He moved backward toward David.

"Gosh, I'm sorry," she said, swooshing the wasps away. "I'll get some Saran Wrap. Be very careful, honey."

"I didn't realize there were so many of those damn things around here," said Roger.

"Yeah, actually they're yellow jackets. They get pretty crazy near the end of summer like this," said David, amused at Roger's wimpiness. David lifted up the lid from the grill, which was lying on the ground, and went over to the board. Three insects crawled happily over the steaks. David waved his hand over them a few times, trying to brush them in a direction away from Roger. When they were dislodged, he placed the grill cover over the board and turned to face Roger with a kind of "voilà" gesture.

"Thanks," said Roger gratefully, taking a sip of beer. "Hate those damn things."

Just as he said this, a yellow jacket hovered over his face, and he let out a little cry of fear, then stood completely still. David saw two more hovering around his arms. Roger seemed to be trying to follow them with his eyes while not moving. Little beads of sweat popped out on his upper lip and around the brow line.

Behind him, party noises, conversation, and laughter, went on. It was as if Roger were suddenly operating in some other, much slower, dimension as the yellow jackets circled him. David felt pulled into it, and was now unable to move himself. He stood there bemused. A few people next to David had noticed Roger was standing completely still and that several yellow jackets were flitting enthusiastically around him.

Sue arrived with a roll of Saran Wrap and stood staring at her husband in horror. "Oh, my God! He's allergic to yellow jackets. I've got to get his adrenaline kit," she said, dropping the Saran Wrap on the bricks of the patio and running back to the house.

"Oh, get them off him!" said a woman.

"Stand in the smoke from the barbecue," volunteered someone else. Roger, however, remained utterly still, like some ceremonial guard. The insects showed no signs of moving on.

"I can't stand this," said a gray-haired woman, sounding angry at their collective helplessness. "Where are those steaks?" she demanded in a take-charge voice.

David, feeling as if he were moving under water, lifted the barbecue lid, and the woman grabbed some meat and approached Roger, clearly hoping to lure the insects away from him.

She ventured toward him slowly with her offering, but the yellow jackets remained in orbit around Roger. There were five of them now.

The party had become very quiet. A circle of onlookers stood equally still and silent around Roger, as if they had all joined David in that peculiar other dimension. At the edge of the circle someone murmured, "What's going on?" and someone else whispered in reply, "Roger's allergic to yellow jackets. He could go into shock."

Roger now appeared to be trembling ever so slightly. Was it with fear, or because he couldn't bear to stand still with these things on him? His face looked terrified. A bead of sweat slid down one side of his face like a teardrop. One insect was now sauntering along his arm, another had landed on his ear. Suddenly, his look of terror turned into a silly grin and he burst into laughter, which seemed to throw him off balance, so that he was hopping on one leg and batting at his ear. The guests took in their breath collectively at the grotesque sight.

The tiny insect feet on his ear were obviously tickling, and the trembling had been his unsuccessful attempt to suppress laughter. Now, he was completely out of control and flailing around in a panic. A few seconds later, Roger yelled, "Ouch," then coughed and wheezed. Suddenly, he collapsed fluidly onto the ground.

He must have fainted, David thought. Everyone crowded around him, and then he heard Sue's hysterical voice behind him. She was pushing her way through the crowd. "Where did you put it?" She shouted at his inert body. "Where did you put the kit!"

But he didn't reply. He was even more immobile than when he had been standing. Sue rushed up and fell to her knees beside him. She said, "Oh, no," over and over again and waved her arms around him to disperse the yellow jackets. They circled around like little airplanes.

David found himself backing away. He heard a man shout, "Somebody call 911!"

Sylvie came up to him and grabbed his hand. "Daddy, what happened?" she said. She looked terrified.

"Roger was stung. He's allergic."

"Matt and Chris still can't find his medicine! Neither can Sue. They can't find it!" Her voice rose, then she looked over at Roger lying on the ground. She stared at him, as paralyzed as he had been, her hands in fists, her face pale, her eyes wide open.

Roger's face had turned red and puffy, with swollen lips. Sue was saying his name over and over again. She knelt beside him with her arms floating gracefully in the air over his crumpled form like a diva in a tragic opera's final scene.

David picked up the rigid Sylvie and took her away, inside the house. He was relieved when she loosened up and fell on his neck. In the kitchen, the two boys were frantically ransacking the place. The younger one was sobbing, but he kept on with his frenzied searching. The older one simply looked serious and determined as he yanked out drawers and pawed through egg spoons and measuring cups.

The woman who had tried to lure the yellow jackets away with steak was at the kitchen phone, apparently having called 911. She turned toward Matt and Chris. "Boys!" she snapped. "What's your address?"

Chris repeated it slowly. The woman shouted it into the phone, adding urgently, "Yes, he's been stung by at least one yellow jacket and he's allergic. He's in shock now, and no one can find his kit. Please hurry. He may still be alive."

LILY AND AMY WERE SPRAWLED AROUND THE downstairs playroom watching a movie and eating microwave popcorn when they heard the sirens approaching.

"That sounds really close," said Amy. "Is that like a fire engine or a police car or what?"

Lily, who had been about to throw some more popcorn into her mouth, stopped in midgesture and strained to determine the source of the sound. As she did, the siren made a kind of hiccuping whoop and fell abruptly silent.

"God, it's stopped right around here!" she said. "It sounds like it's right in our backyard!" She picked up the remote and hit pause. "Let's check it out."

The girls scrambled to their feet and went out past the frozen television screen through the glass doors to the backyard. They both had a look of pleasurable anticipation at the thought that some interesting disaster had struck so close to home. Once outside, they heard the crackle of radios from behind the hedge. They stared at each other.

"Wow! Maybe it's the cops," said Lily.

"Probably someone just choked on a bone or something, and it's the paramedics," said Amy. "That happened to my cousin at Thanksgiving at my aunt's house, and they had those walkie-talkie things."

The girls cantered across the lawn and peered shyly through the opening in the hedge.

There, they saw a lot of adults holding drinks, standing silently around the edges of the yard. They were all watching several uniformed paramedics around the slumped form of Roger. One of the paramedics held up a bottle of clear liquid, with a tube connected to Roger's arm, while the others strapped him to a gurney. Sue, her face all wrinkled up, one arm around each of her sons, stared down at them as they worked. Both boys were crying.

Lily clutched Amy's arm. "That's Sue's husband," she whispered. "Ohmigod, he looks dead."

"He probably just had a heart attack or a fit or something," said Amy, indicating by her disappointed tone that actual death would, of course, have been more satisfactory.

Lily looked around at all the worried faces, but couldn't see her dad or Sylvie. She supposed it would be okay for her to stay there and check it out some more. She led Amy in through the hedge, finding an inconspicuous spot for them to stand and observe. It was all pretty exciting, and she was glad Amy had been here when it happened so she could share it with her. Exciting things hardly ever happened in real life. But at the same time, those boys looked so sad and scared. Lily even felt sorry for Sue.

DAVID HAD BEEN WATCHING ALL THIS FROM THE Heffernans' kitchen window, still holding Sylvie, who was getting very heavy. She had her head on his shoulder, one hand around his neck, and the other in her mouth. She, too, watched the scene below them.

"The medics are here. Everything will be all right," he said to her, but he wasn't sure about that. Roger looked pretty awful, and now David remembered there were people so allergic to bees or wasps they could drop dead from one sting. Roger obviously knew that, too. The half-minute or so, as he had stood there passively waiting for his tiny tormenters to leave or possibly kill him, took on a new horror.

Despite his voluntary paralysis, he had registered a whole range of emotions during those last moments before he collapsed—fear, then sadness with clown-like tears rolling silently down his round face, then grotesque involuntary mirth, and finally, his last gentle moan that sounded both resigned and orgasmic.

David wished he could get away from here, but he could hardly elbow his way past Sue and her kids and go home through the hedge. Just bolting out the front door seemed pretty cold, too.

In the garden, the guests parted as Roger was wheeled away. Soon, the gurney disappeared from David's view underneath the striped awning. Sue and her two sons followed behind with the man with the red toupee. There were keys in his hand. Presumably, he was going to drive them to the hospital. David felt relieved he wouldn't have to help. He didn't think he could handle it. Apart from anything else, he felt drunk and dizzy, and wanted nothing more than to lie down out of the heat and bright sun.

"Okay, pumpkin, we better go home now," he said gently to Sylvie, setting her down with a groan and leading her down the porch steps.

In the backyard, the guests milled around talking to each other in low tones. David heard someone say, "He might not make it." Lily and her friend Amy came up to him, and he was surprised to see them here. "What happened, Daddy?" said Lily.

David explained that Roger had been stung by a yellow jacket, was allergic, and had gone into shock.

"Wow," said Amy.

The gray-haired woman who'd called 911 suddenly raised her voice and waved her arms. "Listen, everybody," she said. "There's not much we can do now. But I think we should clean this all up so when the family gets back here they won't have to."

The others murmured their agreement with this plan. She turned to David. "Maybe you could take these lanterns down."

David patted Sylvie and said, "My little girl is upset. I think I'd better take her home."

Lily piped up, "I'll take her home, Dad. She can watch our tapes with us. And I'll make her a snack." Lily put her arm around her sister, and on the other side, Amy moved in closer to her in a protective way.

"Are you sure?" said David.

"I kind of want to do something nice for somebody," said Lily in a small voice aimed just at her father. "I just feel that way now." David realized she was pretty shook up, too.

"Yes, take me home," said Sylvie.

"Fine, girls," said the bossy woman. Other guests were taking plates of food back into the kitchen.

David couldn't think of any way of getting out of the cleanup committee without looking bad. Resentful but re-signed, he started to take down the Japanese lanterns. Sue had hung them in all the branches, and as he moved from tree to tree, he felt almost as if he were hunting Easter eggs. As he worked, he realized that if Roger were really dead, there'd be nothing more pathetic than Sue and her kids coming home to a festive party scene. He left the lanterns all in a big pile on the buffet table. Presumably, the bossy lady would figure out what to do with them.

After that, he went into the kitchen. Someone had retrieved the Saran Wrap from where Sue had let it fall and was wrapping up hors d'oeuvres. "I think we should put the steaks in the freezer," the bossy woman was saying.

As if he were moving in some sort of a dream, he looked under the sink where he knew Sue kept the garbage bags, pulled one out, and went back outside where he started throwing in crumpled paper napkins, bamboo skewers, and the flowers that had trimmed the tables. He took the bag to the side of the house where Sue kept the garbage can.

There, he ran into a man with an identical trash bag full of clanking beer bottles. "Know where she keeps the recycling?" he asked David.

"I'll do it," said David, sensing a way out of here. The man handed over the bottles and left. David took the bag over to the bottom of the front porch where Sue had a little shingled bench that cunningly hid the three plastic recycling bins the city picked up every week. He could slip away back home after dropping off the bottles and no one would notice.

He emptied the bag into the glass-and-can bin with a crash. Miscalculating the weight of the burden he'd just surrendered, he fell tipsily against the mixed-paper bin, gashing his forehead on the edge of it. With horror, he pulled himself back up and watched as a bright circle of blood splashed on a carefully crushed shredded wheat box below him. His eyes were slightly out of focus, and he willed them to work properly again before he straightened up.

As soon as they were functioning again, he let out a little gasp. He was staring at a whole mess of those horrible striped yellow jackets, crawling over the recycling! He stepped back in horror, his eyes still riveted on the hideous things. But then he realized he was only looking at very realistic life-sized illustrations of yellow jackets on a neatly crushed bundle of recycled cardboard packaging. "Yellow jacket Control Trap," he read in big yellow letters, and underneath, "Make Summer Fun Safe!"

He closed the lid on the bench, touched his head where he felt a wet little gash, and made his way quietly to the sidewalk. As he walked around the block to his own house, the image of the hideous insects with their festive summery stripes hovered in his brain, along with the cheerful phrase he'd just read: "Make Summer Fun Safe!"

But there was no way to make anything safe. The world was a horrible, random, senseless, and often malevolent place, where anything could happen without warning. Roger, despite taking all the precautions in the world, was struck down in the midst of his summer fun barbecue. The traps hadn't saved him.

Then he stopped, puzzled. He'd searched every branch in the garden, taking down all the Japanese lanterns. He hadn't run across a single yellow jacket trap, plastic cylinders that were supposed to hang around the yard, luring the insects to their doom. Yet, in the recycling bin, there was a bundle of the empty boxes the traps had come in. How strange life was, he thought slightly boozily. How random and frightening. Anita could turn on him just as surely as those insects had gone for Roger and there wasn't a thing anyone could do about any of it.

Coming up his own familiar front porch steps, though, he felt that maybe he'd been working himself up into a state. Being home made him feel safer. It was natural, after having seen what had happened to Roger, to become unsettled, but that was no reason to abandon himself to panic. He mustn't let the terrors engulf him. He and Anita would simply have to work out their problems, and of course, they would.

On the porch, he saw that the mailbox was crammed full of the Saturday mail. As was his habit, he stood next to his own recycling bins, jumbled on the front porch rather than stowed in a cunning little bench, in order to ditch the junk mail. He had tossed a couple of catalogs and a package of coupons and was holding on to the gas bill when he saw the long white envelope addressed to him. "Sandy" was typed neatly above the printed return address, "Conway's Home and Garden Center, Corporate Headquarters."

SUNDAY MORNING, ANITA WAITED TO PHONE home until Frank was in the shower. This was definitely the tackiest part, calling her family from the hotel room.

Another bad moment had been yesterday, after lunch. In Chinatown, Anita had seen a store window with adorable Chinese brocade dresses for children and adults—blue and red and green and yellow, embroidered with golden dragons, nicely finished in white piping. She had decided to splurge and buy them for the girls, then she remembered that, of course, she was supposed to be in Denver with her mother and couldn't bring them back any presents like that.

She had tried not to worry last night, but for a moment in that fabulous North Beach restaurant she'd imagined a horrible scenario in which some unnamed bad thing happened to one of the girls, and David called her mother in Denver. As they had arranged, Evelyn would say Anita was out on an errand, and would call back. Then, as the waking nightmare unfolded, her mother called the hotel in San Francisco. Anita was at dinner and couldn't be reached until the child was in the emergency room or something. David kept frantically phoning Denver. Eventually, her mother broke down and surrendered the San Francisco number, and David and the girls would know she was a liar.

She lay back against the nest of pillows and stared up at the ceiling while the phone at home rang. The ceiling sprouted smoke detectors and sprinkler heads. She'd had plenty of that particular view last night, she recalled rather giddily, and a few other angles as well.

Sylvie answered.

"Hi, sweetie," Anita said, trying to sound casual. Steam curled out from beneath the bathroom door. "How are you?"

"Fine," said Sylvie. Anita had long ago become resigned to the fact that children were pretty boring on the phone. They didn't seem particularly interested in finding out what you'd been doing and never could seem to remember what they'd been doing. Still, the main thing was to remind them that their mother loved them, even when she had to be away.

"Are you feeling better?" Anita asked.

"Yeah."

"Did you get lots of rest?"

"Yeah. But a horrible thing happened."

"Darling! What happened?" Anita sat up in bed and her heart began to race.

"We were at Sue's and a wasp stung Roger," she said.

Anita relaxed and her fear turned to anger. "You were at Sue's?" David had promised to keep the girls away from Sue. She couldn't let Sylvie know how irritated she was.

"Did someone put baking soda on the sting?" she said lightly. "That's the best thing to do."

"No, they took him away in an ambulance. He was allergic to wasps."

"I'm sure he'll be all right, darling. Can I talk to Lily?"

"She's asleep with Amy. They stayed up all night watching videos."

"Oh. Well I'll see you both soon," she said.

"Mommy?"

"What, darling?"

"Come home. It was scary what happened to Roger."

"Everything will be all right," Anita said firmly. "Let me talk to Daddy." She had hoped to avoid speaking to David, but he clearly had to be told that Sylvie needed reassurance about Roger and his wasp sting.

"Okay. When are you coming home?"

"Tonight. After dinner. I love you." Anita made kissing noises into the phone.

A clunk meant Sylvie had dropped the receiver down on the table and presumably run off to fetch David. Sylvie never walked when she could run.

When David came on the line and said, "Hi," in a strangely passive voice, Anita resisted the urge to give him hell about taking Sylvie over to the Heffernans'. Instead she said, "Sylvie is upset about Roger getting stung."

"He's allergic. He keeled over. It was pretty gruesome."

"Well, are you reassuring Sylvie? Explain to her that she's not allergic to wasp stings. She needs comforting."

"I need comforting, too," he replied. "It was bad. He may be dead. Sylvie and I may have watched him die. That's pretty strong stuff."

He seemed to be trying to twist the knife, making her feel guilty for not being there. Anita sighed irritably. Why did this have to happen now? It wouldn't have happened if David had kept his promise and stayed away from Sue. In the bathroom, the shower stopped and she heard the glass door slide open.

"Just be extra nice to Sylvie, okay? I'll deal with it when I get back."

"When's your flight? Should I pick you up?"

"Oh, never mind. I'll take a cab."

She hung up as Frank came out of the bathroom naked,

rubbing his hair with a towel. He put the towel around his neck and looked inquiringly at Anita, who knew she must seem preoccupied. "I made my call home," she explained. "Now I can relax." She forced her face into a smile and fell back against the pillows. "God, you're gorgeous," she said. For both their sakes, she had wanted this weekend to be free of any of her domestic worries.

THAT EVENING, FRANK AND ANITA SAT IN HIS car inside the dark, multilevel parking lot at the Seattle airport. "It's very simple," said Frank. "You tell him it's all over and that you want him out of there." Both of them were staring forward through the windshield at a big concrete pillar.

Why, right after the wonderful weekend they'd had, did he have to go on about this? He was spoiling everything. She could tell from his voice that his face had that unpleasant, petulant look of jealousy. She hated him like this.

Anita's own face was a resigned mask, but her eyes were brimming with tears. Wouldn't he notice those tears and be sweet to her and stop making demands?

"Oh, Frank, I hate it. I wake up every night with this horrible sick, trapped feeling, and he's lying there, snoring away. I sleep way over on my side so I won't accidentally touch him. But I told you, I am going to do something. I'm just not sure how or exactly when. Please be patient."

"Jesus! Just throw him out. Tell him to spend his days looking for an apartment."

"It's not that easy. We can't really afford it." Anita hadn't brought this up before. It was hard to talk about money. She had discovered that while she had put David out of her life emotionally, she still felt a joint shame, as half of a couple, about their finances. They lived from paycheck to paycheck and didn't have any savings to speak of. "He'll have to get a job first," she said.

Frank didn't seem to grasp that money could ever be a problem. Sometimes, Anita thought, he just ignored what didn't fit in with his vision of what should happen. "Yes, he'll have to get a job. But don't hold your breath," he said. "Let's face it. He's had a free ride for years and he's not going to give it up that easily. You'll have to get him out of the house first, then maybe reality will set in."

"I think he's pretty scared," said Anita.

Frank grabbed the steering wheel. "You feel sorry for him, don't you?"

"Please, darling, it's all so hard. Don't make it worse. I've never done this before. It's not that easy. I'm doing the best I can. Please believe me."

He put his hand on her shoulder and she turned to him.

"Anita, I'm sorry. I'm possessive. I want you. I can't help it."

"That's why you're so different from David," she said, eager to flatter him and disarm the jealousy. "He's passive. He just wants me to take care of him. You have a kind of masculine ruthlessness. It's scary, but it's exciting. Help me, Frank. Help me ease him out of my life."

"You can't ease him out. You have to kick him out."

"But what if he got custody of the girls? He could say he was the one who stayed home with them."

"I'll get you a good divorce lawyer," he said gently. She was relieved that his anger seemed to have subsided. "The best. Besides, the judge will listen to what they want. Especially the older one."

"Lily," Anita said sharply. The idea that Frank couldn't remember Lily's name irritated her. But then she realized she had consciously avoided reference to her daughters. She was ashamed of that. It was because she suspected that Frank would have preferred that she not be encumbered by some other man's children. Anita had once watched some science documentary on PBS with the girls. Male primates, it said, were loath to take on their mate's offspring by someone else.

"The girls would want to be with you, Anita, wouldn't they?"

"Yes," she said. She had to believe that. But then she added, "Unless they blamed me for a divorce and saw him as the victim."

"They're children," he said impatiently. "They can't possibly understand how marriage works. Or doesn't. Anyway, the trend now is joint custody."

The thought of her girls shuttling back and forth between two homes, both presumably financed by Anita, made her terribly sad.

"Oh, Frank," she said with a little sob, "you must try and understand. If they thought I had abandoned them in any way—I love them very much. Not like I love you. In a different way. I want it all to work." She collapsed onto his shoulder, the gearshift sticking into her knee, and he patted her back and made soothing noises.

"Everything will work out," he said. "It has to. I've been through this myself, and believe me, it seems impossible, and then one day it all falls into place."

Anita knew that Frank's ex-wife had custody of his daughter, Phoebe, and he saw her every other weekend. Phoebe, whom she remembered from Lily's team, might become Lily's friend, borrow her clothes, giggle about boys. It could be fun.

Frank never talked much about his daughter, but he cared about her a lot, Anita was sure of that. It was just that she and Frank were so crazy about each other that their children had to be temporarily put on hold in the brief time they had together. That would change when they didn't have to sneak around like this, she was sure of it.

"Anita," he said. "I want what's best for you. I want to take care of you."

"Oh, my angel," she said. It would be so wonderful to be taken care of.

Frank's voice took on a slightly harder edge, and he disentangled himself from Anita and turned on the ignition. "If he can't move out real soon, Anita, at least get him out of your bed. He can sleep on the goddamn couch. Maybe then he'll get the message." Looking over his shoulder and pulling out of the parking slot, he said, "How shall we work this? Did you say you'd take the shuttle? Shall I drop you off around the corner from your house?"

"I said I'd take a taxi," Anita said, depressed by the shabbiness of subterfuge.

13

THROUGHOUT THE DAY ON SUNDAY, SYLVIE and Lily had looked out the kitchen window over at the Heffernans' house and wondered out loud what had happened to Roger.

"There's no one there at all," said Lily, staring out at the blank windows. "Maybe they're all sitting around his hospital bed. Maybe he's in a coma."

"Daddy, do you think he's dead?" asked Sylvie.

"How should I know," snapped David. "If I knew, I would have told you." Why did children keep asking questions as if adults were omniscient?

"When will we find out?" she persisted.

"I don't know that either," he said. "How could I possibly know?"

The girls left at five-thirty, walking over to the video store in order to make the six o'clock deadline on the tapes Amy and Lily had rented last night. Soon after, he heard someone coming up the back steps. He was confused, because Sue normally came up these steps, but he heard a click, click, click, the sound he associated with Anita coming home from work in her heels.

He opened the door. It was Sue all right, but she wore a dark skirt and blouse and pumps, as if she were off to a funeral. She walked in. "Oh, David," she said with a big sigh. "He's gone. He died instantly. They couldn't do anything for him."

"Oh, no," said David.

"The boys and I spent the night with Roger's boss and his wife. They've been wonderful."

"What a terrible shock," said David. He knew he should offer condolences, but he had no idea what to say.

"I'm flying to Milwaukee tonight. We're taking him back home to bury him in the family plot. It will be easier for the boys to deal with this at their grandparents' house, and I'm not sure I'm strong enough to deal with this alone."

David managed to compose himself enough to say, "I'm so sorry."

Sue's face took on a bleak, hopeless look. "It would have been all right if his kit had been where it was supposed to be. I can't imagine where it is. I searched everywhere." She started to break down, but then, to David's immense relief, seemed to pull herself back together. "I failed him."

"Don't be too hard on yourself, Sue." He realized he might also be telling her to forgive herself for having cheated on Roger the day before he died. He hadn't meant to allude to that, even obliquely, so he hastily added, "Roger must have moved it. Sometimes, things happen because of just plain bad luck."

"Do you think so? I've been wondering if it isn't fate." She sighed. Did she mean she'd been punished for her infidelity? He stepped back nervously.

"Anyway," he said, trying to be of some comfort. "You tried. You got all those wasp traps."

She looked startled. "What do you mean?" she said.

"I saw the boxes in the recycling. Didn't you get some of those wasp traps?" David frowned. "But I didn't see them in the yard."

"Yes, I bought them," she said. "But when I wanted to hang them up, Roger said no. He was afraid the bait would attract even more wasps to our yard. I should have insisted."

"It's all terrible," said David. "I'm so sorry."

Her lip trembled. "Anyway, I was hoping you'd keep an eye on the place and take in the mail." She handed him an envelope. "There's a key in there, and the phone number for Roger's parents in Wisconsin."

"I'm sorry, Sue," David said again stupidly. He wished she would go away. He felt sorry for her, but he didn't know what to say. He was also afraid Anita would come home and give him hell because Sue was over here.

Sue bent her head down and said tearily, "We had our problems. Who doesn't? But we had a wonderful fifteen years and two beautiful children."

"How are the boys doing?" asked Roger. He wished fervently that she'd leave.

"As well as can be expected. We have a lot of hard work ahead of us, and it will be difficult to raise them without a male role model. I just have to be brave. For them. It's what's keeping me going."

Sue checked her watch. "Listen, I have to go and pack a few things. Roger's boss is taking us to the airport." She gave him a chaste embrace. He managed to give her a few stiff pats on the back. Then, she turned and went back down the steps. He watched her walk across the lawn and through the hedge.

As soon as he closed the door, he heard another pair of feet coming up the front steps. Sue had left just in time. This must be Anita, but the soft, squishy footsteps sounded like Sue.

When he reached the front hall, Anita had already come in, wearing sneakers and jeans and carrying her little bag.

"What happened to your head?" she asked.

He touched the reddish mark where he'd hit the Heffernans' recycling bin. "I tripped," he said vaguely. "Listen, I just found out Roger Heffernan didn't make it. Dropped dead at his own barbecue. One yellow jacket sting and he was gone."

"That's awful!" said Anita. "Those poor little boys."

"Sue's taking them back to Wisconsin tonight," he said.

"For good?"

"I suppose so. After all, they only moved out here six months ago because he was transferred. She doesn't have a job here or any real ties. They have family back there, and I can't imagine she'll want to stay in the house where he died."

"Have you told the girls?"

"They're returning videos. They'll be back soon." David closed his eyes and caressed the skin in the middle of his forehead with an air of deep emotion. "I'm afraid I feel kind of blown away by all this. The idea that tragedy could just descend on a family and destroy it like that!"

"I'll tell the girls," she said. "But it would have been a lot easier if Sylvie hadn't been there to see it."

"I suppose you're criticizing me for accepting a neighborly invitation," he said sourly. "How can you trivialize such a terrible tragedy? Well, you won't have to obsess about Sue anymore, now that she's going back to Wisconsin."

"Oh, let's not start," snapped Anita.

"Thank you," he said with dignity. "Frankly, I was pretty traumatized myself. I actually saw the poor bastard die. It was a graphic lesson in how close mortality can be. It makes you think about what's really important in life."

He dragged himself toward the stairs. "I think I'll go lie down." A few seconds later, he called down over the banister, "Sorry the place is kind of a mess. What with Roger and all, I just haven't had the heart to do anything."

Upstairs, lying on the bed, David congratulated himself on how he'd handled all that. Surely Anita could see the poignancy of Roger's death. Maybe it would put everything into perspective for her, and she'd realize how important it was to keep a family together.

Downstairs, Anita sat down heavily on the sofa. She reran the conversation they'd just had in her mind. As usual, David had managed to twist everything around for his own benefit. By dwelling on Roger's ghastly accident he'd tried to deflect criticism from his broken promise about staying away from Sue. He'd made a pitch for family unity and tried to make Anita feel guilty about being miserable with him. He'd cast himself as the sensitive guy who was moved by tragedy.

He'd also managed to give himself an excuse for letting the house get trashed. On the coffee table in front of her she saw a scattered pile of the Sunday paper, a collection of beer cans, a few Pop-Tart wrappers, and a Barbie doll.

Wearily, she rose and started picking it all up. Underneath the newspapers, she discovered an unopened gas bill and an opened envelope addressed to David. The return address said, "Conway's Home and Garden Center."

Without any compunction, she let the newspaper fall back onto the table and read the letter.

Dear Mr. Jamison,

Sorry not to get back to you sooner, but things have changed here at Conway's, and we won't be taking bids for our advertising. The fact is, my niece Jennifer, a recent communications graduate, has just accepted a position as account executive with Skip MacDougal Associates. Because we are a family business, we felt it would be a win-win situation to work with this agency.

I'm sure you can understand that this is an excellent fit for us. A member of the Conway family will have creative input and be able to assure that we get the best advertising possible from a prestigious, full-service firm.

My brothers and I really enjoyed meeting you and listening to your ideas. We all wish you the very best in your future endeavors.

Sincerely,

Sandy Conway Smith
Director of Marketing and Consumer Affairs

Anita flung the letter on the coffee table. Damn David, she thought with disgust. This would just make it harder to do what she wanted to do.

THAT NIGHT, LILY LAY IN BED, THINKING ABOUT Roger being dead. When she and Sylvie had come home from the video store, Mom had sat down with both girls and told them that things like this hardly ever happened, and because something tragic had happened to the Heffernans that didn't mean it had to happen to them, and how no one knew why bad things happened and how they shouldn't worry about stuff they couldn't do anything about, but that their parents would take care of them.

"It's important," she had said, "to tell me how you're feeling about this. Tell me if you're scared or whatever." She sounded so calm and in charge. Lily liked that. It reminded her of when she was little, even though now she understood that her mother couldn't really stop bad things from happening.

Lily also knew she couldn't tell her mother the truth about her feelings. Because the truth was, the idea of something really bizarre happening to the weird Heffernans was kind of cool. They acted like this perfect family, with Sue always pretending everything could be so wholesome and all-American like people on TV, and then her husband drops dead at a barbecue. In a way, it almost served Sue right for thinking she could make life perfect.

But Sue was majorly weird herself, exactly because of the way she pretended to be so normal. That's why, in a way, Lily wasn't really surprised that something had happened over there. Those weirdness vibes probably pulled bad luck right into the Heffernans' patio.

Lily felt kind of sorry for the boys, though. She had never particularly liked Matt and Chris. They were stupid little kids with blank faces. Probably because their mom controlled their lives totally and they'd been turned into miniature zombies. Still, it would be pretty horrible to have your dad dead. Lily couldn't even imagine having your mom dead.

She fluffed up her pillow, turned over on her stomach, yawned, and realized she should sleep. She had to get up early for school tomorrow, but she was all wired from thinking about Roger.

Suddenly, she heard her parents' raised voices from their room. They sounded angry. The vaguely pleasurable excitement that she'd been feeling vanished immediately. Now she felt weak and sick and like someone in an elevator that went down jerkily and too fast.

She lifted her head from the pillow and strained her ears, like an animal in the forest. Dad was saying, "This is so sudden. We've got to work this out. I'll get a job, and you'll be happy, okay? You can't just throw me out! Where will I go?"

And then Mom said in a sobbing, apologizing kind of voice, "I think it's too late. Don't you get it? My feelings have changed. I never thought they could. Anyway, you don't love me anymore yourself. All you can say is, 'Where will I go?' You're only thinking of yourself, David."

"You never even warned me!" Dad shouted.

"I tried, but you wouldn't listen. You've taken me for granted for too long, and it all died, inch by inch. You should have seen it coming and done something about it."

She couldn't believe Mom was saying this. Lily put the pillow over her head. She didn't want to hear any more. She felt herself shriveling up, snakily twisting and distorting like something plastic thrown on a fire.

IN ANITA'S TOP DRAWER, UNDERNEATH HER COLlection of lacy underwear, she had hidden a large paperback book called *Leaving: A Woman's Guide to Ending a Nonproductive Relationship.* The cover of the book depicted a wedding ring rolling off toward a hazy, hopeful, dawn-like horizon.

During the next week, she read the book in several secret sessions in the tub, smuggling it into the bathroom under a towel. Lowering herself into the warm water and reading the soothing, conversational prose became a comforting ritual. She imagined the author's voice—a steady, measured, big sister kind of voice—and rejoiced with the author at her own successful efforts to ditch a crabby, critical, controlling husband who demeaned her.

Be good to yourself, the author said. Take time out to

pamper yourself. Buy yourself little presents and treat your-self to a new haircut. There were other passages that offered more practical advice. Don't bother telling the guy what was wrong with him. Just say, "It's better this way," or, "I think this is the way it's going to have to be."

Anita had already laid into David in their bedroom after the girls had gone to sleep, justifying her desire to get him out of her life with a long whispered tirade about his passiv-ity, his inability to take charge, his sloth. None of it really worked. He'd just snapped back that she was being unfair. Besides, hashing out what was wrong with him seemed to give him the idea that they were still negotiating. It had gone beyond that.

There seemed to be a great deal of advice for the woman who'd slaved away at home while her husband made all the money, and who feared a threadbare life as a displaced homemaker. No need to read those sections, Anita thought bitterly. Although maybe David could use some of the re-entry to the workplace tips and résumé writing advice.

The chapter that she saved until last, because she felt so guilty about it, was the one about telling the children. But even here, the author managed to make it all sound sensible and easy. Maybe it wasn't so awful. Lots of people did it, after all. Frank and his ex had done it. The chapter told her she couldn't be a good mother if she was stuck in a miserable marriage. She clung to that thought. And if the children went off the deep end, said the author, professional counsel-ing could put everything into perspective for them, too. Anita's health insurance would cover it.

Once the horrible knowledge was finally out in the open, and the girls knew, the logical next step would be to get David on the sofa and then into an apartment somewhere.

Anita relished the thought of the time when she'd come home to just the girls. She'd want to come home then, she

really would. The book described the heady feeling of liberation that was the payoff for having the guts to take charge of
your life.

The final chapter promised that there were new men out
there—no matter how beaten down and shell-shocked you
were. It was just a matter of meeting them, developing honest, intimate relationships with them, and learning to trust
and love again. It was important not to repeat the same bad
judgment that got you tangled up with Mr. Wrong.

In one way, Anita felt rather smug about this chapter.
She'd already got a leg up on that situation. But she also
wondered how patient Frank would be, and how long he
would wait. Once, just once, he'd really scared her when he
said, "Anita, I don't know how long I can wait for you to take
care of your problems."

There were plenty of women who had waited for years,
thought Anita. Everyone knew about those old-fashioned
secretaries who had spent a decade waiting to see if the boss
would ever get around to leaving his wife. Spending Christ-
mases alone, losing their looks, being brave and not complaining. Everyone thought those stoical, old-time mistresses
were fools. Men could be crazy and impetuous when it came
to love, but they seemed much less willing to be long-term
fools for it. If only there was somewhere for David to go.

The solution to the problem came to Anita all at once, a
few days later, while she was sitting in front of her computer
at work, looking at inventory data. She felt physically transformed, as if her bones had become straighter and stronger.
She could almost believe her blood was racing faster through
her veins. She realized suddenly that it was all possible.

Anita remembered the day her mother had charged like a
bull at a hideous old floral-patterned armchair they'd hauled
with them through all of Daddy's postings. "I've talked about
getting rid of that damned thing for years, and, by golly, I'm

going to do it right now," she'd said. Anita had watched, fascinated and thrilled, as her mother muscled the offending piece of furniture out onto the porch, and then, panting into the phone, called the Salvation Army to take it away. Now, she knew just how her mother had felt.

She couldn't wait any longer. David must leave. It simply had to be done. There would be no more of those horrible whispered conferences at night in their bedroom, with her pleading with him to leave and his scornfully refusing to even consider it. She had to confront him immediately, and without the children around.

If he raised the old objection that they couldn't afford two households, she had her answer. Why hadn't she thought of it sooner? Sue's house was just sitting there, empty. As far as she knew, it hadn't even been listed. It might take months to probate Roger's will, and David could live there rent-free until he got his act together. Sue would probably be relieved to have a house-sitter, and David would be close to the girls, so they could get used to the idea of the divorce.

Anita rose, got her purse, and told Marilyn the receptionist she was taking lunch early today. Setting out of the building into the street, Anita felt like a movie heroine about to seize control of her destiny. She imagined purposeful music behind her as she pushed open the heavy glass door with brass trim and walked boldly through a clump of scavenging pigeons on the sidewalk. They flapped away from her feet at the very last minute, and she took satisfaction in forcing them to scatter.

The number sixteen bus was strangely empty at this hour of the day. There were a few little old ladies with fuzzy white hair and glasses and plastic shopping bags and cheap raincoats, and some kids with bad skin trying to look tough with funereal clothes and tattoos and savage haircuts.

There was also a shabby, unshaven, middle-aged man carrying a dirty old backpack. He was presumably homeless. A lot of homeless people rode the buses in the free zone downtown. Usually, Anita tried not to look at them or think about their lives. It was too sad.

This man didn't look sad, though. He was sitting with one hand resting on his chin, looking out of the window of the bus with a pleasant, interested expression. Anita mentally cleaned him up and put him in a suit. He could have been any respectable person, really. He was actually quite good-looking. Cleaned up, he was someone you would want to talk to at a party. She realized he was about her age. David's age.

Is that where David would end up? For a minute, her courage drained away. But then it came surging back, and she heard Frank's voice explaining to her with thinly veiled frustration that David would simply have to get a job. Lots of people had jobs.

She wasn't sure just what kind of a job he could get. Advertising agencies wanted buzzy, young people. Everyone had heard horror stories of laid-off middle-aged managers who couldn't get decent jobs and ended up doing menial and embarrassing things. Anita worried about it herself. Just last week, Pam had told her she thought the colors she'd ordered for fall were "kind of older-looking."

But why should she feel so sorry for David? Had he cared how tired she got of retail, and Pam, and ambitious younger buyers making snide remarks about her markdown rate? Suddenly she took a malicious pleasure in the sight of David wearing an unattractive polyester uniform with a button that said, "Ask Me About Frosty Freezes," or something, and leaning into a microphone, saying, "May I please take your order?"

The bus pulled up to her regular stop with a squeak of brakes, and she began to walk home. It wasn't just the number sixteen bus. The street where she lived also looked and felt different in the middle of the day. There were practically no cars parked here, and with the exception of Ed and Laura Margolin, who were outside mulching a garden bed with grass clippings, the street was deserted.

She remembered pushing Lily in her stroller up this street in the spring when it was deserted and quiet like this, back when she'd been home and David had worked.

What a wonderful time that had been. How astounding it had been then to fade into a ghostlier version of herself, as if the troubling vivid color were leeching out of her. In place of herself, there was Lily, who had sprung into the center of the world, a completely enchanting creature, blinking in the sun as she was pushed up this street, reaching out to objects that caught her eye with a small, dimpled hand.

If Anita had been told back then that she'd walk down this same street fourteen years later to tell her husband to leave, she would never have been able to imagine it.

Right after she gave birth, Anita had been thunderstruck by Lily's charm and by how much pleasure could be had from admiring her. And, she had been astonished by the ease—no, it was more than ease, it was relief and gratitude— with which she had felt her own persona fade away. How liberating it had been to forget oneself.

Of course, as the girls grew older, and became more independent, Anita had felt herself coming back. And now Frank, ah Frank, had brought her back with a vengeance. She hadn't felt so alive since her own adolescence.

But coming back was different. Its satisfaction lay in the thrill of rediscovery. She felt vivid and lively, but without the painful preoccupation with self that had cast a shadow over everything up until the babies came.

Turning into her own yard, she took a deep breath. She could do this. She knew she could.

She discovered David sprawled on the sofa reading *People* magazine and still wearing pajamas and bathrobe at noon. He looked up, clearly amazed to see her here in the middle of the day.

"Anita!" She stood in the doorway to the room and looked down at him. He hadn't shaved, and there were more white hairs in his stubble. He wasn't as handsome as she had once thought. In fact, he looked kind of weaselly around the jaw and the mouth. Why hadn't she seen that before? She had been completely blind for years. She'd actually thought she'd been happy.

"David," she said very calmly, placing one hand on the inside of the doorway in a gesture rather like a bit of old-fashioned stage business, "I want a trial separation." Frank had told her it would be easier to ask for a separation than a divorce, and that David would be more likely to leave the premises, which gave him less of a chance of getting the house.

"I think you should stay at Sue's. I'm sure if you call her she'll say that's okay. We can tell the girls about it tonight. We can tell them together, if you want." The book had said you should tell the children with both parents there, but Anita expected him to bail out—seeing as he was such a coward about unpleasantness.

"Forget it, Anita," he said irritably, tossing the magazine aside. "I've told you before, I'm not going anywhere. If you want out, you leave. You find an apartment somewhere. Or maybe you have a lover you can move in with." He gave her a look of disgust. It was the first time since Mother's Day that he'd mentioned that.

"Oh, please!" she said. "Let's not start in about that."

"It might have some bearing on a possible divorce and custody arrangement," he said in a triumphant tone.

"You're just speculating," she said. She didn't add that

Frank had told her it wouldn't make much difference, anyway.

"Roger Heffernan saw you, Anita! Necking in public. In some restaurant."

"That's ridiculous. I never spent more than ten minutes with Roger Heffernan in my life. I doubt he would have been able to recognize me in some restaurant. Look, David, think about the future, not the past. You should think about getting a job."

David's face scrunched up and he looked suddenly pathetic. Anita closed her eyes. "I can't believe this," he said in a hopeless tone. "Why, Anita, why?"

She took a deep breath, and remembered the stock phrase the book recommended. "I just think this is better for everybody," she recited. "If you won't move into Sue's, I'll have to get a lawyer to get you out of here. Either way, I'm going to tell the girls tonight that we are separating on a trial basis."

She opened her eyes again. His face was still crumpled, and he looked like some kid cowering in front of the playground bully. It was awful. She was afraid she'd burst into tears. She trembled and said, "I'm sorry. I'm so sorry. I never wanted this to happen. Really, I didn't."

He sat up and leaned forward as if he were going to rise, take a step toward her, and embrace her. She turned and fled from the house.

DAVID HADN'T MOVED FROM THE SOFA WHEN, AN hour later, the phone rang. It was Anita. He hoped she'd called to say she was sorry she'd lost it like that, and to withdraw her ultimatum. Instead, she had come up with a few details.

"I think you should take what you'll need for now over to

Sue's before the girls come home, so they won't have to see you packing. I know you'll want us to do everything we can to make the transition easier for them." She spoke in an imperious, impersonal way. "And you can be in the house after school for the girls until I come home. I don't want them over at Sue's. They should feel they have their own familiar space."

Then, in a sad voice that broke his heart, she said again what she had said at the house earlier: "I'm sorry. I'm really sorry." She seemed to both loathe and pity him in turns.

Maybe it wasn't such a bad idea, he thought. If he spent a week or so at Sue's, Anita would have to realize how stupid this was. The girls would be terribly upset. He counted on them to back him up, and she cared about what they thought.

It had occurred to him that he could pretend he'd called Sue to get her permission and she'd said no. Then Anita would have to let him check into a motel on the overburdened Visa card.

Of course, Sue would never say he couldn't stay at her house. Even Anita couldn't deny that Sue was always generous and helpful, which is why he didn't think he actually needed to call that number in Wisconsin and get her permission. Plus, he didn't want to discuss his marital problems with Sue, nor did he care to hear about her troubles right now.

He went upstairs and flung his suitcase in the middle of the unmade bed, then grabbed clean pajamas and jeans and underwear and socks and threw them in. This all reminded him of the time he was eight and went with his little plastic Fred Flintstone suitcase over to the neighbors' for a few days. That time, his mother had just vanished from the face of the earth, only to return with a new baby sister. A sister who'd grown up and turned on him, scooping up the priceless antiques from Aunt Martha's house and shipping him the Tupperware and old alarm clocks and a collection of *National Geographics*, for God's sake.

He looked around the bedroom where he'd woken up for so many years. Would he ever sleep here again? He was used to everything here. It was so unfair to be sent away like this. So humiliating.

He yanked a few shirts off their hangers. Anita's clothes occupied three quarters of the closet. Now, presumably, she'd spread out and take over the whole thing. She'd always complained about the closet space in this house. Well she'd figured out how to solve that problem, hadn't she?

He got dressed from some of the clothes he'd packed, then went into the bathroom to get a razor and his toothbrush. He threw the final items into the suitcase and tugged crookedly at the zipper. He cast a look around the bedroom, narrowing his eyes at the sight of Anita's bathrobe lying over a chair. Suddenly, he had an urge to tear it to pieces.

He took a deep breath and strode out of the room. Despite the fact that there was no audience, he attempted to make a dignified exit from the house, going down the stairs with a measured tread, walking through the kitchen without looking around, closing the door gently behind him, striding toward that inviting opening in the hedge.

WHEN HER MOTHER STOOD AT THE BOTTOM OF the stairs and called up in a nervous, kind of fake-casual way, "Girls? Can you come down here, please?" Lily was pretty sure she knew exactly what was going to happen.

She put down her homework, pushed her hair behind her ears to keep it out of her face, and sighed. On the way down, she rapped on Sylvie's door. "Better come down now," she said. "Mom has something important to tell us." If she didn't do that, Sylvie would stall the way she always did and say, "Just a sec, just a sec," and Lily and Mom would be sitting there waiting for the big climax and it would all be kind of embarrassing. Lily just wanted it to be over fast.

She opened her sister's door and looked in to see Sylvie sitting on her rug, in a litter of toys, her legs wide apart. She held a Barbie doll in one hand and a pink plastic comb in the other. "Just a sec," she said, proceeding to attack Barbie's hair with so much enthusiasm that the doll's smiling head was almost snapped off.

"I think you'd better hurry up," said Lily harshly. "I think it's like a really big deal." Sylvie looked up at her sister with wide eyes, and Lily could see she was frightened. "Okay," she said, dropping the comb and the doll and scrambling to her feet.

Lily put an arm around Sylvie. "It'll be okay," she said, giving her a little squeeze.

She knew she was right when she saw Dad sitting next to Mom on the sofa in a stiff, formal pose, like a family photo. It was right out of some old seventies sitcom, except in those soothing reruns, families had little meetings to discuss nice things, like where to go on vacation.

"Sit down, girls," said Mom with a brave little smile. It was all so phony. The four of them never sat here in the living room like this. Here it was. The big announcement. It was so obvious.

Lily couldn't stand it. "You're getting a divorce, right?" she said impatiently.

THE FIRST NIGHT DAVID SPENT IN SUE'S HOUSE, Anita felt festive and giddy with relief. She hadn't appreciated the enormity of her burden until it had been lifted. The weight of it had sneaked up on her, getting heavier and heavier by small, nefarious increments.

After tucking in the girls, reassuring them and, as the book recommended, resisting the urge to apologize about the separation, she went to her own bedroom. She closed the blinds tightly, shutting out Sue's house, and tried not to imagine what David was doing over there right now. Was he sleeping on the sofa? In Sue and Roger's bedroom? She didn't want to think about any of it.

She slept nude, in the middle of the bed, sprawling out luxuriously. Her body felt light and buoyant. For the first time in ages, she felt optimistic. She imagined David coming to her and telling her that he understood perfectly, that he had found a job, that he would be sending her support checks. In her fantasy, David looked more like his old self and less weaselly, and he said, "If you hadn't initiated this separation, I never would have pulled myself together. I would have ended up an old, cranky man, resentful of you for my dependence. Now, I have a new life."

She imagined having Frank over to dinner, introducing the girls, stirring something fragrant on the stove while he chopped parsley or grated cheese, his starched cuffs rolled up over his forearms. She imagined the four of them at the dinner table, laughing and having a good time, and later, Lily teasing her slyly about being in love and giving her tacit approval. She was getting old enough to understand.

Sylvie's unselective habit of ingratiating herself with everyone and disliking no one had frustrated Anita in the past. The way Sylvie had bought into Sue's heavy-handed overtures had been particularly upsetting. Now, though, as it became time to introduce Frank, this aspect of Sylvie's character would be a real blessing.

She imagined traveling with Frank, exploring the world

together, spending lazy weekends with him. She imagined the time when the girls were older and away at college, and all the time she could have just to be with Frank. She imagined the girls' weddings, with both David and Frank in attendance, everyone amicable and mature and relaxed.

Anita told herself that everything would be all right. She wasn't sure she deserved it, though. Maybe she'd be punished for all the years she had spent thinking badly of women who had affairs, who left their husbands, who disrupted their children's lives, and who didn't have the fortitude to hang in there for better or for worse. She swore never again to judge anyone. She knew that no one outside a marriage could possibly understand what went on inside it. After all, hadn't she spent years lying to herself about her own marriage? She hoped that now, finally, she was able to view her own life without blinders.

Anita also thought about all the years with David. She had to admit that they had loved each other—at least she was sure she'd loved him. She'd been so happy when the babies were small. It would have been wonderful if it had worked out differently, if David had taken responsibility.

That's what it all came down to. When he ceased contributing, she lost respect and desire for him. She had fought it, pretending to herself that money wasn't an issue, that careers weren't important enough to undermine a marriage. But damn it, it *was* an issue. She felt overburdened and betrayed. Helplessly, she'd watched him get slack and dependent and lazy and frightened about competing out there in the world. She would never admit it to anyone, not even her mother, but she now believed that when a man just gave up, like David had, and let his wife take care of him, the whole core of the relationship was damaged. Love and affection had been battered away by anger and resentment. And desire was even more problematic. Desire meant surrender, and it was impossible to surrender to someone you could no longer respect, someone you didn't think would ever change.

THE SURPRISING THING WAS THAT, AFTER THE initial shock, David didn't really mind the new arrangement. His days were much the same. He especially liked lounging around in the Heffernans' bedroom, knowing that no children would come pounding up the stairs demanding something. In the rest of Sue's house, the furniture was arranged differently than at his own house, but the way this room was shaped, there really was only one place for the bed, and it was in the same place his and Anita's bed had been, with bedside tables and twin lamps in the same position, and a chest of drawers by the window. He felt quite at home, really.

In a few short days, he'd developed a pleasant routine. He slept in as long as he liked, then checked the want ads in the morning paper on the off chance there might be something he wasn't overqualified for. After that, he did the crossword puzzle. Then, he'd read or maybe take a stroll up to the Honey Bee for a little lunch, or walk over to the supermarket for something for dinner. After school he put in a few hours with the girls, but he certainly didn't feel obliged to do any laundry or cleaning. Being an unpaid baby-sitter was enough. He wasn't Anita's maid, too.

He cleared out just before she got home. He didn't have to go through that nervous little moment after her arrival wondering whether she'd be pleasant or critical. Back at Sue's, he'd enjoy some wine and a bite to eat, watching the news and prime-time TV in nag-free peace.

He had also spent a lot of time daydreaming. He fantasized about Anita's having an abrupt change of heart—coming to him and putting her hands on his shoulders and saying with tear-glazed eyes, "Darling, I must have been out of my mind. Please forgive me," then collapsing with a shudder of surrender against his chest.

After this touching scene, he imagined a second honeymoon in some tropical place. Anita's mother could take the kids, and he and Anita could go to Maui or something and fuck their brains out and forget all about their problems. Problems that David felt were really Anita's problems inflicted on him and the girls in a completely selfish and pathological way.

The trouble was, he couldn't come up with as much enthusiasm for the reconciliation scenario as he would have liked. Try as he would to imagine himself soaping down Anita in the shower, or giggling with her over the Chablis in the hot tub, or sucking her toes beneath a palm tree, it came out empty and false and plain unexciting, like some cheesy resort brochure he might have worked on back in his copywriting days.

The truth was, he couldn't fantasize positively about Anita because he was beginning to resent her with an intensity he never could have imagined. Anita had always seemed too dependent, falling apart too easily when things went wrong around the house and then blaming him. Now he had come to the conclusion she was a superficial, selfish woman who only cared about money, and who put him down because he didn't make enough of it. Well, actually, he didn't make any at all, he admitted to himself, but there were extenuating circumstances.

Really, how in God's name could he go out there and be a world beater when she was so emotionally unsupportive? And didn't his contributions to raising the children count? Why had he ever thought she'd be able to deal with his being a househusband? She was too conventional, just like her mother, to accept anything less than a stereotyped relationship with the man as the provider.

Maybe that's why their sex life seemed to have collapsed. She lost interest because, on some primitive level, she saw sex as something a wife provides the breadwinner. God knows, Anita hadn't been interested in sex for its own sake for years—not since the babies had come along. Why hadn't he seen it? She had really only come across like a young juicy thing when he first met her because she'd wanted babies.

Babies and a meal ticket. He had never completely believed it when men said that's all women were after, but maybe where Anita was concerned there was a lot of truth to it. All on a subconscious level, of course. Anita had probably managed to convince herself she loved David for himself.

And why hadn't he been able to face the fact Anita was having an affair? She wouldn't have thrown him out if there hadn't been someone else in the picture, he was sure of it. David had been in denial about this, partly because he didn't think Anita cared enough about sex to bother. With his new insights, though, he realized she was motivated by some crass need to be taken care of.

David might have had his own little lapse with Sue on the sofa, but that was different. That was passion. God knows there hadn't been much of that in his marriage for years. So when the opportunity presented itself, David had done what any normal, red-blooded, sexually-deprived guy would have done.

No, it was impossible to fantasize about reconciliation. David had another set of fantasies that were more satisfying. These concerned Anita's sudden death, and always made him feel cozy and calm. The death itself happened offstage. It was abstract and without emotional content, just a prelude to the good part.

He imagined a phone call from Anita's office. Someone delicately telling him about a freak accident. A bus running over her or something. He didn't dwell on the grim details. In the fantasy, he took the call calmly, exuding a quiet dignity, graciously making the nervous person at the other end feel better.

He'd tell the girls gently and expertly. Of course they'd be upset at first. But the poor things didn't know how bad the alternative would be—the messy divorce, then a ragged life with a succession of Anita's sleazy younger lovers hanging around.

He would arrange for a tasteful, dignified funeral, no expenses spared. Anita had never shown much interest in religion, although she once confided that she prayed occasionally. Maybe the Unitarians could come up with something nonsecular but spiritual.

Then he'd get on with his life. He wouldn't even have to get a job. Part of Anita's benefits package included a two hundred thousand dollar life insurance policy. That would tide him over until he got back on track with his career. And the mortgage insurance would pay off the house.

There was no doubt about it, Anita's death would definitely be more convenient than a divorce. As for getting back together, forget it. There was no way he could ever trust her again. He couldn't trust her not to make unreasonable demands. He couldn't trust her not to tell him what to do all the time, like not seeing Sue. Above all, he couldn't trust her not to screw around.

Who was the guy, anyway? David conjured up a picture of some flashy Skip MacDougal type with a Lexus and capped teeth and Armani suits. That's what Anita would go for. It was repulsive.

God, for all he knew she could end up HIV positive. A quick death underneath the wheels of a bus would be infinitely kinder than a lingering, painful, shameful, and costly disease. It was really the most compassionate thing to wish for her.

One evening, after he'd been at Sue's for about a week, David was lounging on the bed in the Heffernans' bedroom mindlessly channel-surfing. He was enjoying the fact that he could do so without Anita saying, "Please find something, I don't care what, and stick with it!" from behind a magazine. The phone rang and he hit the mute button on the remote. It was Sue.

"David! I called your house and Anita said you were at my house. Is everything okay?"

"Everything is okay with your house," he said. "But Anita and I have kind of split up. I've been spending nights here. I hope you don't mind. It's just temporary. We thought a little time out would help."

"Oh, David, of course I don't mind. I'm so sorry. How are you holding up?"

"Not too bad, really. Listen, Sue, I suppose I should have called you and asked you if I could stay here, but I didn't want to bother you at a time like this." David felt suddenly shabby. Here he was, all stretched out on her bed. He even had his shoes on the white lacy coverlet, and he was glad she couldn't see what a disaster area the kitchen was.

But Sue was completely understanding. "I'm just sorry things have been going so badly for you. How are the girls handling it?"

"Better than I expected. But tell me how you are."

Sue let out a weary sigh. "It gets a little easier every day. The funeral was very moving. A pretty little white Methodist church, with a good choir and some simple flowers from people's gardens on the coffin. He's buried in his family plot. I think he would have liked it."

David hated hearing about Roger's funeral. To change the subject, he asked about her sons.

"They're doing better. I think they'll want to come home soon."

"Home?"

"Yes. I think their routine at school and everything will help them adjust."

"Oh. I kind of thought you might just stay back there."

"I don't know what we'll do eventually. I don't want to rush into anything. But I think they should finish out the school year, don't you?"

"I suppose so," said David. "Want me to forward your mail or anything?"

"No, not yet, anyway. I'm making decisions little by little. I'll let you know."

"All right, Sue."

"David?"

"What?"

"Look, I know it's not really any of my business, but I'm worried about the girls. Do you really think it's best for them that you move out? Shouldn't Anita be the one to move out? After all, you're the primary caretaker."

"Anita doesn't see it that way," said David. "And I'm sure if we actually did decide to split up permanently, God forbid, she'd expect the house and custody of the girls."

"But that's all wrong!" Sue sounded agitated, and David was touched at her loyalty.

"Well, I'm pretty sure we can patch things up," he said confidently. He suddenly forgot all his fantasies and found himself hoping fervently that they could. Because if they didn't, when Sue and the boys came back, he'd be homeless.

14

ONE OF THE LUXURIES OF THE NEW REGIME from Anita's point of view was that she was able to talk to Frank on the phone for as long as she liked after the children were in bed. As she did in her office at work, she whispered into the phone. She was always nervous the girls would ask her who she was talking to, or, worse yet, linger outside her door and overhear something.

"It's been a whole week," she told him. "I just feel so relieved. I didn't know how miserable I was."

"Well, it's a good first step," said Frank.

"A huge step for me," she said defensively. "And for the girls."

"The key thing is not to let him back in. That's very important."

She wished Frank wouldn't lecture her like this. And why

wasn't he giving her some credit for being brave enough to throw David out in the first place? Instead, it was as if she hadn't gone far enough. "He hasn't even mentioned coming back. I'm just so grateful to have him out of here. And I'm grateful to you for giving me the courage to do it," she added.

"Do you think he's looking for a job?"

"I don't know. I haven't spoken to him for a couple of days. I can't even look him in the eye. It's all so painful."

"Eventually, you're going to have to come to terms with the finances. Are you going to give him an allowance? This should all be negotiated. I think it's time you see a lawyer."

"Can't I have some time to regroup?" Anita said plaintively. "I'm mostly thinking about the girls right now. They're going to need some time to adjust to all this." Frank didn't seem to give the girls' feelings a moment's thought. Didn't he realize that for Anita this was the most agonizing part of all of this?

"I'm just trying to tell you this could all blow up if you don't plan now," Frank went on. "He may be getting legal advice himself. And if he does, that advice would probably be to consolidate his position by moving back in. You mustn't let that happen. It could mean handing him the house on a plate. Maybe even the girls, too."

Anita was irritated. Frank might know all about the law, but he hadn't lived with David for almost twenty years. "Believe me, I know David. He's too passive to do anything like that. He'll just wait and see what happens."

"It sounds like that's what you're doing." Frank's voice had taken on a condescending crispness, as if he were trying to get through to a not-very-bright client. "I think you should be ready in case he tries to get back in. I can set up something for you with a very good guy in my firm."

"Please don't pressure me like this. I can only do so much at a time. So far, it seems to be working out." She'd done what he wanted. She'd thrown David out. Didn't he know how hard that had been?

His voice softened, for which she was grateful. "I just want to make sure you're all right. I want you to be prepared in case things get ugly."

THANK GOD, DAVID REFLECTED, SUE HAD PHONED again, to let him know she was arriving tomorrow. Her once immaculate house was looking pretty scruffy. The sink was full of dishes and David had let dirty clothes pile up in the bedroom. Before getting ready for bed, David collected all his dirty laundry, took it down to the washing machine in the basement, and started a load. He'd dry it in the morning while he cleaned the house.

On the phone, Sue had explained she'd only be in town for a few days, signing some legal papers arising from her husband's death, and would be leaving again to return to Milwaukee until the boys were ready to come back to school. "Use the house for as long as you want," she had said. "I feel safer knowing you're keeping an eye on things. It's one less worry for me."

Sue turned down his offer to meet her at the airport. Roger's boss was going to pick her up, she said, and take her straight to the office, where some details of the insurance settlement would be handled.

David was looking forward to seeing her. He'd had a week and a half now without any significant adult companionship. Maybe the two of them could have a quiet meal together before he had to go back to his own grim household to wait out the few days she'd be here.

One of the first heavy rains of the season was batting against the windows, and the house felt cold. It was hard to believe that only a few weeks ago he'd been sweltering at that barbecue. Soon the first frost would come, killing off the last of the yellow jackets.

After undressing, he realized he'd thrown all his clothes in the washer and he didn't have anything to wear to bed. He'd just have to sleep nude, the way he always had before the kids came along. Once under the covers, though, he realized his chest and shoulders were cold. For a moment, he considered going downstairs and turning up the thermostat, but Sue had some complicated digital device that was preprogrammed. He imagined himself puzzling over it, naked and shivering.

What the hell, he thought, flinging back the covers. There must be something of Roger's he could wear. He went over to a tall chest and pulled open the top drawer. He caught a faint smell of lavender. The drawer was full of women's underwear. Feeling slightly voyeuristic, he picked up something in red see-through chiffon with black lace. David was shocked. Sue seemed like the last person in the world to own such a garment. It was right out of a porno magazine. He pawed around some more and discovered a black stretch-lace bodysuit and a green satin Merry Widow arrangement.

That time on his own sofa, Sue had been wearing sensible white cotton underwear. He could only assume this stuff was Roger's idea. If David had been some kind of a lingerie fetishist himself and asked Anita to dress up for him, would she have agreed? He fingered the cups of the green satin number and imagined it propping up Sue's ample breasts. The results would be pretty startling.

Feeling sleazy, he resisted the urge to explore further. He reluctantly folded all the stuff back up and tried to remember where it had all been. As he smoothed it back down in the drawer, he felt something square and rigid. He peeled back more lingerie and discovered a flat, kidskin box, tied with a pink satin ribbon.

He stared at it with fascination. As a boy, he remembered once discovering a packet of letters tied with a similar ribbon underneath his mother's utilitarian JCPenney's bras and girdles, along with a peculiar round case that contained a strange rubber object he later learned was a diaphragm. The underwear drawer was the classic female repository for secrets.

He hesitated for just an instant, and then assured himself that no one would ever know what he was about to do. He loosened the ribbon and lifted the lid. Inside he encountered a flattened, browned orchid—presumably once a corsage— and some snapshots of people he didn't recognize. In one, there was what appeared to be a teenaged Sue in Bermuda shorts leaning against a vintage Mustang with some wholesome-looking boy and, beneath it, a collection of handwritten letters on three-hole-punch-ruled school binder paper folded into quarters. Relics of high school romance didn't live up to the promise of the kidskin case with its elegant ribbon, and David had no interest in reading the letters.

He was more intrigued by a small red plastic box. He turned it over in his palm and saw a prescription label with the name "Roger Heffernan" on it. David flipped open the box. Inside, there was a small glass ampule, a syringe, and a pair of tablets.

With trembling hands, he put everything back as he'd found it, making sure to tie the pink ribbon along the old creases, and crept back into bed, entirely forgetting how cold he was.

He lay in the dark, his mind in turmoil. Could she have put Roger's kit there and then forgotten about it? But why would she put it there at all? Surely, the logical place was in the medicine chest, not in her secret hideaway. On the other hand, it was absurd to think that Sue had deliberately withheld the means to save her husband's life. There had to be a perfectly simple explanation, but unfortunately, he would never hear it because there was no way he could ever admit that he'd been going through her lingerie in the first place.

The next morning, he had another idea. Maybe Roger himself put the kit there. David couldn't imagine why, but it seemed the only possible answer. Roger may not have been such a terrific husband, but Sue had never come right out and said she was unhappily married. And even if she were, there wouldn't be any reason to just let him die, leaving the boys she loved so much fatherless.

He went to the grocery store and got some fresh pasta and ready-made sauce and a couple of bottles of wine. A quiet dinner with Sue might give him the opportunity to probe a little and find out just how she did feel about Roger. He had felt kind of queasy ever since his discovery.

At lunchtime, when he figured Anita would be away from her desk, he left a message on her voice mail. "Sue's back for a few days, so I'm coming home for a couple of nights. Don't worry, though," he added bitterly, "I'll sleep on the sofa."

He was back at his own house and the children were both downstairs in the playroom watching TV when he heard Sue's familiar tread on the backstairs. He opened the door and there she stood, smiling at him, just as soft and serene and snub-nosed and rosy as ever. She couldn't possibly have let anyone die. There must have been some horrible mistake.

She seemed to be evaluating his appearance, too, because the first thing she said was, "Oh, David, you look terrible. You must be going through hell!"

He shrugged, embarrassed. "Yeah, well, things are pretty rocky, no doubt about it. I pretty much avoid Anita. In fact, I was hoping we could have dinner at your house tonight. I bought some stuff."

"That would be great!" she said with evident relief. "I'm not ready to be alone, to tell you the truth."

The door from downstairs opened and Sylvie's voice called out, "Who are you talking to? Is Mom here?" Her head emerged from behind the door.

"Hello, Sylvie!" said Sue enthusiastically, holding out her arms. Sylvie, looking slightly confused at Sue's sudden reappearance, walked slowly over with a shy smile and allowed herself to be embraced.

"So what are you going to be for Halloween this year?" asked Sue in a businesslike way.

"A princess," said Sylvie. "I want to be a princess."

"Is your costume ready?"

"No. Mom's been too busy."

Irritated, David interjected, "We've got three weeks, Sylvie."

Lily's heavy footsteps became audible on the basement stairs, and she too emerged into the kitchen. She stared at Sue with a surly look. Why couldn't she be more gracious, David wondered crossly. "Hello, Lily," said Sue, disentangling herself from Sylvie. Lily turned away and went back down the basement steps, slamming the door behind her.

"She certainly doesn't seem too happy," said Sue sadly.

"We've all been pretty stressed out," said David, checking his watch. Anita would be back soon. "Let's go over to your place. I'll pour you a glass of wine and make dinner."

"Bye, Daddy," said Sylvie, giving him a kiss. Sue knelt down in front of her and said, "I've missed you, sweetheart. Soon, I'll be back and we can be together a lot, okay?"

"Okay," said Sylvie.

Back in Sue's kitchen, David filled two glasses. Sue sat at the kitchen table while he got the water boiling for the pasta and began washing gourmet salad mix at the sink.

"Have you finished all your business?" he asked. "It must be rough, going over all that at a time like this."

She sighed. "Yes. But I tell myself to count my blessings.

Roger had a very generous insurance policy set up. He's taken wonderful care of us. I have an income for life, so I never need to worry. I can still be at home with the kids— and there's enough for the boys to get a good education, too." She sipped her wine.

"That's wonderful, Sue." David suddenly felt envious. Why couldn't Anita just drop dead like Roger? Then he could get back into the house, and cash in on the insurance besides. He looked out the window over the sink and saw Anita in her kitchen, their kitchen, setting the table.

"Tell me how you feel about the separation," said Sue. "Like I said, you look like you've been through a very bad time."

He sighed deeply. "I'm sure she'll come to her senses eventually." He didn't want to get into all of Anita's complaints about his not working. It was too humiliating. "Maybe there's another guy. She won't discuss anything with me."

"Roger thought so," said Sue solemnly. "And, David, there's something I never told you before. Remember last Mother's Day when Anita was sick and I took her that plate of food? I didn't want you to think I was eavesdropping, and I didn't want to interfere, but I overheard her talking to someone on the phone."

"Oh?" said David. He kept staring over at his own house. The girls were sitting down now, and Anita was carrying something large and cylindrical to the table. It looked like a big cardboard bucket of deli fried chicken.

"I'm only telling you this because I don't think Anita has any right to throw you out," Sue went on calmly. "You have to take care of those children."

David turned away from the window with its view of his estranged family and looked at Sue. She was gazing at him with what he assumed was pity.

"What exactly did you hear?" he asked.

Sue closed her eyes, and said in a reluctant voice, "I heard her say, 'I love you.'"

David felt as if he'd been kicked in the gut. He let go of the colander with lettuce and held on to the sink with both hands. "Jesus!" he said. "Everything's so screwed up. How did this happen? I can't believe it. My whole life is falling apart, and there isn't a damn thing I can do about it."

Sue scrambled to her feet and went to his side. She put an arm around him. "None of it's your fault, David. None of it. You're a wonderful person. A wonderful parent. A wonderful lover. You don't deserve this." She stroked his forehead. "The girls don't deserve it, either."

LILY, GNAWING ON A DRUMSTICK, LOOKED UP from the table and stared into Sue's kitchen. There was Daddy, standing right next to Sue, framed by the window over the sink. She had one hand on his shoulder and his head was kind of drooping. She was stroking his forehead, and then she kissed it! Lily tried not to let her mother see her reaction, but it was too late. It was hard to hide anything from her.

Lily had stared back down at her plate and stirred up her coleslaw, but Mom's head swiveled in the direction she had been looking. Lily heard her breath suck in, real fast and short.

Sylvie, who had her back to the window, stared at Mom. "What is it?"

"Nothing," said Mom, pulling the cord that closed the curtains. The little metal hooks made a horrible sound on the rod, like teeth. Mom gave Lily a warning look, a look that meant, "Don't tell Sylvie."

Lily felt kind of sick at the idea of Dad getting all gushy

with Sue. It was so gross. But at the same time, she was glad Mom thought she was grown up enough to protect Sylvie from the horrible truth. Lily also felt, in some strange way, relieved. Now she understood why Mom and Dad were separated. It was because of Sue. Her dad and Sue had been fooling around. Lily felt ashamed, as if she were contaminated by her father's behavior.

"YOU'RE REALLY UPSET. IT'S NATURAL," SAID Sue, gently leading David away from the sink to a chair. "Just sit down and I'll take over." She patted his hand and went back to the sink to fetch his wineglass for him.

"God, Sue, I'm sorry. It's just that all this has been so hard." He felt weak and foolish falling apart like this.

"Of course it is," she said in a calm voice as she continued the salad preparations. "And, it's all Anita's fault. I don't think you really understand just how destructive she is, David. She's busting up a family for her own selfish reasons. If she cared one bit about the children, she couldn't do what she's doing. What right has she to throw you out? You, who've looked after those girls for years."

"Oh, I'm sure she loves the girls. It's me she hates."

"Sounds to me like she's just found someone else she thinks is more interesting. But you're the father of her children."

"There's more to it than that, Sue. We've had a lot of tension in the marriage for a long time." He felt suddenly too tired to put up a front. "She's wanted me to get a job for a long time. I don't know why I didn't. Now it's probably too late. The truth is, I stayed home for six years, and now I feel unemployable and useless."

She turned to him and said urgently, "Don't you see? She

wore you down. She systematically undermined your confidence. You're talented and resourceful, but she didn't give you the support you needed. It's not your fault."

"Maybe not, but the fact is, I'm in a pretty bad position. No job. No income. No home. I never told you this, but this slimy guy who used to work for me, Skip MacDougal, stole the Conway's account by hiring one of their kids right out of college."

"Oh, no," she said sympathetically.

"I swear to God, Sue, I've sometimes wondered what will become of me. I never believed she'd throw me out."

Sue put the pasta into the boiling water. "She should be the one to leave, not you. You should get the house and the children. Breaking up your home was all her idea." Sue seemed to be bristling with anger on his behalf.

"The sad thing is," he said, topping up his wine, "even if she did take me back, I've gotten to the point where I resent her so much I don't think I could stand living with her. She's betrayed me. Turned on me. God, Sue, I've even been fantasizing about her dying. It would be so much easier than this."

He suddenly realized how tactless this was. "Oh, Sue, I'm sorry. I was so preoccupied with my problems, I didn't think about you and what you've been through."

"That's all right," she said in an oddly satisfied tone. "You're angry. Justifiably angry."

"I've been going on and on," said David, seeing an opportunity to bring up the subject of Roger. "Now tell me how you're feeling. About Roger."

"I still can't believe what's happened. I keep thinking he's away on a business trip or something. The idea that I'll never see him again, that we won't get to see the boys grow up together—" She began to cry.

"Oh, Sue, I'm so sorry," said David. It was all right. She was crying. She wouldn't do that if she'd cold-bloodedly let him die. David felt a huge surge of relief.

WHEN MOM CAME AND TUCKED LILY IN, THEY didn't talk about what they'd seen in the Heffernans' kitchen window. Maybe they could later, when Sylvie wasn't around, but now she might hear them through the wall. Anyway, Lily didn't really want to talk about it. It was too creepy. Lily gave her mom a specially hard hug and kissed her about five times and said, "I love you, Mom."

Later, Lily lay awake and promised herself to be nice to her mother and help her every way she could. She'd actually blamed her mother for the separation. Dad had hinted that it was all Mom's idea, and Lily had even heard him begging her not to go through with the divorce when they'd had that fight late at night. As a result, Lily had been cold to her mother, and even tried to get her to take Dad back. But Mom had just cut her off and said, "We'll talk about this later. It's very painful for us all, but it's something the adults will have to work out. Please trust me."

From now on, Lily would. Totally. She fell asleep feeling a heady mix of disgust and fascination with her new knowledge.

SUE WAS FINISHING THE DISHES AND DAVID WAS working on the second bottle of wine in the living room when the doorbell rang. He heard her go into the hall and open the door, then to his amazement, he heard Anita. "I have to talk to David," she said in a cold, mean voice.

"Do you want to come in?" Sue asked pleasantly.

"No. I just need to talk to him," Anita replied.

Sue walked into the living room, and said very calmly, "Anita wants to talk to you."

He rose and went into the hall.

"I got your phone message at work," Anita said. "I think it's better that you don't come back tonight. I was going to suggest you stay in a motel or something, but then I saw you and Sue getting all cozy at the sink, so I thought maybe you'd want to stay here." She lowered her voice and said in a hoarse whisper, "Lily saw you, too!"

"You've got a lot of fucking nerve peering in windows and making insinuations like that!" he said. "Especially considering what you've been up to."

Anita turned very red, then silently handed him a long white envelope.

"What's this?" he demanded. The envelope was unsealed. He removed the contents, a thick bunch of sheets, stapled together and full of typing.

"It says you left voluntarily, that you can't come back, and that we're separated," Anita told him.

"What!"

"I'm sorry, David," she said, turning and running down the wet, concrete steps. He watched her go, saw her narrow little back, the bend of her neck, her crisp dark hair. She stared at the ground keeping her face out of the rain, and seemed to be panting, each breath leaving a warm cloud in the frosty air. He almost ran after her, but then Sue came and stood at his side and put a hand on his forearm. "What is it?" she asked.

David stood there, staring down at the papers. It seemed to be some legal document. "I don't know," he said. "I don't know what to do."

He went back into the living room in a daze and collapsed

in Roger's big armchair by the fire. Sue poured out the wine while David looked at the document in the flickering light. It was headed *"Jamison v. Jamison."* He got as far as the part that Anita Jane Reynolds Jamison was the plaintiff and David Scott Jamison was the defendant before he flung it aside.

"Let me see that," said Sue. He drank deeply while she skimmed the papers, her forehead wrinkled with concentration. He let his gaze drift back to the fire.

"She can't do this," Sue said. "She can't have the house and the children."

"I don't even want to think about any of this," he mumbled in a shaky voice.

Sue came over and sat on the arm of his chair. She stroked his hair. "Thank God I'm here," she said. "Thank God you're not alone at a time like this." He let his head fall against her breast while she kept stroking him. "Oh, Sue," he said, the will to keep his dignity intact hopelessly disintegrating. "I feel like such a loser."

"No, David, you're not a loser." Her tone was gentle but unequivocal, and he felt her lips on his forehead. His face was turned away from her because he felt like crying. His eyes were bunched tightly closed, but he moved his arm around and found her waist and pulled her closer.

She put her cheek on his forehead and said haltingly, "I wanted to tell you about Anita before. If I hadn't heard what she said—I wouldn't have let myself—you know. It made it seem less—"

"Don't talk," he whispered. He put one hand on each side of her head and pulled her face down to his, then kissed her on the mouth.

His admonition not to talk seemed to excite her. She dug her nails into his shoulder and her fat tongue was back in his mouth, tasting of wine this time instead of peanut butter.

Before he knew it, she was straddling him in the armchair and moving her pelvis so that he felt her pubic bone grinding slowly into his cock.

She remained obediently silent as he slid down onto the floor, held her by her lovely curved hips, then rolled her over onto her back beneath him. Her silence and the way her body moved under his hands, allowing him to arrange it just the way he wanted, created a wonderful surge within him. Long-latent feelings of power and capability came tumbling back, and he felt like his true self again.

She helped him undress them both, still kissing him, still silent, her small hands expertly undoing buttons, his belt, sliding fabric smoothly down arms and legs, pushing elastic around waists and over hips and thighs.

This task completed with a minimum of awkwardness, he hovered above her, took a second to admire her white flesh lit peachily by the fire, ran a hand roughly over her breasts, used his knee to flip apart her thighs, which fell to either side like petals falling off a flower. Then, he slid his cock inside her, and watched her face melt into unguarded and total surrender.

ANITA WAS SHAKING WHEN SHE GOT HOME. SHE locked herself in the bedroom and called Frank. "I did it," she announced. "I gave him those papers. I doubt he'll go to a motel. I think he's going to spend the night with Sue. Lily and I saw them at the kitchen window, practically groping each other."

"Perfect," said Frank. "It's even better that they're spending the night under one roof. And that Lily saw them. This can help solidify your position, custody-wise."

"And Frank," added Anita, her heart still thumping, "he knows about us. He seemed very certain."

"I don't think that's a problem," he replied after a moment. "We've been discreet. We certainly haven't flaunted it around in front of the kids."

"I guess it all goes back to Roger's having seen us that time," said Anita.

"Roger's dead," Frank pointed out. "Anyway, it's not a big deal. Try and relax, darling. Things are working out fine. It will all turn out for the best, really it will."

DAVID REMEMBERED MURMURING GOOD NIGHT right afterward as he lay on his back in a haze of sweat and well-being, and then, emotionally and physically exhausted, falling quickly asleep. He was dimly aware, at one point, of Sue gently spreading a quilt on top of him. He felt its delightful, delicate warmth, just the right amount, on his cooling skin.

When he next woke, it was dawn. For a second he wasn't sure where he was. A yellowish-gray light penetrated gauzy curtains that he recognized as Sue's. He sat up and looked around the room. He'd never seen it from this low angle before, but it slowly took familiar form. At eye level, he saw the wine bottle and two glasses on the coffee table next to the document Anita had delivered last night.

That memory sent him crashing back down onto the carpet. Then he smelled coffee. Wearily, he rose, wrapped himself in the quilt, and went into the kitchen where Sue sat at the table drinking coffee and wearing a fuzzy pink bathrobe.

He went over to her and dutifully kissed her forehead. She didn't seem to notice, which was a relief. He couldn't have stood it if she'd been all lovey-dovey.

"I've been thinking," she said. "I've been thinking all night, David."

He glanced nervously over at the windows. His house was

a dark shape in the misty dawn. No one was up yet over there. He didn't want to be seen through the window wrapped in this silly quilt. He sat down heavily at the table and said, "What time is it?"

"Five-thirty." Sue got up to get him some coffee.

"You haven't slept all night?"

She waved her hand impatiently as if that were an inconsequential detail. "I never need much sleep. I usually get by on four hours or so." She placed a mug in front of him. "David, I've been thinking," she repeated.

"I'm not sure I can," he said gloomily, staring down at his coffee.

"I know you can't. That's why I've been doing it." She gave him an intent look, leaning down over the table in the chair across from him to catch his eye. With reluctance, he looked back at her.

She smiled sadly. "I don't think you want to give up everything you have. You have two children. They need two parents."

He grunted assent.

"What would be gained by splitting that all up? Would you be better off?"

Of course I wouldn't, he thought bitterly. I'd have to find a job flipping hamburgers and spending half of my miserable paycheck on child support. I've screwed up my whole life and I'll end up living in a trailer. What he said was, "I suppose you're right. I wish Anita would let us try counseling."

She was silent for a moment, then she said, "David, I thought about what you said last night. About wishing Anita were dead. I've had the same idea."

He was too startled to reply. "It would be perfect, wouldn't it," she went on in a soft voice. "We could help each other raise our children. I even fantasized about having a new baby. I'm still young enough. We'd both be financially se-

cure. I had that daydream, too, and I'm not ashamed of it."
She sighed. "But it isn't right."

That was a relief. For a moment he wondered if she'd gone
around the bend, and was proposing murder and marriage.
He supposed he should be flattered that Sue found him so
desirable. But it wasn't a topic he wanted to dwell on.

"Realistically," she went on, "I think you have to get back
into that house and give your marriage a chance. At the very
least, you have to get her to move out."

"Anita isn't going to let me back," he said. "She made that
pretty clear last night."

"I've thought about this all night, David."

"You're very sweet," he said.

She seemed impatient with him. "Listen, I want to talk to
Anita," she said urgently. "I want to tell her there's nothing
between us. Because there can't be. I want to plead with her
to give your marriage a try. I think I can get through to her.
As a mother."

"Oh, Sue, I don't think—"

"I'll cancel my flight to Milwaukee and talk to her after she
gets home from work tonight. We have to do something
now, before it's too late. I want to convince her to let you
back into that house with your girls. It's the only way I can
live with myself."

David sipped his coffee groggily. "But, Sue, Anita won't
listen to you. She's resented you from the start. It's very kind
of you to want to help, but right now the nicest thing you
can do is just let me stay here."

"Of course. As long as you like."

"Thanks, Sue. I really appreciate it. Just until I get myself
organized. It's all been such a blow."

"I know," said Sue. "It broke my heart to see your spirit
crushed like that." She gave him a cool, candid look. "David,
I tried to give you some of your confidence back last night."

He felt as if he'd been slapped. What was she saying? That last night had been an exercise in developing his self-esteem? "And I really want to have a talk with Anita," Sue concluded stubbornly.

"I think it's a bad idea," he said.

"I think you might be very surprised," she answered with a strength that he found threatening. "If we can just arrange for you and the girls to be somewhere else tonight, I'll tackle her one on one."

"Look, Sue, it's hopeless, it really is. I appreciate your letting me stay here. I appreciate your kindness. But I don't see what you or anyone else can do about the fact that my marriage has fallen apart."

She leaned over and grasped his arm tightly. "But, David, we can't just crumple. There's so much at stake. Lily. Sylvie. Especially Sylvie. I love her like a daughter. I refuse to abandon her to Anita."

"But Anita's her mother," David pointed out.

"Let's face it, David, the only way this can ever really work is if there were just us and our children. That's how it's meant to be."

A sleepless night must have left her overwrought, thought David. Why was she so concerned about all this, anyway? She had her own kids to think of. Maybe she'd been driven crazy by Roger's death. Maybe this was some way to displace her grief. Or maybe it was because he'd fucked her. She was so intense, he thought, panic rising.

Despite all that, he knew he needed her right now. He also needed somewhere to stay while things sorted themselves out. "Just try and calm down," he said, patting her hand. "Your boys will be missing you. Don't worry about me and the girls. I'll have to work this through somehow." He realized he was eager for her to go back to Milwaukee. Once she'd left, he could relax in this pleasant, empty house and think about his next move. The first thing was to get himself a lawyer. "I appreciate your concern," he said. "I know you're a caring person. I know you want what's best for other people."

"Yes, I do," she said. "And I know what that is. Just trust me and everything will be all right."

15

AFTER BREAKFAST AND THE PAPER, DAVID wanted to be alone again. Sue was kind and well-meaning, and it was good to hear from a neutral third party what a bitch Anita was, but at the same time, Sue's intensity was beginning to get to him. Sure he was getting a raw deal. Sure he deserved the house and the girls. Sure Anita should have to be the one to leave. But what could he do about it, really? It all seemed so hopeless.

And he wished he'd never fucked Sue. Women always believed that after you'd done that, they had some kind of emotional hold on you. That was the last thing he needed right now.

Once he saw that Anita and the girls had left, he made some excuse about having to go look through some papers in his desk at home. "I may be a while," he said. He intended to take a quiet nap on his old bed.

At home, David went upstairs and lay down on the bed, trying to pretend he still lived here and that Anita had never kicked him out. After a few minutes, it occurred to him to see if Anita hid anything in her underwear drawer the way Sue and his mother had. He went over to it, rummaged around, and came up with a how-to book on dumping your husband.

He seized it with the thrill of a general discovering the enemy's battle plans, and settled down to read. It was full of a lot of cheap-shot male bashing, taking it as a given that the woman was always some pathetic victim. David was disgusted to see that Anita had actually used canned language from the book to avoid any real honest communication. "It's better this way," she had said, whenever he'd tried to discuss what was happening to their family. There it was, straight out of chapter three.

He skimmed a lot of bullshit about being good to yourself while you ruined your husband and children's lives, and went straight to the chapter on alimony, child support, and custody. "Remember, even if you aren't working, you're entitled to support for you and your children, as well as the money to get good legal representation." That cheered him up. So did a section on how to make sure you got the house. The book pointed out that it was less disruptive for the children to stay in the same house with their primary caretaker.

Sue was right. He should get the house. The kids, too, of course, although he wouldn't really want to be on call twenty-four hours a day. Probably he could have every other week off. According to the book, Anita should support all of them. He shouldn't have to suffer because he'd stayed home with the kids. On the contrary. He should be compensated for having sacrificed his career.

David suddenly felt motivated to get himself a lawyer and start fighting right now. Anita had had a head start, and he'd better catch up. He got on the phone to the general practice lawyer he'd hired to write some nasty letters to his mother and sister when they'd been fighting about Aunt Martha's estate, and said he was looking for a divorce lawyer.

"Is it pretty straightforward? Have you already agreed on some things?"

"No," said David, fired up by the advice in the book. "The situation is that I'm a househusband and she works. Seeing as I'm the primary caretaker, I figure I'm theoretically entitled to alimony and child support and the house."

The lawyer sighed. "Theoretically, maybe. But unless your wife is interested in giving you custody, don't expect too much sympathy. A lot of judges won't come out and say it, but they still figure a guy should have too much pride to go this route. Unless you're disabled or something, the court's probably going to wonder why you aren't working. I think you need someone who specializes in divorce. I'll transfer you to Linda. She can give you a few names. Good luck."

David was so upset he just hung up the phone before Linda got on the line, and fell back down on the bed, feeling completely helpless again.

Sue came over at lunchtime and invited him to her place for a meal. He wanted to say he was too depressed to eat or talk or anything. Instead, he followed her, zombie-like, across the lawn.

"I figured you needed some comfort food," she said, dishing up some wonderful lentil soup with circles of sausage in it. Surprisingly, the steaming bowl of soup did cheer him up a little. He forgot about his earlier resentment of Sue. She seemed calm now. At least someone was being kind to him.

After lunch, she showed him what she'd been doing all

morning. She'd made a princess costume for Sylvie, white fluffy chiffon with gold stars sewn on it.

"How nice of you to think of something like that when you're going through so much," he said, trying to sound more enthusiastic than he felt.

"I always feel better if I keep busy," she replied, smiling.

"I'm so depressed I can't move. I feel as if my spirit is completely broken." He heard his own voice, a lifeless monotone.

"Oh, David," she said. "Everything will be all right eventually. I just know it."

He let his head fall into his hands and began to shake. "I just talked to a lawyer. He practically came out and said there's no way I can get back in that house. Everything is completely fucked up. My life is ruined."

"David, I think I can appeal to Anita's feelings as a mother," said Sue. "I wish you'd trust me."

"Oh, we've been over this, Sue."

"I want to try," said Sue. "Please. Let me try. What do you have to lose?"

"Nothing, I guess," said David, feeling completely defeated.

"She gets home around five-thirty, right? Well, there's a matinee at the Metro Cinema at four-thirty. Take the girls to that, and then go out for a Coke or something until seven. By the time you get back, I think your problems will be over, I really do."

DAVID SAT AT THE END OF THE BAR AT O'BRIEN'S, drinking a pint of a microbrew called Auld Lang Syne, and eating pretzels. O'Brien's was supposed to be an old-time Irish pub, but David remembered when it had been a discount electronics store, and could never completely give himself over to the ornate, darkly varnished Victorian bar, the stained-glass windows, and the heavy lace curtains, all of which were supposed to give the impression the place had been here for years.

Still, he liked O'Brien's. It was a friendly, neighborhood place with a dartboard over in one corner and lots of Guinness posters around. Maybe he'd been missing out all these years by hanging out at the Honey Bee when he wanted to escape instead of coming here. The Honey Bee was so wholesome. By contrast, there had seemed to be something decadent about drinking beer in a place where smoking was allowed and kids weren't, where the occasional couple actually sat at the bar and gave each other smiles and kisses in the dim light, where instead of tasteful chamber music, the baseball play-offs blared in the background.

For the last six years, he'd lived in a kid-dominated world. He'd felt guilty if he even thought about straying into an adult environment. Why had he allowed that to happen? And what good had all that devotion to family life and clean living done for him? He'd ended up here, anyway, hoping despondently that Sue could shame his wife into taking him back.

At the last minute, he'd decided to skip the movie. It was some fantasy about kids in outer space, with a lot of special effects. He had simply dropped the girls off at the theater and told them he'd pick them back up at six-thirty. The thought made him look at the clock. Like everything else here, it was a fake antique with a big oak case and gilt numbers. The sweeping second hand and the cord coming out of its side, however, revealed more recent technology. He vowed to wait at least ten minutes before allowing his eyes to glance over there again. He didn't want to think about the scene between Anita and Sue that was about to take place.

When he next looked at the clock, less than sixty seconds

had passed. Anita wouldn't even be home for another twenty minutes. He sighed and sipped his beer. The longer he waited, the more he realized how stupid he'd been to go along with Sue.

He must have been out of his mind to think her little scheme would work. It had seemed worth a try this afternoon when he'd been so completely demoralized. Then, he actually believed that Anita might agree to taking him back on a trial basis. Now, it all seemed kind of nutty. He must have been influenced by the fact that Sue, who was so practical, was so adamant about it.

But Sue had other aspects to her character that he hadn't previously imagined. He remembered her face when they'd made love on the carpet in front of the fire, that wild, open look. He felt a little rush, remembering it. He felt his spirits crash again when he recalled what she'd said early this morning in her kitchen about trying to restore his self-confidence. Did that mean she'd been faking it, too?

That conversation at dawn had been unsettling in more ways than one. Had she really worked out a whole scenario where she got together with David and they raised all four kids and even went on and had another! Maybe she was in love with him. He'd assumed she was just a good, unselfish friend who needed some good sex and was willing to give some back. If she did love him, and wanted to raise children with him, how could she be so calm about helping him patch things up with Anita? He'd always thought Sue was so straightforward and uncomplicated, but there was so much he didn't understand.

Come to think of it, why did she have to come to Seattle to sign papers, anyway? She could have signed them in Wisconsin and sent them by Federal Express. But she hurried back here as soon as she'd heard Anita and David had split up. Was she that crazy about him?

The waitress, a vivacious brunette with puffy hair and big round earrings bobbing from her ears, came by. "How about another one?" she said cheerfully.

"Sure," he said with a wan smile, pushing his dirty glass toward her across the varnished bar. He glanced up at the clock.

Two of hers, two of his, and one of theirs. Jesus. That would make five kids. Well, if anybody could handle all that, it would be Sue. Apparently, she didn't even sleep more than four hours a night.

But what the hell was she talking about, having a baby? She'd told him she'd had her tubes tied, for Christ's sake, so it must all have been a daydream. Still, it was weird. What about Roger? How come she was fantasizing a new family when she was supposedly grieving over him?

Once again, he remembered the hidden adrenaline kit. What the hell was all that about? Roger's death had been excruciatingly painful to watch. It had taken so long for that yellow jacket to finally sting him, and while he stood there, knowing he might die, every emotion had crossed his face for all those gaping people to see. He had seemed so naked and open, just as Sue had seemed during sex. Unless, of course, she hadn't been faking it to bolster his self-esteem.

His second pint of beer arrived, and David told himself to calm down. He knew he should be grateful to Sue for trying to help. She was the kind of person who could fix everything. Her life was always incredibly well-organized. She carried off everything graciously and without a hitch. Each meal was faultless, each room perfectly decorated. That barbecue had been like something out of a magazine.

Except of course for its ghastly finale. She hadn't been able to plan that. David couldn't think of any other aspect of Sue's life that hadn't been planned. Up to then, this had been

a woman who controlled her own environment. Yet in the
end, even Sue had been defeated. By an insect.

David took a deep draught of his beer. He'd been pretty
smashed that afternoon. He was feeling this second pint
now, and he remembered the same light-headed feeling he'd
had as he clambered around the Heffernans' backyard, re-
moving those Japanese lanterns from the trees.

Sue's party came back to him in brightly lit vignettes: the
steaks lying on that board, the flowery drinks, Sue rubbing
sunblock all over her husband, the man with the red toupee
joking about it.

He glanced at the clock. In fifteen minutes, Anita would
trip up the porch steps in her high heels. Click, click, click.
Sue was waiting for her.

Anita had always gone for heels because she was short and
they made her taller. Poor thing. She'd never had much confidence. What a contrast with Sue, who wore comfortable
shoes that encased her square white feet with their straight
toes. Anita's toes were all wrenched sideways from those
heels. The baby toes were almost completely deformed,
small triangles of flesh. He'd always thought they looked a
little pathetic.

There had always been a row of her small, high-heeled
shoes in the closet, a neat row of Italian shoes in shiny calf-
skin with vampy straps and all kinds of colors. David had
once found them sexy, symbols of the suffering she was willing to go through to look attractive.

Would Anita listen to Sue? Or would she yell at her and
tell her to get out of the house? No, Anita hated confrontation.

David sipped some more beer and watched the dark-
haired barmaid swishing a white towel over the bar and
laughing at something a sallow man with a ponytail said as

he lit a cigarette. No, Anita wouldn't cause a scene, especially not with someone who'd just been widowed in a tragic accident.

The barmaid turned down the ball game, and music suddenly surged from a stereo speaker above him. The song was a golden oldie. In fact, it had been a golden oldie when he and Anita had been young. "In the Still of the Night." Anita loved that song. She knew all the words.

He remembered, on one of their first dates, how startled he had been when she'd put her head back on the cracked red leather seat in his old MG, closed her eyes like some lounge singer, and begun to sing along with the radio in her sweet soprano voice.

Then she'd opened her eyes and, still singing, looked at him obliquely, as if gauging his reaction. He had been so startled and excited. This was the first time she seemed to have relaxed around him. But she wasn't just relaxed. She was also wondering how he took her languid pose and her pretty little voice, singing its teenaged song of longing for his benefit.

That had been the moment he knew for sure that she would go to bed with him. He could still remember the feeling of triumph leaping inside his rib cage, a reckless, dizzy, confidence; excitement, but relief, too.

He gazed at himself in the bar mirror, and was amazed to see how old and tired he looked. Overcome with the memory of that date with Anita, and the power of the soupy song, he felt the sting of a tear in his eye.

At the end of the bar, a glass broke, a woman laughed. The waitress grabbed a broom and hustled away from the man with the ponytail. The sound of breaking glass followed by nervous female laughter reminded him of something that seemed important. His head snapped back up.

Anita, who had sung for him that summer night long ago,

would be pulling up to the house about now. He saw her dim form in the dark, heard her heels clicking up the steps.

His brain searched laboriously through the beery buzz for that elusive thought brought on by the sound of breaking glass. What did it remind him of? And why was it so important?

He remembered. The glass breaking at the barbecue, the woman laughing, Sue rubbing sunblock on Roger, then turning away from her husband and rushing past David the way the waitress just had. But the waitress had a broom. Sue had been carrying the plastic bottle of sunblock.

He set his beer down, suddenly sober with fear.

David had removed those Japanese lamps from every tree and shrub in the place. There hadn't been a single yellow jacket trap hung up anywhere in the yard. Sue said it was because Roger didn't want them used. But she'd bought them, anyway. A lot of them. He'd seen the wrappings in the recycling bin. Those yellow jackets, which should have been lured by the traps that weren't there, were all lured by Roger instead. Could Sue have mixed the attractant from those missing traps into the sunblock she smeared all over her husband?

David looked up at the clock. Twenty-eight past five. Anita might be home by now. He frantically hailed the waitress. "I gotta go," he said, tossing some bills on the bar and pointing to the clock. "I'm late!" He realized his voice was too loud.

"Relax," she said. "That's bar time. It's set fifteen minutes fast so we can clear the place out at closing time." She waltzed away, collecting dirty ashtrays with no idea she'd said something miraculous.

David scrambled off the stool and pulled his keys out of his pocket. He had just enough time to get home before Anita.

In the car, it occurred to him that all this was another bad fantasy. The idea of Sue cold-bloodedly killing her own husband was ridiculous. No one would believe it for a moment. Even if it were true, no one could prove it. But if it were true, Sue would have to be crazy.

He couldn't leave Anita alone with Sue. He'd tell Sue he'd had second thoughts about that woman-to-woman talk.

He remembered what Sue had said this morning. How the two of them could raise those kids together if Anita and Roger were both out of the picture. That they would have plenty of money. He'd said he wished Anita were dead. And Sue had said she would take care of everything.

The light changed. He clumsily pushed the car into gear and lurched through the intersection, his tires squealing. He suddenly didn't care if Anita loved him or not. She was his wife. He had to protect her. "Anita!" he called out.

Startled at the sound of his own voice when he was all alone in the car, he told himself to get a grip. He must be fantasizing all this, rescuing Anita, making everything better again. It was pretty pathetic, casting sweet, nurturant Sue as a crazed killer, just so he could be the good guy.

The house was dark. Anita wasn't home. But if Sue was waiting for her, why wasn't there a light on? Why would she sit in the dark? Clinging to the porch railing, he felt his way up the stairs and had a hell of a time finding the lock. Finally, he found the cold metal circle with his thumb, then jammed the key into the lock and pushed his way inside.

The house was silent. Where was Sue? He felt for the light switch, and flipped it. Nothing happened. Damn. The circuits must have overloaded again, the way they did when too many things were running at once—like two hair dryers and the dishwasher or something. But no one was here.

He felt his way through the hall and over to the basement

door, heading for the fuse box at the bottom of the stairs. Maybe Anita had come home early and was down there messing with the breakers. He called her name timidly, but there was no answer.

He'd have to get the lights back on, then call Sue and tell her the whole plan was off. He set off down the stairs as he had a hundred times before. He would feel for the smooth metal door of the fuse box, open it, run his finger down the plastic switches until he found one on the wrong side. But this time, it was all different.

He tripped and fell and felt himself plummeting help-lessly, hurtling headfirst down the steps, banging his head against the concrete wall. He tried to put both his arms out to break the fall, but instead he landed on his head at the bottom of the steps, one arm bent underneath him, the other twisted behind him.

He lay there moaning quietly in the dark. What the hell had happened? He'd only had two pints of beer, for God's sake.

Then, the lights came on and a booming voice started talking about a medicine for really big headaches. David took in his breath sharply, instinctively turning toward the TV set to confirm where the voice was coming from.

But there was someone else there, too. In person, not on TV. "David!" Sue was stepping back from the fuse box a few feet away from him. It was the voice of a disappointed mother.

"For really big headaches!" the announcer repeated.

David tried to focus, which proved difficult, and push himself up off the floor, which was impossible. His right arm, underneath him, hurt like hell, a stabbing, unremitting agony.

"I think I broke my arm," he said. He let his head flop back down again and closed his eyes. He knew his thinking was slow and fuzzy, but he knew besides feeling pain, he also felt fear.

"Don't move," said Sue. The commercial was replaced by some sitcom with a laugh track. He felt her hand on his shoulder. "Which arm is it?"

She reached out and touched the hand that wasn't pinned under him. Her hand felt cold and rubbery. With great effort, David lifted up his head a few inches and stared at Sue's blurry face. "You have to go home," he mumbled. "Anita will be here anytime."

He realized he hadn't imagined that strange touch. Sue was wearing the yellow rubber gloves he'd seen her wear when she did dishes. In one hand she was holding a large, cast-iron skillet, part of the junk he'd inherited from Aunt Martha.

"What's going on?" he asked in a feeble voice.

Sue knelt in front of him, as if approaching a wounded animal. "I was only trying to work everything out for all of us," she said.

Her face was blurry again. To try and get his focus working again, David looked over her shoulder. Behind her, on the third step from the top, he saw a gleam of something. It slowly came into focus: a thin line of copper wire.

"Pull yourself together, David!" she said urgently.

Yes, he had to do that. She stepped away from him and he tried to push himself up. Mercifully, the TV stopped blaring. "Don't hurt Anita," he said. With a great effort of will, he managed to prop himself up with his good arm.

"Anita wants to throw you out," said Sue, coming closer again and setting the skillet down beside her. "Didn't you read the papers she handed you? She wants the house and the girls."

"Get away from me!" he screamed suddenly. "You're crazy!"

"That's a horrible thing to say," she said.

He felt his little burst of strength fading. "You were going to kill her, weren't you?" he said. "Like you killed Roger?"

"Roger deserved to die," she said. "He betrayed me."

"He betrayed you?" David repeated. What was she talking about?

"It may interest you to know," Sue went on in a prim little voice, "that Roger got a vasectomy without telling me. Before I had a chance for a daughter. He ruined my life. He left me unfulfilled."

"So you killed him?"

"He had a bad accident. So will Anita. Just like you said you wanted," she said in a reasonable tone of voice. "You're not thinking clearly. Let me help you." She reached under his arm and tried to lift him up.

"Don't hurt Anita."

"It's the only way," she said, suddenly tender. "Because we love each other. And because of the children. Two boys, two girls. Maybe even another baby, if we're lucky. It has to be this way."

David closed his eyes and collapsed against the cool concrete wall. "You're crazy," he said. "Just go home. Get the hell out of here, okay?" He began to weep slowly, aware that this was all part of his woozy, weak, feeling. God, his arm hurt. "I must have been out of my mind to let you take over my family."

"No, David," she replied. "We're supposed to be together. That's how it's meant to be."

"No, it's not! Go away! Leave me alone. Leave my family alone!"

"I'm your family now, David."

"No! I don't want you. I don't want you around. I don't want you around my kids. I don't even want to fuck you. I never did. I just felt sorry for you."

He sank to the bottom stair, and his head fell forward. For a moment, he felt very peaceful, then he felt his head explode. He knew he should try to get up and do something about it, but it seemed so terribly hard. It had always seemed easiest to do nothing, and that is what he did now, slipping into the blackness.

WHEN ANITA CAME HOME, THE HOUSE WAS completely dark. Where was everyone, and why hadn't they left the porch light on for her? She felt her way up onto the porch and discovered that the door was unlocked. She walked in and fumbled for the light switch, which was in the on position. She flipped it up and down a few times, but nothing happened. The breakers must have tripped again.

She called out, "Is anyone home?" trying to sound brave but producing a tentative voice. "Girls?" she said more sharply.

She sighed and went down the first couple of steps to the basement, feeling her way along. She crept down two more steps. Could there be a burglar lurking around? Listening intently for a telltale sound of stealthy movement, she took a deep breath and went down one more step.

"Damn," she said as her foot encountered something that rolled away and went *blonk*. The girls had left toys on the stairs. She had to proceed very carefully.

She had just opened the door to the fuse box when her foot came up against something large and solid. She screamed and clawed at the breakers until she found the right one and pushed it back.

The basement was flooded with light. Beneath her, David was scrunched over at the bottom of the steps, his familiar springy hair clotted with something wet and sticky and dark. There was a Pyrex measuring cup next to his head. That must have been what she knocked down with her foot. He was surrounded by greasy-looking cast-iron pots and pans. One skillet lay upside down beside his head. The light caught a gleam of blood, much redder than on David's hair, around the base. Next to him was an open cardboard box on its side, spilling out more unfamiliar kitchen implements: an aluminum hard-boiled egg slicer with a little grid of wires, and a potato peeler with a green painted wood handle.

Moving carefully on her high heels, Anita sidled down next to him. She touched his back, which was bent over in the attitude of a Moslem at prayer. He was warm.

"David?" she ventured. She pushed him a little, feeling a bizarre comfort in the familiar feel of his shoulder blade, then shook him. There was no response.

Anita clattered upstairs as quickly as she could, ran to the phone in the hall, and punched up 911. While she waited for two rings, she realized that all those kitchen things must be Aunt Martha's. A box of the stuff must have fallen on his head. A calm woman's voice answered, and trying not to scream, Anita said, "Come quick! There's been a horrible accident."

After she answered all their questions and hung up, she went back down and squatted on the stair above David. She touched his shoulder and whispered his name, but there was no answer. He looked so helpless that she began to cry, and then she heard the sirens and went back upstairs. A man and a woman in blue uniforms rushed in, and with great relief, she led them to David.

There was no room for her on the crowded stairway. She stayed in the kitchen and listened to the businesslike voices of the paramedics floating up the stairwell, without being able to make out what they said. The woman came into the kitchen. "We're taking your husband to Harborview," she said. "It's the very best place for a trauma like this."

There was a sharp rap on the kitchen door, and Sue walked in wearing one of her flowery smocks. "I heard the sirens," she said with a worried expression. "Is everything okay?"

The medic said, "Her husband is hurt. We're taking him to the hospital. Are you a neighbor? Maybe you could drive her down there."

"But the children," said Anita. "I don't know where the children are."

"I gave them some passes to the movies," said Sue. "David was going to pick them up at the Metro." She looked at her watch. "About now."

"Okay," said the medic brusquely, pointing at Sue. "Can you pick up her kids and take care of them for a while?"

"Of course," said Sue breathlessly. "Anything I can do to help—"

The medic interrupted her and turned to Anita. "You can ride with us. He still has a chance. Your neighbor here is getting the kids."

16

WHEN ANITA CALLED HER MOTHER IN DEN-
ver from the pay phone near the nurses' station, Evelyn
picked up with her usual cheerfully modulated officer's wife
hello. "Oh, Mom!" said Anita, bursting into tears.

"Honey! What is it?"

"There's been a terrible accident. David is dead. It looks
like he fell or something on the basement stairs. His skull
was fractured. I'm at the hospital. He died on the way here."

"My God!" said her mother. "I think I'd better come out."

"Yes. Please. Oh, Mom, I feel so guilty. I guess he was
organizing his aunt Martha's things. It looks like a box of
them fell on him in the dark. If I hadn't thrown him out—
well, it would never have happened."

Her mother's voice slid down to the baritone she reserved

for the most important pronouncements. "It's not your fault, Anita," she said.

"But I feel so guilty," said Anita. Her voice rose. "I hated him. Lately, I've actually wanted him to die."

She became aware that a young man in a gray suit with thick, wavy dark hair and remarkably blue eyes was standing right next to her, looking at her intently. "Mrs. Jamison?" he asked softly.

"Mom, I have to go. There's someone here—"

"I'm getting a flight out of here as soon as I can, Anita. I'll get a cab from the airport. Just take care of the girls, honey. I'm on my way."

"Was that your mother?" asked the stranger, gesturing to the phone.

"Yes," said Anita, feeling and looking frightened. Who was he? Was he some hospital administrator?

He handed her a business card. "I'm Paul Flynn. Seattle Police Department. I know it's a difficult time, but I wonder if I could ask you some questions."

"Detective?" said Anita, staring down at the card.

"It's just routine." He cleared his throat and said, "I'm sorry about your husband."

"The children will be worried. They don't know what's happened. I should be with them."

"I'll drive you home, Mrs. Jamison."

Anita obediently followed Detective Flynn's gray suit down the corridor.

"How did this happen?" he asked once they were in the car.

"I don't know," said Anita. "I just got home. It was dark. I went downstairs to the fuse box. He was at the bottom of the steps. The medics just said he had a very bad—they said his skull was crushed."

It began to rain, and Flynn turned on the windshield wipers. To Anita's relief, he wasn't one of those drivers who looked at you while he drove. Anita didn't have to maintain eye contact. She could just flop back on the seat like this, vaguely aware of red streaks of taillights in front of the windshield through the rain. "What time did you get home?" he asked.

"Five-thirty, I guess."

"Those things that fell on him. Where were they positioned?"

"In a kind of stack at the bottom of the stairs. I guess he fell against them in the dark, trying to get to the fuse box."

They drove in silence for a while.

"But why are you involved?" Anita said.

"The medics call us when there's an accidental death. We have to make sure it really was an accident."

"I'm just so worried about the girls," Anita said, turning away toward the side window. Outside, lights and shapes and cars slipped by in an abstract landscape. Anita felt panic and despair, and as if her soul might become detached from her body and fly out into the night on some random trajectory. Nothing was certain anymore. Perhaps it never had been.

By the time they got home, Anita's anxiousness to see her daughters had become a physical craving. Thanking Detective Flynn perfunctorily, she ran through her house, out the kitchen door, and through the hedge.

She knocked hard on the Heffernans' back door, and waited impatiently. There was no answer. By the time she decided to knock again, Detective Flynn was hovering in the yard at the bottom of the porch.

Finally, Sue appeared and opened the door a crack. "How is he?" she asked.

"He died," said Anita. "Where are the girls?"

"They're resting," said Sue. "Oh, Anita, I'm so sorry.

Maybe I should just keep them for the night. Wouldn't that be better?"

"Where are they?" demanded Anita.

"Downstairs, watching a video," said Sue, looking startled at Anita's tone.

Anita pushed Sue aside and plunged into the house.

Detective Flynn walked up onto the porch and introduced himself. "It's nice of you to help," he told Sue, as if apologizing for Anita's brusque behavior. "Naturally, she's pretty upset."

"How come the police are involved?" asked Sue.

Flynn shrugged. "We check out a lot of accidents. It's kind of routine. Are you pretty close neighbors?"

Sue sighed. She crossed her arms, tilted her head to one side, and said in a confidential tone, "I try to keep an eye on the kids. Things have been dysfunctional over there. A lot of fights. They were in the middle of a messy divorce. Poor little things, they've been through so much. To be honest, I really think it would be better if the girls stayed here tonight. Could you arrange that?"

"She seems to want them back pretty badly," said Flynn. "After all, they are her kids."

"GO AWAY," ANITA MURMURED WHEN SHE HEARD the doorbell early the next morning. She'd only had an hour or two of sleep. Detective Flynn stood on the doorstep. "May I come in?"

"Oh, please no," said Anita. "The girls and I were up most of the night. This is such a terrible shock. Can't you give me some time?"

"I'm sorry, Mrs. Jamison, but I must talk to you. Are the girls asleep?"

"Yes."

"I think it would be better if we talked before they woke up. We have some questions that have to be answered about your husband's death."

"Questions?"

Flynn stepped into the hall. "Can we talk in here?" he said, indicating the living room.

"I suppose so," said Anita, feeling sick and helpless. Why wasn't her mother here yet?

"I understand you and your husband were in the middle of getting divorced," he said.

"That's right."

"Was it a pretty tough one? Were you very angry with him?" he asked her in a kind way, as if he were her friend.

"We were doing our best to keep it civilized, for the sake of the children," she said stiffly.

"Had trouble with the breakers before?"

"Yes. Our wiring is terrible." From upstairs, Anita heard Lily moving around in her room. She half rose, but Flynn held out a hand.

"Look," he said, "why don't you come downtown and make a statement. That way we can take care of this without bothering the girls."

"No! I can't just leave them."

"Maybe your neighbor, what's her name, Mrs. Heffernan, could keep an eye on them while we go downtown," said the detective.

"No, please!" said Anita.

"Mrs. Jamison," he said firmly. "I strongly suggest you come downtown voluntarily. All I need is a statement from you. We need to get all the paperwork squared away."

"But my mother's on her way from Denver," said Anita. "I don't see what the problem is."

"Mrs. Jamison, we believe your husband was murdered. I don't think you want the girls around while we discuss this.

Will you come downtown with me and answer some questions there? We have a lot of questions. After all, you found the body."

"Let me tell Lily I'm going," said Anita in a panic. If they thought David was murdered, they probably thought she did it. There had to be some mistake. She'd answer their questions and clear everything up. It was so obviously an accident. She wished she could call Frank, but the last thing she wanted now was for the police to know about Frank.

She ran upstairs, and found Lily lying listlessly on her bed. "The police want me to go downtown. I want you to take care of Sylvie until Grandma comes."

"What?" said Lily, sitting up. "Police? Mom, what's going on?"

"It's about Daddy's accident," said Anita. "Just some boring paperwork."

"I just remembered," said Lily. "When I woke up, I forgot, and I went to pick an outfit, but then I remembered about Daddy." She began to cry and Anita held her for a while.

When her mother left with the detective, Lily walked her to the door, in her pajamas and robe, gave her a huge hug, and said, "Come back soon."

"Of course, I will, darling," said Anita. Lily felt her mother trembling and she squeezed her extra hard to stop the shaking.

ANITA SAT ACROSS FROM PAUL FLYNN IN A SMALL glassed-in room overlooking a sea of messy desks. Between them was a big fake wood table that contained two Styrofoam cups of coffee, a small black tape recorder, and an $8\frac{1}{2}$ by 11 manila envelope that Flynn had flung on the table with a flourish.

"There are a few things I want to show you," he said,

pointing at the envelope. "We know a lot about what happened to David." He opened the envelope and drew out some black-and-white photographs. Anita cringed. Surely he wouldn't show her pictures of David's body. Anita turned her face away.

"Here's one we took of the third step from the top," he said in a matter-of-fact tone. Anita squinted at what looked like a close-up of a piece of wood. There was a little ruler propped against the surface.

"Notice anything?" said the detective.

"The ruler?" said Anita, shrugging. She felt stupid, as if she should know the right answer.

Flynn pointed at a corner of the photograph. "See that little hole there?" Anita saw what appeared to be a dot. "It's a screw hole. There's one just like it on the other side."

"I don't understand," said Anita.

"If someone wanted to run a wire across the step and trip someone, they'd screw something into the wood right there to fasten the wire to. Do you know anything about that?"

"No!" said Anita, startled. This was why they thought there was something suspicious about David's death? "But it's an old house. There are a lot of flaws in the woodwork. Those little holes could have been there for years."

"We don't think so. There are traces of sawdust underneath them."

"Maybe they're termite holes or something," said Anita.

"We don't have termites here," said Flynn. "Termites are in California."

Anita just shook her head, dazed.

"There's another problem," he went on. "The problem is the medical examiner says that a bloody frying pan found near him couldn't have done that much damage falling on him."

"It couldn't?"

"No. For one thing, he was struck at least four, maybe more, times."

"My God," said Anita, feeling queasy.

"Let me show you a picture of the TV down in that basement," said Paul Flynn, pulling another photograph out of the envelope. "Look. He traced a circle over the picture. "That line of blood matches the bottom of the pan we know was the murder weapon."

"I can't believe this. There must be some mistake," said Anita.

"It's clear to us that somebody tripped him with that wire, struck him over and over again with the frying pan when he was down, and then"—here the detective leaned forward and gave Anita an intense look—"maybe because their arms were so tired from hitting him over and over again, or maybe because they wanted to take away the wire, or check and see if he was really dead, they put the pan down on the TV for a moment, before throwing it back over there, trying to make it look like the box fell on him."

Feeling faint, Anita gripped the edge of the table in front of her. Could any of this be true?

"If you know what really happened, it would be better if you tell us now, Anita." Before, when he'd been less antagonistic, he'd called her Mrs. Jamison.

"I can't believe this," she said.

He leaned over closer to her. "Let me tell you something. It's pretty hard to get away with murder. You're in big trouble and you can only make it worse by refusing to cooperate fully at this time."

"But I didn't kill David!" she heard herself shouting. Would that make her look guilty? She had to stay calm.

"I want you to think about your girls, Anita. Tell us what happened. Get it off your chest. It'll be easier for them. You can probably get out on bail. You'll have a lot of time to make arrangements for them. I want to give your family all the support I can. That's why I didn't arrest you this morning in front of the girls, okay?"

"But I didn't do it," said Anita. "I didn't."

"Maybe you were under a lot of pressure," he said. "Maybe things were so bad between you, it seemed like there was no way out."

"No. It wasn't like that at all."

"Maybe he was abusive," said Flynn. "You can tell me about it. It might make things easier."

"No. No. He was passive. He never hurt anyone."

"You told your mother you wanted him dead, didn't you? On the phone at the hospital. You really wanted him dead, didn't you Anita?"

"No. He was the children's father."

"Somebody killed him, Anita. If it wasn't you, who could it have been? Who else could get into the house and set it all up?"

"The only person," said Anita slowly, "who had easy access to our house is our neighbor."

"Mrs. Heffernan?" Paul Flynn rolled his eyes in a give-me-a-break way. "Is there any reason she would wish harm to come to your husband?"

No one would ever believe Sue could do anything like that. Anita couldn't believe it herself. Could she tell the detective she thought David and Sue were having an affair? Or would it make her look jealous, and likely to want to kill David? She wasn't sure what to do.

"I don't know," said Anita.

"Were either of you seeing anyone else?" asked Flynn.

"I want to call a lawyer," replied Anita.

17

SYLVIE WAS STILL ASLEEP. LILY WENT BACK UP-
stairs and sat on her bed, looking out the window. It was
raining, and the drops of water coated the branches and
remaining leaves of the cherry tree and dripped off the tips
like beads of glass. She liked the sound the rain made, a
familiar sound she'd remembered from when she was just a
little kid and before she knew her dad was going to be dead
when she was just fourteen.

From the window, she also saw Sue coming out of her
house. Was she coming over here? Lily's heart sank as she
watched Sue crossing their lawn wearing her stupid flowery
smock and carrying a big ham.

She'd try to get rid of her all by herself, but it would have
been easier for an adult to do it. Sue was pretty hard to get

rid of. God she wanted Mom or Grandma so bad! Lily went downstairs just in time to see Sue's face smiling sadly at her through the glass of the kitchen door. Lily hated Sue more than ever. A horrible thing, like Daddy dying, was just the kind of thing phony nice people like Sue loved, because it let them act all supportive and perfect.

Lily decided she wasn't going to let her in the house and that was that. She put the chain on the door before opening it a crack. Sue said, "Oh, honey, I'm so sorry. How are you all doing?"

"I don't know," mumbled Lily.

"I brought you this ham, because it's hard to think about cooking at a time like this. Let me in."

"Bring it later, okay?" said Lily. "Mom isn't here. I'll tell her."

"She isn't?" said Sue sharply. "You girls are all alone?"

"Just for a while," said Lily. "My grandma's on her way."

"Where's Sylvie?" demanded Sue. "You girls shouldn't be alone at a time like this. What was your mother thinking?"

Lily bristled at the criticism of her mother. "Sylvie's asleep. We'll be okay."

"Where is your mom?" persisted Sue.

"She had to go downtown with the police. She'll be back soon. Look, I don't want to talk now, okay?" Lily leaned against the door and managed to shut it, despite Sue's pressure against it from the other side. She clicked the dead bolt shut.

Sue pounded on the door and yelled, "Let me in. I won't leave you here by yourselves."

Her heart racing, Lily yelled back in a pleading tone, "Just leave us alone!" She ran into the front hall and made sure that door was locked and the chain was on. Sue was still pounding and yelling on the kitchen door. Lily dashed breathlessly into the basement, avoiding the spot where Daddy had fallen. She checked the latch on the glass doors that led out into the backyard, then went back up the stairs to the living room and sat on the sofa, her arms wrapped around her knees, her eyes shut tightly.

She heard footsteps on the front porch. "Please go away," she whispered over and over again. The front doorknob was rattling.

Finally, the noises stopped, and feet went back down the front steps. Lily's heart was still racing. She told herself to take a deep breath and calm down. I did it, she thought with a kind of gratified surprise. I got rid of her.

Then, she heard a noise down in the basement. It sounded like breaking glass. Once, Dad had said a burglar could break in there really easily by smashing a pane of glass and reaching in to undo the bolt. Mom told her not to worry about it. But Mom wasn't here. Lily ran to the door that led to the basement steps and leaned against it. Someone was coming up the steps. "Please go away," Lily shouted.

Sue's voice said, "Lily?"

Lily leaned as hard as she could against the door, bracing herself against the wall. "Leave the ham if you want, but just go away."

Sue pushed the door open and stepped into the kitchen, cradling the ham like a baby. "I can't do that," Sue said briskly, muscling past her. "It would be irresponsible."

"Don't fucking push me!" yelled Lily as Sue deposited the ham on the counter with a thud.

"Oh, Lily," said Sue sadly. "If only I'd had more time with you. I think you'd be a very different young lady. Your father often said the same thing."

Lily shouted, "Don't talk about my father, you fucking slut." She burst into tears and began her usual rat-in-the-maze retreat, pounding noisily up the stairs, running into her room, slamming the door behind her, and locking it, before flinging herself on the bed.

A moment later she heard Sue's voice outside her door. "I've tried, Lily. I've tried to be your friend."

Lily buried her head under her pillow, but she could still hear the doorknob rattling. "Let me in," called Sue. "All families have problems. We can talk this through."

Lily shouted, "I can't hear you!" then cranked up the radio next to her bed as loud as she could, blasting out rock music.

In the next room, the music woke Sylvie up. She jumped out of bed, and as soon as her bare feet hit the floor, she was startled to see Sue come into her room. "Where's Mom?" asked Sylvie.

Sue sat down on the bed. The wall was throbbing with the music from Lily's room. "I have some very sad news," Sue said. "You'll have to be a brave little girl, and I'll help you. You see, Sylvie, the police have arrested your mom. She put something on the stairs to make your daddy trip and die."

"It was an accident. Mom said so," said Sylvie.

"I'm afraid she lied to you. She hated your daddy and wanted to divorce him, didn't she?"

"Mommy's in jail?" said Sylvie, her eyes growing wide, her body rigid. "But who will take care of me?"

"I will," said Sue. "Your daddy wanted me to. You see, our family was supposed to be you, me, Matt and Chris, and Daddy. And maybe even a new baby brother or sister." She touched her stomach and smiled.

"I don't understand," said Sylvie, beginning to tremble uncontrollably. "I want Mommy."

Sue put her arms around her and stroked her hair. "We'll have to go away for a while," said Sue. "Matt and Chris are waiting for us in Wisconsin. It's pretty cold there, so we'd better pack some warm clothes. And make sure you pack all your favorite toys. Like Barbie and the Velveteen Rabbit." Sue rose and began going through Sylvie's drawers, selecting items of clothing.

"But what about Lily?" asked Sylvie, looking away dazedly.

"Lily doesn't want to come."

FRANK PICKED UP ON THE THIRD RING.

"Darling!" he said when he heard Anita's voice. "Let me just close the door. Phoebe's here this weekend." In the background Anita heard Frank call out, "Don't disturb me, sweetheart. This is a business call."

"Frank," she said, turning away from the glass wall. Paul Flynn had left the room, but he was standing a few feet away, scrutinizing her. "I'm at the Public Safety Building downtown. Someone killed David, and they think it's me."

"What!"

She gave him a quick account of David's fall, of his skull being crushed, of the trip-wire holes, and the bloody skillet.

"Are you under arrest?" he asked.

"No. I'm making a voluntary statement."

"Don't do that!" said Frank. "I'm getting you the best defense lawyer in town. Tell them you have nothing more to say until you talk to him. They can't hold you unless they arrest you. Tell them you'll only answer their questions with an attorney present. And for God's sake, don't take a polygraph. Anita, from what you've told me, you're in a very bad position."

"They asked if I was seeing someone else," she said, trying not to sob. "That's when I said I wanted to talk to a lawyer."

"Jesus! Don't tell them about us. It will only make things worse."

"Can I tell them about Sue and David? She's the only

person who could have done it. I don't know why. It all seems crazy."

"Don't tell them about Sue and David. It just gives you a motive. Tell them you are leaving. Tell them they'll have to arrest you if they want to keep you there."

"I can't say that! What if they do arrest me? The girls are all alone."

"You have to. It's better to get arrested than answer any more questions without an attorney present. You can always get bail and go home later."

"Frank, I didn't do it!" she said.

"Listen to me, Anita. Until you're in the clear, we can't see each other. I know that's what your lawyer will say. I want to be with you right now and take you in my arms and comfort you, but right now, I can't. I want you to understand and believe that I love you, whatever has happened. I'll be with you again as soon as I can without putting you in jeopardy. I have to hang up now and get on this right away. Anita, this is very serious."

Anita was shaking when she hung up. Frank had actually sounded as if he thought she might have killed David— bludgeoned him to death. If the man who loved her thought that, it was no wonder the police did.

Flynn came back to the little glass room.

"My lawyer says I can go home," Anita told him.

"Your lawyer doesn't decide when you go home," said Flynn. "I do. If I have probable cause, I can arrest you. I think I do. I think my boss will agree."

"I'll only answer questions with an attorney present," she said in a quaver. "I'm sorry, but I have to take my lawyer's advice."

"Okay. Who's your lawyer?"

"Well, I called a corporate lawyer I know. He's finding a criminal lawyer for me." She didn't want to give him Frank's name, so she quickly changed the subject. "Listen, I want to call my children," she said in a pleading tone. "Please let me call them. I have to know they're all right."

Flynn shrugged. "Okay," he said. "Dial nine to get out like before. But don't promise them you'll be home right away."

18

"Jamison residence," said Sue as she answered the phone.

"Sue?" said Anita, startled. "What are you doing there?" There seemed to be loud rock music in the background.

"You left them alone," said Sue. "You shouldn't have."

"Let me talk to Lily," demanded Anita. "Right now."

"She's sulking in her room. I came over here to bring you a ham. It's so difficult to think about planning meals at a time like this. I was horrified to find you'd left them alone. What happened? Have you been arrested?"

"No!" shouted Anita. "I'm coming home. My mother is on her way, too. Tell the girls. And *please* go home and get out of my house."

"All right," said Sue in a dead calm voice. "I'll take care of the girls at my house. They'll be happier there." She hung up.

Anita slammed down the receiver. "I want my girls now," she said to Flynn. "They're with Sue. And since you asked a while back, yes, she might well have had a reason to kill David. They were having an affair, but he wanted to get back together with me."

Anita didn't care if telling him this made her look guilty. She just wanted to get to the girls. "You gave my daughters to this woman who might have killed their father!" She was almost shouting now, and the loudness of her voice thrilled her. "She gave them passes to the movies yesterday. Maybe she was getting them out of the house so she could kill David. Or me. Maybe she really wanted to kill me. You'd better take me to her house so I can get my children back from her right now."

Flynn squinted one eye and tilted his head. He looked as if he were mulling it over.

SUE RAN BACK UPSTAIRS WHERE SYLVIE WAS LA-boriously tying her shoes. "Sweetheart, we have to hurry."

"I want Mom," said Sylvie.

"Your mom's in jail," said Sue harshly, shoving Sylvie's hands aside and tying the shoes herself. "We have to hurry and catch our flight. Otherwise the police will take you away and put you in a foster home." Sue was pushing Sylvie's little arms into her jacket and she grabbed her backpack and Hello Kitty suitcase.

"But what about Lily?" said Sylvie, looking frightened.

"I told you. She doesn't want to come. She's staying with Amy for a few days. We'll call her as soon as we get to Wisconsin. She'll join us there later. Now stop asking questions, and hurry like a good girl. Come on, darling." Sylvie was still half-asleep and seemed completely perplexed. In a confused daze, she allowed herself to be led out the back door, across the lawn, through the hedge, and into the Heffernans' silver van. Sue buckled Sylvie into the front passenger seat. "Precious cargo," she said, smiling.

"When are we coming back?" asked Sylvie.

Sue patted her arm. "Not for a while, honeybunch. Not until we get all the custody issues resolved." Sylvie had heard Mom and Dad talk about custody, too. She wasn't sure what it was, but she knew from TV it had something to do with being in jail. "Now just wait here while I run inside and grab my purse and my coat."

"Will we be in Wisconsin for Halloween?" said Sylvie, sounding panicky. She started to cry.

Tenderly, Sue brushed away her tears with her fingertips. "Don't cry, sweetheart. How silly of me to forget." She checked her watch. "I'll go back and get your princess costume. Will that cheer you up?"

"I guess so," said Sylvie listlessly. She stopped crying and Sue looked relieved.

"Just in case, get down," Sue said, unbuckling Sylvie's seat belt. "Lie down on the bottom of the car and don't move. If someone comes by, they might be the police to take you away to the foster home. Lie there until I come back. It's important! Don't worry. I'm locking all the doors."

Whimpering and perplexed, Sylvie obeyed, scrunching down onto the floor of the van. Sue patted her and tucked her pink backpack in next to her. Sylvie closed her eyes tight and heard the sound of the car door slamming and the locks clicking.

It was cold and dusty down here. Sylvie's face was next to a mat that smelled greasy and funny. "Mommy!" she whispered, then unzipped the backpack and reached inside for Velveteen Rabbit.

SUE MUST BE GONE BY NOW, LILY THOUGHT. She turned down the music and stood at the door to her room, listening. Everything was still. She quietly opened the door and went to Sylvie's room. She hadn't thought about that when she first cranked up the music. She had just wanted to drown out Sue. But she probably woke up her sister, too.

She opened the door and panicked when she saw Sylvie's empty, unmade bed. She ran downstairs, called out her sister's name in the empty house, then ran back up to Sylvie's room, hoping somehow that she would have miraculously reappeared. The room was still empty. And Velveteen Rabbit was gone.

Sue had probably taken Sylvie over to her house. That wasn't right. Mom wouldn't like it. Lily was supposed to look after Sylvie. She stared out the window onto the lawn. There was Sue walking away from the house trailing Sylvie's fluffy white princess costume with its shiny gold stars behind her like some kind of banner.

Bathrobe flying behind her, Lily ran breathlessly downstairs and caught up with Sue right before they got to the hole in the hedge.

"Give my sister back," she shouted.

Sue didn't reply. Instead, she gave Lily a forceful push. Lily fell down on the wet, cold grass, but she scrambled up as fast as she could. Sue had turned away and kept walking, but Lily grabbed the collar of her smock. "I said don't fucking push me."

"You little monster," said Sue. She twisted around to face Lily, but Lily held on to her collar. Sue pulled her arm way back and gave Lily a hard slap across the face. Lily felt her eyes jangle as Sue delivered the blow, and the collar slipped out of her grasp. Her face was burning.

"You're a fucking psycho!" said Lily, her voice rising. "I know you're crazy."

"You're messing everything up!" said Sue, smoothing down her hair. "Go back home."

"Give Sylvie back!" said Lily. She flew at Sue, grabbed her shoulders, held on tightly to them, and kicked at her shin with her own sturdy legs.

With a little cry, Sue fell sideways and Lily held on, landing on top of Sue, enveloping her with her open bathrobe, trying to pin her down. The two of them were nearly motionless, just squirming a little in their effort to dominate one another. Sue was stronger, but Lily had the advantage of her position on top, using her knees to hold Sue down. Lily felt Sue's fast breathing in her face. A gust of wind lifted up the princess costume for a moment and set it down again on the wet grass.

Finally, with a grunt of effort, Sue flipped Lily off of her, rolled away, and got to her feet. She went back to where Lily lay slightly dazed and lifted one foot to kick her in the ribs. Lily grabbed her raised ankle and pulled Sue off her balance. She fell with a grunt, tumbling down sideways next to Lily.

They both scrambled to their feet and faced each other about two feet apart, like a couple of wrestlers. "You know, Lily, this is no way to solve anything," said Sue, panting heavily. She gave Lily a sad little look, as if she felt sorry for her.

"Give back Sylvie!" shouted Lily, springing at Sue, grabbing the top of her smock and shaking her.

Sue flapped her arms in Lily's face to get free. Lily managed to get a new hold on the smock lower down, grabbing both big pockets. Sue tried to wriggle away, but Lily held on until she felt the stitching breaking and heard a tearing sound. As one of the pockets ripped off, a small object flew out of it and landed next to Lily.

Sue suddenly stopped struggling. Lily saw that she was staring down at the thing on the grass, looking very scared, with her eyes wide open and her mouth and jaw tight. Lily had never seen Sue look frightened before, and the sight exhilarated her.

Sue swooped toward the object, which appeared to be metal, but Lily was quicker and snatched it up with a little cry of triumph, then ran toward her own house clutching it. It felt cold and hard.

Sue came running after her, yelling, "Give me that!"

Lily had no idea what it was she had, but Sue seemed to want it very badly. She tried to run to the phone and call 911, but Sue was too close. Instead, Lily took her usual route, careening up the stairs and running into her room, where she slammed and locked the door.

Sue was pounding on the door again, and saying urgently, "Give it back. Give it back, Lily. I need it."

Lily knew full well how easy it was to open these bedroom locks. She had chased Sylvie to her room a million times, and when Sylvie had slammed the door and pushed that button in the middle of the knob, Lily had easily opened it with a nail file from the bathroom. Now, she heard Sue's feet running down the stairs, presumably in search of some suitable tool.

Maybe she should run into Mom and Dad's room now, lock herself in, and use the phone there. But Sue was already coming back up the staircase. Lily went over to the window, which led out onto the kitchen porch roof, and slid it open. She'd been out here before to get balls and Frisbees. Sue wouldn't follow her out here, would she? Maybe she could climb down the drainpipe. Lily had wanted to try it once, but Mom wouldn't let her. Then she could run to a neighbor and call 911.

She opened the window and sat on the ledge, looking behind her just in time to see Sue swing open the door. She was holding a paring knife, which she must have used to open the door. She started toward Lily, knife in hand.

Lily screamed, "Get away," and climbed out the window.

SYLVIE'S HEART BEGAN THUMPING WHEN SHE heard the car pull up. Then she heard the car door slam and a man's voice saying, "We'll take care of it, just relax." It was the voice of that policeman who'd brought Mom home last night. Sue was right, he was here to get her and put her in a foster home! Sylvie tried to smash herself as far into the floor mat as possible, clutching her rabbit.

ANITA STOOD ON THE HEFFERNANS' FRONT porch with Paul Flynn and pushed the bell for a second time. He had seemed pretty skeptical when she'd told him that Sue and David had been having an affair. Sue would deny everything perfectly plausibly, and Anita knew she had no proof. But at least the girls would be out of Sue's clutches.

No one was answering the door, but the silver van was parked right in front. Anita tried not to get hysterical, but in a low, angry voice she snapped, "I want my girls!" at Flynn.

"Try and remain calm," he said. "I'm sure they'll be all right." Just then they heard a cry from the back of the house.

"That's Lily's voice, I know it!" said Anita. "Lily!" she called back, like a mother cow lowing for its calf. She ran around the house, Paul Flynn following.

When she got into the Heffernans' backyard, Anita saw Lily standing precariously on their own kitchen porch roof in her robe and pajamas, her arms held out for balance. One of her hands was open, the other was in a fist.

Anita tried not to scream. Lily looked as if she'd fall off the roof at any minute, down onto the concrete below. Sue was climbing out the window after her. Anita saw a knife in Sue's hand.

Sue looked down at Anita and Flynn. "I had to use this to open the door," she said, setting the knife down on the window ledge. She turned to Lily and said in a sweet voice, "I'll come and get you back in. It's very dangerous out here."

"Don't move!" Anita told her daughter. "Sit down, be careful!"

"Mom!" said Lily jubilantly. Lily waved her closed hand and almost lost her footing. "Whoa," she said with teenaged bravado.

"Lily!" screamed Anita.

SCRUNCHED DOWN IN SUE'S VAN, SYLVIE SAT up. She was sure she'd heard Mom's voice yelling, "Lily!" Her small hands fumbled with the childproof locks, but she couldn't defeat them. She'd have to crank down the window and climb out that way.

SUE WAS COMPLETELY OUT OF LILY'S BEDROOM window now, sitting on the steep roof, inching her way down the slope toward Lily. "I'll get her," she said. "She's very distraught. I'm afraid she's been through too much."

"Get away from me!" shouted Lily, stepping closer to the edge of the roof, arms outstretched, eliciting a scream from Anita.

"Get back, Mrs. Heffernan," said Flynn. "Lily, sit down! I'll get you."

Keeping an eye on Sue, Lily slowly lowered herself into a sitting position and shouted, "Get away from me, bitch!" She threw the object in her hand down at Flynn. "She wants this real bad," she said. "It was in her pocket."

It bounced off his shoulder.

"She's hysterical," said Sue. "She said she might jump! I'll save her."

"Mrs. Heffernan! Get back!" repeated Flynn.

But Sue kept moving toward Lily, crawling on her stomach and reaching out to grab her. "I'm coming, sweetheart," she said to Lily in a calm voice.

Flynn leaped up onto the porch. Anita saw him looking down at the concrete and knew he was calculating how bad a fall would be.

"Goddamnit, please get back!" he yelled to Sue.

Lily held up her arms to ward off Sue.

"I've got her," yelled Sue triumphantly as she seized Lily's wrist.

Lily let out a scream and rolled toward the gutter.

Anita looked on in horror as Sue, prone, kept holding on to her daughter. Sue, who hadn't taken her eyes off of Lily all this time, didn't seem to be aware that Flynn was climbing on the porch railing to help the girl down.

"Get back!" screamed Anita at Sue.

Lily was on her stomach now, too, with her legs hanging off the roof. Flynn, now that he could see Lily's feet, scuttled over to where she hung and reached up for her.

"It's okay, sweetheart," he said softly. "I've almost got you." Lily wasn't sure he could catch her. She tried to shake off Sue, but Sue wouldn't let go. She was making it look like she was trying to save her, but she was pushing as hard as she could. Now she was twisting Lily's wrist, and it hurt a lot.

Suddenly, Lily felt someone grabbing her knees. When Flynn managed to reach Lily's waist, he gave her a terrific yank. Finally, Sue's hands were dislodged. Lily felt herself being taken into Flynn's arms just as she heard the scream from Sue above and then the horrible sound as she slid off the roof and hit the concrete headfirst.

Mom screamed, too, and Detective Flynn lowered Lily onto the porch and held her close so she couldn't turn her head around to see Sue. Without even thinking, she wrapped her own arms around his torso and held on to him, burying her face in his chest. Flynn gently disentangled himself and handed her over to her mother, who had rushed up onto the porch. He dashed over to where Sue lay, facedown.

Evelyn Reynolds, an alert, curious expression on her face, emerged from the side of the house. She carried a suitcase. "I rang the bell over and over again. What's going on?" she demanded. Lily and Anita unfolded to include her.

"But where's Sylvie?" said Anita in a panicky voice.

A small figure carrying a pink backpack came through the hedge and ran across the lawn, past the sodden white and gold costume on the grass, over to her family. "It *was* you, Mom!" Sylvie shouted jubilantly.

While the four of them embraced to a sound of mingled weeping, laughing, and explanation, Flynn felt Sue's neck for a pulse. There didn't seem to be one. He wasn't surprised. She had landed on her head, and the impact had been horrendous. From the way she was lying, it seemed clear her neck had been broken.

The pool of blood beneath her grew, fingers of red running steadily in three directions across the concrete. One of them led directly to the object that Lily had flung at him. As he radioed for the medics, he noted that the object was a length of copper wire, attached to two eye-bolts, wrapped into a neat package.